D0398041

sharpshooter

A SUNNY McCOSKEY NAPA VALLEY MYSTERY

sharp shooter

Nadia Gordon

CHRONICLE BOOKS
SAN FRANCISCO

ACKNOWLEDGMENTS The author wishes to thank the many people who generously offered their advice, input, and expertise on the matters of food, wine, and human nature throughout the course of the writing of this book. Special thanks to my brother G., who schooled me in the ways of Assault Golf, a noble game which should rightly be known as his own invention and not that of Wade Skord. I am deeply indebted to my wonderful mom in so many ways, but particularly with respect to this project. Without her enthusiasm and support, this book would not have been completed. I would also like to thank R. S. for his many contributions. Whenever I saw that fiendish look light up his face, I knew his brain was about to disgorge a thought of great usefulness. Further thanks to Mark for comparing the manuscript against his extensive personal archive of facts; to R. C. for her culinary prowess; to L. L. for the same, and for starting it all; and to J. W. for his sassy wit and *savoir-boire*. Thanks also to Norm for sharing his experiences and expertise; to Leslie J., whose joyful spirit and love of good food are inspiring; to Nik for his friendship and frank opinions (less of that next time, please); and to D. C., who read and listened and was there like a true friend. Thanks also to my editor, Jay S., for his patience, good judgment, and innumerable contributions at every stage. What succeeds best in this book is there thanks to Jay, who makes work fun. And last but not least, my thanks and fond appreciation to Jay L., who provided instruction and motivation by his good example. *Santé!*

Library of Congress Cataloging-in-Publication Data available.

ISBN: 0-8118-3462-X

Printed in the United States of America

Book and cover design by Benjamin Shaykin
Cover photo by Rebecca Floyd
Composition by Kristen Wurz
Typeset in Miller and Bodoni 6

Distributed in Canada by Raincoast Books
9050 Shaughnessy Street
Vancouver, British Columbia
V6P 6E5

10 9 8 7 6 5 4 3 2 1

Chronicle Books LLC
85 Second Street
San Francisco, CA 94105
www.chroniclebooks.com

For Lauren, Rebecca, and Jonno

Give the tardy fruits the hint to fill;
give them two more Mediterranean days,
drive them on into their greatness, and press
the final sweetness into the heavy wine.

–Rilke, translated by Robert Bly

PART ONE

Murder by Moonlight

I

In the black of the early morning, *Silvano Cruz drove his pickup truck under the fieldstone and ironwork archway announcing the Beroni Vineyards Estate. He drove slowly, leaning forward in his seat to maximize the view of the road and swath of vineyard illuminated by the truck's headlights. The slightest changes in the land were duly noted—a new growth of stinging nettle near a culvert, a cluster of ragweed, a pockmark indicating a gopher's presence. As vineyard manager, he found it all of interest. The truck's approach startled a cottontail foraging at the side of the road and it froze in the headlights, then darted into the truck's path and back again. Silvano stopped and turned off his lights. After a few seconds he turned them back on and watched the rabbit scramble up the embankment.*

At the winery, he pulled into his regular parking spot and got out to stretch. The cool morning air soaked quickly through his work shirt and he buttoned up his denim jacket, glancing up the hill at the Beroni mansion overlooking the vineyard from the top of the driveway. The sky had turned a deep blue and he could see the outline of the palm trees that flanked the big Victorian, and the round tower of the reading room that made the house look like a castle in the dim light. Silvano grabbed his Thermos and headed for the little John Deere tractor parked just off the road. He pumped the throttle twice, turned the key, and it rumbled awake, more than he could say about himself at this hour. One beer too many at last night's barbecue had left his mind feeling sluggish, half trapped in the dreams the alarm's buzzer had interrupted. He poured himself a cup of coffee from the Thermos and sat listening to the engine's deep-throated purr. The sound was both comforting and disquieting, in part because he couldn't hear anything else. It was like his wife with the vacuum cleaner. He'd often startled her out of a meditative daze as she marked the carpet with neat lines, oblivious to him calling her name.

The tractor settled down to a softer idle and Silvano put his Thermos away. He turned up his collar and rubbed his hands together before slipping on his work gloves and easing the tractor forward. He gripped the black wheel and squinted, watching for obstacles in the predawn light as the tractor chugged down the dirt track toward the base of the vineyard. He wanted to have a look at the irrigation system down there before the seasonal crew arrived later that morning. They were slated to start harvesting portions of the Cabernet Sauvignon grapes being grown in the lone oak region, what Silvano referred to as C7, area C, section 7 of Beroni's vast holdings. They were getting a late start, but nevertheless he planned to have the day's harvest in by noon or earlier, before the sun had a chance to heat up the sugar in the fruit.

Up ahead he could see the artificial lake at the bottom of the Zinfandel acreage, its colors shifting from somber blacks and grays to oily blues and greens as the sky began to lighten. Silvano's boss, Al Beroni, often told the story of how, forty years earlier when his wife, Louisa, had agreed to marry him, she'd told him that she dreamed of a lake for rowboats and a gazebo for watching them, sheltered from the strong sun. It was a fantasy better suited to the lush gentility of the south of England than the arid wildness and scrub pines of the northeast of the Napa Valley, but he'd built them for her, along with a three-acre rose garden behind the main house. No one had ever taken a rowboat out on the lake—more of a pond, really—as far as Silvano knew, and the gazebo didn't get used much except for the occasional wedding. There had been times when he'd seen a group of visiting Beroni cousins and in-laws standing in the empty gazebo like exotic birds in a cage, or one of Louisa's ladies' clubs gathered for a picnic, a flock of women in knee-length skirts clutching flutes of champagne and trying not to let their high heels sink into the lawn. The lake was pretty enough, but it was still a waste of valuable farmland in Silvano's opinion, though it did serve in drought years as a reservoir for irrigation water. Still, what was now underwater could have produced two hundred cases of wine a year, maybe more.

As he continued down the narrow track, he stared at the gazebo gently lit by the pink and gold glow of sunrise with a mixture of contempt and awe. It had six equal sides and a peaked roof crowned with a white dove lifting off in flight. On five sides a fine white lattice formed a waist-high skirt; the sixth was open and faced the lake, with three crisp white stairs leading down to the small, kidney-shaped lawn. Silvano glanced at the stairs and then back again. He released the throttle and let the tractor settle to a halt. A wake of dust billowed up around him, then subsided. Cautiously he looked again, then turned the key and killed the motor, staying seated until he was sure of what he saw. He wanted to be sure, because a thing like that could rattle a man if he wasn't prepared.

With the tractor quiet, the trill of a red-winged blackbird cheered what promised to be another warm Indian summer day by the afternoon. Silvano got down off the tractor. He left his gloves on the seat and walked around to the edge of the dirt track. The gazebo stood less than fifteen yards away. There, on each of the freshly whitewashed steps, he saw long, narrow pools of blood. Raising his eyes reluctantly to the floor of the gazebo, he crossed himself and muttered, "Sweet madre de Dios."

Sprawled across the floor and long since drained of blood lay Jack Beroni—son of Louisa and Al Beroni—now dead, surely dead. Silvano climbed the stairs at one edge and inched his way around Jack's body, careful to avoid the blood spread out around it as if this affliction were somehow contagious. He knelt and held his hand in front of Jack's nose and mouth. He didn't feel any breath, which didn't surprise him. He hesitated an instant, then took up Jack's hand and wrist, pressing his fingers to the place where the pulse should have been. The hand was cold and lifeless, the vein still. Jack's silver Rolex, chilled by the night, seemed to burn Silvano's fingers and he let the hand drop suddenly. The resulting thud made him jumpy and he looked over his shoulder, half expecting a man with a gun to be watching him. There could be no doubt about it, Jack Beroni was definitely dead. The thing had been done, the breath was gone, the blood had run out all over his mother's floor and down the steps to the manicured lawn, freed from his body through a bullet wound to the chest.

Silvano stared. Jack's normally robust complexion had drained to an industrial shade of bone, the color of computers and cheap telephones. Only his black hair still displayed the vigor and distinguished bearing of its owner's former self. He lay awkwardly, head turned to one side, legs twisted, eyes wide and mouth a horrible grimace of shock and surprise. He'd fallen with one arm wedged underneath him. Most awkward of all were his feet, sticking up at odd angles in their lustrous black oxfords. The silk jacket of his tuxedo lay open, displaying a white shirt that Jack had worn unbuttoned in fashionably rogue contrast to the formality of its tailoring, and which was now pierced with a neat round hole over his heart. A dark crimson stain seeped out around the hole. Suddenly the smell of blood seemed to be everywhere, heavy and thick at the back of Silvano's throat. He hurried back to the tractor, started it, then changed his mind and ran back up to the winery fighting a wave of nausea that finally overwhelmed him as he neared the structure.

By noon the C7 Cabernet Sauvignon harvest was not in; in fact, it had not even begun. Instead, a string of patrol cars had nosed to the side of the road near the lake, fouling Silvano's neatly sculpted drainage ditch in several places. Half a dozen St. Helena police officers combed the area around the gazebo, which had been roped off with yellow crime-scene tape. Al and Louisa Beroni had come down from the house and now stood off to the side while the police worked. Their arms linked, dressed in neat but conservative attire, he in khakis and a chambray button-down, she in a blue cotton skirt with appliqué pockets and a cream-colored sweater set with pearl buttons, Al and Louisa watched in a dazed state of grief, unable to leave the scene in front of them, as though if they watched long enough the tragedy would reverse itself. Police officers moved methodically away from the gazebo in concentric circles, their steps shortened and eyes downcast in the search for evidence.

2

Sunny McCoskey pulled a woolly, sea-green sweater over her T-shirt and stepped into a pair of clogs. In the bathroom, she rubbed a tiny dab of pomade between her hands and smoothed her bangs into place, then poked small silver hoops through the holes in her earlobes. She'd been up since four reading yesterday's newspaper over coffee and oatmeal with raisins. Rationalizing what she suspected was behavior verging on the not quite normal, she reasoned that she was merely making good use of one of the few fringe benefits of living alone, the freedom to indulge her occasional insomnia. Is it a crime to get up in the middle of the night and make chocolate chip cookies and cinnamon twist bread? To wake up two hours early for work in order to catch up on inconsequential personal correspondence and read several newspapers? Only if someone else is trying to sleep, and there was certainly no need to worry about that. She thought wistfully of the Jack Russell puppy she'd seen at the animal shelter last week. If she'd brought him home, there would be the heartwarming *clickity clack* of toenails on the hardwood floors. And probably a yellow puddle in the corner.

She poured the second half of a pot of coffee into her Thermos and added a generous splash from the last of an open bottle of Spottswoode Cabernet Sauvignon left over from a splurge of notable excess the night before. She had no business drinking such expensive wine, but how could she help it if Monty Lenstrom was going to offer her his wholesale discount and make it seem like such a bargain? Sunny heard more than thought, *Never cook with wine you wouldn't drink,* one of Catelina's many admonitions and a convenient one for justifying the café-con-vino practice that plenty of people in Napa Valley would consider a daily blasphemy against both the bean and the grape. Why make a perfectly good pot of coffee and then ruin it with an inferior wine? Life is short. Good wine or bad, Monty gnashed his teeth whenever he saw her do it, even though she had patiently explained on more than one occasion that a key compound in red wine, the phenolics responsible for the tannic flavor, were also abundant in coffee. The common note drew the two beverages together in a symphony that took some time to get used to, she admitted, but that was exceptionally satisfying once properly appreciated. And since phenolics were rumored to prevent heart disease, her morning quaff was practically health food. She could think of certain French farmers who would be sure to approve.

A string of Nepalese tin bells sewn down a red rope chimed noisily as she shut her front door and went out. The morning was cool and a layer of dew frosted the front yard. The front of her clogs darkened with moisture on the way from the front porch across twenty feet of overgrown grass to the crooked little arch that faced the sidewalk. The sky was just tinged with the first yellow light of dawn. Sunny drew the wet, late-September air into her nostrils. Fall, harvest, damp-leaves-on-the-ground air. It filled her with joy. Sunny, born Sonya, was wry by nature and preferred autumn's stoic good spirit in the face of winter's decline to the brighter ebullience of spring and the arrogance of summer. Most of all she was glad today was Friday. Whenever she looked at the balance in her checking account, she thought about keeping her restaurant, Wildside, open on nights and weekends. Then Friday would come around and she would remember why she liked to keep overhead low and her hours reasonable. Too many restaurants closed because their owners burned out on eighty-hour workweeks, staggering home at two in the morning every night.

She made her way up the street to where her pickup sat waiting, its enormous bed slightly cockeyed with age. Her father bought it new from the Ford dealership in Napa in 1978 and sold it cheap when Sunny said she wanted it a couple of decades later. The root beer–colored side panels and scratchy upholstery reminded her of childhood so forcefully that it still gave her a small spike of excitement each time she hopped into the driver's side instead of sliding into the middle, her designated riding position most of the time when she was growing up.

She eased out of the sleepy neighborhood and onto Main Street. Even at the crack of dawn, cars were already pulling in and out of parking spaces on the main drag. St. Helena, despite appearances of fashionable wealth, was still essentially a farm town and it woke up early. She studied the cars out front of Bismark's and the coffee drinkers seated with their newspapers in the window. If Monty or Wade were there, she'd stop and have a scone, but she didn't recognize anybody and drove on toward her restaurant.

Wildside's parking lot was empty and she took the furthest spot like always, noticing that somebody had staple-gunned a wanted poster to the fence that lined the back wall of the property. HAVE YOU SEEN THIS INSECT? it demanded in bold type, illustrating the question with grainy snapshots of the glassy-winged sharpshooter in all its life stages, including larva, various nymph forms, and voracious, sap-sucking, mud-colored adult. Though it had yet to make an appearance, the glassy-winged sharpshooter was the latest in a long line of hungry visitors to threaten the valley. The wine business—and everyone who depended on the wine business, which was the whole valley—was understandably alarmed about the problem, and they watched the sharpies' progress with dread as they made their way steadily northward county by county. They called them the SUVs of leafhoppers, which were considered trouble to vineyards at any size since they vectored Pierce's disease, lethal to grapevines. Those in the know said Pierce's disease would make the industry's recent bout with phylloxera look like a case of the vineyard sniffles. Every day the local newspapers covered the crisis. A glassy-winged sharpshooter spotted in San Mateo, too close for comfort. A shipment of ornamental shrubs from Southern California, rife with eggs, narrowly intercepted. A case of Pierce's disease suspected in Fresno. The valley continued to prosper, even as its inhabitants ground their teeth at night, worrying.

Sunny went around back through the restaurant's tiny garden and opened the heavy door to the kitchen. Inside, she put on a CD of Brazilian jazz and set to work preparing for the day's lunch. At seven-thirty she heard footsteps coming down the path and Rivka appeared, clad in her usual white tank top and jeans, no matter what the weather. Her hair, long and wavy when it was down, had been braided and wound into two tight buns behind her ears. Rivka had a face like a Mayan temple carving. Her eyebrows arched above almond-shaped eyes in two bold lines and her nose was well-defined and punctuated with two shapely half-moon nostrils, the left one pierced with a tiny silver stud. She had full lips that curved up in a demure smile even when she was feeling sour or bored. She swayed to the music and said, "This new boy of mine does not know how to dance."

Sunny said, "He doesn't know what he's missing. He's probably been spending all his nights cooking grapes in test tubes."

Rivka lifted her black eyes. "I wish that was a joke. I'm a wine widow and we aren't even married."

Sunny whistled. "The M word! That must have been some date."

Rivka tied the strings of a long white apron around her waist. "Actually it was pretty low-key. Cheap food, worthless movie, no sex. If it wasn't for his sweet face, it wouldn't have been worth the time."

"No sex?"

"Rule number three. No sex after ten o'clock unless I'm drunk."

"I've never understood that one," said Sunny.

"Too sleepy. Conditions not conducive to optimum performance."

"At least you have the option. Why is it the date-free zone every weekend at my place? I have another hideously wholesome weekend planned. Sports, Riv. I have been reduced to the mind-numbing practice of sports. Why don't I live in the city?"

Rivka looked incredulous. "You mean San Francisco? You've got to be kidding. The numbers are better up here in the sticks. You just keep channeling all that romantic frustration into the cooking and it's all going to work out fine. Thirty-two is old, but not that old. There's still time."

"Excuse me? Thirty-two is only old if you're a twenty-four-year-old lassie all full of 'tude. These things are relative."

"Maybe so, but you've gotta get it in gear one of these days. Use it or lose it."

Sunny reduced a mound of parsley to a heap of tiny bits with expert precision, the knife moving at terrific speed. "Why don't I live in Alaska, where the man-babes are plentiful? I hear they're falling off the man-babe trees, lying around on the ground just going to waste by the basketful."

"Because you would freeze your ass off," said Rivka. She slipped into the walk-in and reappeared with an armful of white tubs covered in plastic wrap. "I probably shouldn't tell you this."

"What? Tell. Don't toy with me, Chavez, I've been up since four."

"Not again."

"Yep. Dish, please."

"Okay. Alex told me that he would have asked me out a long time ago, but he thought"—she stopped to laugh—"he thought you were my partner."

"He thought we were a gay couple."

"Yes!" Rivka bellowed with laughter.

"Well, I guess that explains it."

"There's more."

"Oh, good. I can't wait."

"He also thought Wade Skord was your boyfriend. That's how he figured out we weren't a couple."

"That's lovely. And do we have any idea how widespread this concept is?"

"No idea."

"Not that I don't love Wade."

"I hear you."

Sunny stood over the sink in back and pulled the rough skin off a steaming-hot roasted beet, revealing the slick sanguine flesh underneath. Beet juice stained her fingers and purpled the calluses lined up across her palms at the base of each finger. Blood-red splashes hit the white sink. The back windows stood open wide in front of her, framing a view of the lush vineyards and sea of green, gold, and red leaves that stretched to the east behind the restaurant. Up valley she could see a portion of Howell Mountain. Gusts of cool air brushed her face while she worked, and soon she was lost in thought, remembering previous harvests. The first time she'd worked a harvest, reaching overhead to pick clusters of Sauvignon Blanc for eight hours that felt like sixteen, then the all-night party . . . The old black phone on the wall behind her jangled. Very few people had the kitchen number; it had to be either her mom, Monty, or Wade.

"Hello?" she said cautiously.

"Sunny?"

"Wade?" Sunny cradled the receiver and rubbed at her stained hands with a towel.

"Hi, Sun. Listen, do you think you could come over here to my place?"

"Right now?"

"If it's not too much trouble."

"Are you okay?"

"Yeah, I'm fine. I just want your opinion on something."

"What kind of something? Are you sick? Are you okay?" Rivka gave her a curious look. Sunny raised her eyebrows and shook her head, listening.

Wade said, "Sick? No, no. It's . . . Well, I'll explain when you get here. It won't take long."

"Okay. I guess I'll be there in, um, fifteen or so."

"Great. Thanks, McCoskey."

Sunny hung up the phone and turned to Rivka. "He says it won't take long."

The road twisted through live oak, digger pine, and bay on its way up into the hills. After a few miles, sturdy trunks of Douglas firs rose out of the red soil, and the hills became Howell Mountain. Sunny rolled down the window and stuck her head out, catching the sweet breeze and picking out the plant smells. It had been a long, hot, dry summer and the turn to fall was welcome. Soon it would rain and there would be chanterelles on the lower slopes where the oak did better than the pine. It was pleasant to be called away from the kitchen unexpectedly, even if it meant the morning would be a crunch when she got back, even if the tone of Wade's voice worried her. Still, these sorts of alarms were almost always false. He probably didn't want to say what he wanted in case she wouldn't come. The time was right for bottling last year's harvest. It had been aging in barrels for a year now, and Wade would need to free up those barrels soon for this year's wine. Probably he'd made two or three different blends and he wanted her opinion. She reasoned that if it was a real emergency, he would have said so on the phone.

At the crest she made a left onto a narrower paved road and soon passed the turnoff to the stone pillars and wrought-iron arch that announced BERONI VINEYARDS ESTATE, Wade Skord's formidable neighbor. The road wound around a bend and along the edge of a steep ravine. At the black mailbox with SKORD MOUNTAIN VINEYARD hand-lettered on the side, she took a right onto a dirt road that curved precipitously down a slope lined with dense forest. As the grade flattened out, her truck emerged from the trees into bright sunshine, and grapevines took over where forest had left off. The deep ruts that had scored the steep part of the road were replaced by even deeper potholes and a luxurious layer of fine dust. Sunny slowed the truck to a crawl, hoping to minimize the wear and tear on the shocks, not to mention the cloud of copper-colored dust. The vines that lined the road threatened to engulf the truck. Purple clusters of matte-finish grapes hung in graceful bunches every few inches and leafy tendrils arched skyward. Gnarled silver-gray stocks plunged into dark soil. Between the rows, dry weeds made a shaggy straw-yellow carpet.

After a gentle turn at the bottom of the hill, the cabin came into view. It had been built in the thirties after Prohibition, the same time that several acres of the slope above were planted to Zinfandel. Those vines still produced some of the best wine in the valley. Wade had added a large bedroom and kitchen to the original cabin, the exterior of which had weathered to a shade of silvery gray that made it blend into the surrounding forest so well, it was possible to stand on top of the ridge and take in the view without noticing the house at all. A redwood deck, another of Wade's modifications, extended off the southwest side, looking toward the winery.

Wade was waiting on the deck when Sunny pulled up. He'd taken off his boots to go in the house and now he stood in his white gym socks watching her walk toward him. He had on a gray wool work shirt over a white thermal shirt and dirty jeans and stood there, smiling weakly. Sunny kissed each cheek and looked at him. There was an awkwardness about him, a stiffness and hesitation that hadn't been there before. "What's up?" she asked.

He rubbed his belly and scratched at the stubble on his neck. "Oh, the usual. Just sitting around watching the grapes grow. You want a cup of coffee?"

Sunny followed him inside. The kitchen glowed with soft golden light streaming in the windows and Sunny stared at a bowl of pomegranates sitting on a countertop. They were beautiful, their skin looking a deeper shade of red against a mint-green ceramic bowl. A collection of the season's first fall leaves was spread out across the scarred wood of the kitchen table. Wade poured her a cup of coffee and Sunny sat down, gently stacking the leaves to one side and waiting for him to join her. He lifted an open bottle of Zin but she shook her head. Wade settled into the chair across from her. She could hear the clock above the refrigerator ticking.

Finally he said, "Steve Harvey came by early this morning." He looked up at Sunny to see what the police officer's name meant to her, if anything, then went on. "I heard a car drive up and when I saw who it was I figured Beroni had lodged another complaint against me. My existence is disturbing their precious peace, my mailbox needs mending and is bringing down the property values, I drive too fast, I didn't wash behind my ears. Same old bull."

Sunny waited. When he didn't go on, she said, "What did he want?"

"That's just it, Sunny. It wasn't a complaint this time. The last two times the cops have come out, it was because Beroni called them about me playing Assault Golf in the evenings. I guess they can hear the shots up there and it gets Al's undies in a bunch. But it wasn't that. We worked all that out. I never play after ten anymore, you know that. Anyway, I asked Steve to come in, but he wouldn't sit down. He just stood there looking at his shoes. He asked me right off the bat where I was last night. I said here, like always. Then he asked me if there was anyone with me, what I was doing, what time I went to bed, did I make any phone calls, all kinds of stuff. I told him I was home alone after about seven. That's right, isn't it?"

"Seven, seven-fifteen maybe. I was home by eight and I stopped at the store."

"After you left I did some work in the office. I made a couple of fried eggs and toast around eight-thirty, played the guitar for a while. Then I went to bed. I don't know what I thought he was after when I was telling him all this. I was just answering what he asked. I should have told him right away I'd have to call my lawyer. Anyway, he asked me if I heard anything unusual last night, if I saw or heard anybody creeping around. I told him I was sound asleep by ten and didn't wake up until five-thirty this morning."

"You dog," said Sunny. "I woke up at four and couldn't get back to sleep."

Wade ignored her comment and went on. "Then he says, 'Wade, do you own a rifle?' and that's when the hairs on the back of my neck started to stand up. I said, 'What's this about, Steve?' and he says, 'I just need to know if you own a rifle.'"

Sunny stared at him and he met her gaze, nodding very slightly, affirming that there was more. "I said I didn't feel right answering any more questions until he gave me some idea of what this was about. I was still thinking it was probably about Assault Golf, because he'd been out here before about that, but he was acting strange. I knew just by watching him that something bad had happened. Besides, he knows I own a rifle. He's even seen it a couple of times. In fact, I fired it once when he told me to so he could hear for himself how loud it was up at the Beroni place, and he agreed it wasn't loud at all. All they could hear was a pop, very faint.

"Anyway, it struck me as odd that he would be asking me about it now. It just didn't seem right. I could tell something was upsetting him. That's when he told me that Jack Beroni was dead. They found him this morning in that little gazebo over by the lake. Somebody shot him last night."

Sunny gaped. "Jack Beroni is dead?"

"Shot in the chest. With a rifle, sniper style from a distance."

"Are they sure? It has to be some sort of mistake, right?"

"Oh, they're sure, all right. They found the body. It's pretty hard to make a mistake about that."

"I don't believe it." She thought of the chipper little gazebo standing beside the artificial lake over at Beroni Vineyards. She'd seen it often enough in the distance on the walks she and Wade liked to take at dusk. There was nothing menacing about the frilly white structure and the emerald lawn around it. It was hard to imagine anything bad happening there.

"He told me it happened last night, late. Like maybe around eleven o'clock. Jack had been out somewhere. He was still wearing a tuxedo."

"What was he doing down at the gazebo at night?"

"Who knows."

"So then what happened?"

"Well, he told me how Silvano Cruz, the guy who manages the vineyard up there, found him first thing this morning. He'd been dead for several hours, probably most of the night. They didn't find the gun that was used, or at least they haven't yet.

They're combing the forest by the lake right now. But they could tell by the way the bullet mushroomed out that it was fired from some kind of high-velocity .22. That could be any of the center-fire rifles everybody and his dog owns. Anyway, we stood there for a minute staring at each other and then Steve says, 'If you don't mind, I'd like to have a look at that gun of yours,' and that's when I knew I'd already said way too much. I told him that he'd need a search warrant to go any further into my house and that I wanted to talk to my lawyer before I answered any more questions. He was like, 'You sure you're sure about that?' and I said, 'Damn right I'm sure.' Then I told him he'd better leave."

Wade stared up at Sunny across the table, his hands cupped around his mug of coffee. His wild gray hair, cowlicked in a dozen directions, stuck up all over his head, and his cheeks were grizzled with salt-and-pepper stubble. His face was deeply tanned from long days outdoors during his fifty-seven years, and his clear blue eyes shone at her, firm but questioning, looking for some confirmation that he'd done the right thing.

"The gun we use for Assault Golf, that's a .22 caliber rifle, right?" said Sunny.

"Ruger M77 bolt-action .22 Hornet," said Wade.

"The same kind that was used to shoot Jack."

"It's possible."

Plenty of people in Napa Valley had guns. Guns were used to shoot skeet and, in Wade's case, golf balls. At worst they were used to shoot gophers, deer, or quail. It never even occurred to her that one might be used to kill someone she knew, someone practically everybody knew. There wasn't a person for thirty miles who wouldn't recognize Jack Beroni.

"I think maybe I should give Harry a call," said Wade.

"I think that's probably a good idea, just in case."

Harry was Wade's lawyer. He'd helped him out when the Beronis tried to put in a road that ran three feet over onto Wade's side of the property line. He also did all the paperwork when Sunny opened Wildside. "I'm sure it's just routine," she said. "I mean, it makes sense for him to come here, for Harvey to cover all of his bases. You might have heard something." Sunny put a hand to her mouth and nibbled at a rough corner of one of her nails.

"I hope you're right. It rattled me. Steve standing there giving me the third degree, telling me Jack Beroni has been killed within a mile of here. Everybody knows how I feel—felt—about Jack, but I certainly never wished him dead. Well, maybe once or twice, but not seriously, of course," said Wade.

"You and half the valley. You were just more vocal about it. If they're going to talk to everyone who had it in for Jack, they're in for a lengthy investigation. Still, I'd call Harry and get his take, just to be sure." Sunny tried to sound unconcerned, to actually be unconcerned, but the facts were alarming. Jack Beroni was dead. His nearest neighbor—and Sunny's closest friend—had a long history of legal battles, animosity, and outright fights with both Jack and his parents. Wade had been home alone, hadn't spoken to anyone. In other words, he had no alibi. And Steve Harvey had already been here poking around, asking about Wade's gun. That could only mean Wade was a suspect. A terrible thought occurred to her. "Wade, you didn't happen to play Assault Golf last night?" Her stomach turned over when she saw his face.

"I played a ball around nine o'clock," said Wade, his worry interrupted by a conspiratorial flicker of pride. "Sank it in two shots."

Sunny winced. As harmless as it was, she had never thought Assault Golf was a good idea. What good could come of firing a gun at night? Still, she had to admit it was fun. Wade had invented the game years ago. It started when he used to like to practice driving golf balls across the ravine onto the grass in front of the winery. Then one day he got the idea of using the balls for target practice before he walked down to pick them up. Soon after that he sank an old coffee can next to the compost heap on the edge of the meadow and Assault Golf was born. The idea was to use the old eight iron Wade had bought at a garage sale to hit the ball toward the compost heap, then switch to the rifle for no more than three shots to move the ball along the ground toward the coffee can. A player scored ten points every time he made the ball move without hitting it. If he succeeded in getting the ball into the coffee can, he scored an additional fifty points. Actually hitting the ball, and therefore ruining it, earned a fifty-point penalty. After a while, he was so good at it, it wasn't much of a challenge anymore. Then the day came when Wade found glow-in-the-dark golf balls on the Web, and after-hours Assault Golf was born. Sunny had played half a dozen times and Wade played a ball or two nearly every night before bed. It was exactly this sort of behavior that made Sunny question the virtues of living a solitary life.

She finished her coffee and pushed back her chair. "I'm not sure there is anything we can do about this right now other than worry," she said, giving Wade an ironic smile and standing to go. She glanced in the sink. Two plates were stacked on top of the frying pan with a spatula, a fork, and two knives. There was also a wineglass with dark purple residue in the bottom. There were crumbs on the top plate and there would be crumbs and olive oil from the eggs on the one under that. Eggs and toast for supper. Toast with canned sardines for breakfast. For someone who had such good taste in wine, he sure didn't put much effort into what he ate when he was alone. *Food's just something to put the wine on, anyway,* he'd joke.

Wade walked her to the door. At the truck, she gave him a hug and, trying to sound casual, made him promise to call Harry right away.

Driving back to Wildside, she tried to get used to the idea that Jack Beroni had been killed in a way that left only one possible conclusion: There was a murderer at large in the valley. She drove on, hardly noticing the beauty of the surrounding countryside, a sight that normally still caught her attention every day. The idea that Steve Harvey suspected Wade Skord was simply ridiculous. Harvey must have just been checking out every possible source of information. It sounded like that was all he was doing—until he asked if Wade owned a rifle. No, thought Sunny, when a man is shot and a policeman comes to the door asking to see a gun, it's not a routine visit, it's a criminal investigation. Sunny gripped the steering wheel and pressed the gas pedal, racing back to the restaurant as though that would help.

The chirp of a siren interrupted her thoughts. Steve Harvey's patrol car filled her rearview mirror. She tipped the truck off the side of the pavement at the next turn out and waited for Harvey to walk up. His muscular shoulders bulged under the khaki shirt. Harvey was a stocky guy. A healthy crop of sun-bleached hair glistened on his forearms as he came over. He took off his sunglasses and smiled at her.

"Hi, Sunny."

"Hi, Steve."

"Where's the fire?"

"Fire? Oh, just in a hurry. I'm running late."

"Are you headed to the restaurant?"

"Yes."

"Mind if I follow you? I'd like to talk with you for a few minutes if that's all right."

"Of course, my pleasure."

He gave her a perfunctory smile. Sunny watched him walk away in her side mirror, then pulled slowly back out onto the highway and drove the short distance to the restaurant, the patrol car tailing her at a polite distance. At Wildside, they got out of their cars and walked around the back of the restaurant and through the kitchen into Sunny's office without speaking, the stiff leather of Steve Harvey's holster creaking loudly.

3

Sunny's office at Wildside looked significantly smaller and messier with Sergeant Harvey standing in it. Suddenly the room that had always felt perfectly spacious and efficient seemed cramped and crowded with furniture and papers. The walls needed painting, the two windows were dusty and fringed with cobwebs in the sunlight, and the walls and desk and even the standup metal filing cabinet were littered with several years' clutter. Postcards from traveling friends, mailers from wineries and kitchen suppliers, snapshots, souvenirs, shift schedules, supply lists, and long-forgotten reminders were tacked, taped, and held up by magnets in drifts. A bent and corroded metal rooster bought at a flea market in Provence perched on top of the filing cabinet. Every flat surface including the floor was stacked with cookbooks. On the desk next to an old typewriter from the thirties was a piece of driftwood that someone thought was shaped like a trout. There was a ceramic pig from Mexico, a primitive mask from a Burning Man costume made out of an empty bleach jug painted turquoise blue and neon green, and, displayed on the windowsill, a collection of dried chicken feet.

The comfortable disarray seemed to indicate not a colorful personal history and eclectic interests, but shoddiness and negligence when Sunny saw it through Steve Harvey's eyes. She glanced at the photograph of the smiling blond woman, a Bordelaise in a deep V-neck sweater holding a seductive armload of Cabernet Sauvignon fruit. The picture, which had once seemed to epitomize the sensuality and abundance of harvest, now looked vaguely incriminating, as though it signaled a bent toward the lascivious or some other warp in character.

Sunny pushed one of the windows open for fresh air, kicked a bag of dirty gym clothes aside, and dragged her desk chair around toward the coffee table, suggesting that Sergeant Harvey take the more comfortable seat on the couch. He declined. Instead he grabbed a small wood and cane café chair from the corner, which turned out to be, like the rest of the room, far too small for him. He perched on the edge of it stiffly, like a trained bear. It occurred to Sunny that he felt as uncomfortable as she did. He said, "I hate to bother you in the middle of a busy morning, Sunny."

"Don't worry about it. I have a hunch I know why you're here."

"Do you?" said Steve, suddenly stern instead of apologetic. Sunny felt the sting of authority in his voice, and the wooden resolve it always provoked in her. It was like being in the principal's office or her father's study all over again, only this was her office, her space, the place she'd spent years getting to. She felt the tingling sensation of rebellion rising up. She told herself to relax, he's only doing his job. She said, "I was on my way back from Wade Skord's house when you pulled me over, but I think you know that."

She thought she caught a flicker of surprise in his face, maybe even a little amusement. He'd assumed she wouldn't notice him staking out the base of the turnoff to Howell Mountain. He said, "Then you know about Jack Beroni."

"Only that he was found this morning in the gazebo. That someone killed him. Do you have any idea who did it?"

"We have some leads. It was done sniper style, at night, by somebody who was a good shot with a high-powered rifle." Sunny thought of Wade, standing up behind the house with his .22 Hornet, using the night-vision scope to sight the glowing yellow golf ball lying in the grass across the ravine. Steve Harvey leaned forward and rested his elbows on his knees, provoking a vision of him on the toilet. Sunny stifled a giggle. "Are you sure you wouldn't be more comfortable on the couch?" she said.

He sat upright again. "No, thanks. Was there a particular reason for your visit to Wade Skord this morning?"

"He called and asked me to come over. Your visit and Jack's death had his nerves all jangled. He just needed to see a friend."

Steve nodded. "Did he tell you what he did last night?"

"Yes, but I don't feel right about speaking for him. I'll tell you what I know directly. Wade can speak for himself."

Steve shot her a hard look and said, "Okay. We can always talk about that stuff later." He looked around the room as though it were evidence. His eyes settled on the blue and green mask. Fringe made from strands of painted plastic wrap hung down half a foot from the bottom. He said, "Tell me about your day yesterday. You worked here at the restaurant?"

"Yes."

"Until what time?"

"Around five."

"And then what did you do?"

"I drove over to Wade's place to have a look at the harvest. It's getting close up there. He'll bring them in any day now."

"What's he got up there, Zinfandel?"

"Yeah."

"So the two of you were out in the vineyard tasting grapes? What time was that?"

"Probably around five-thirty. We tasted fruit and took samples from each segment. He has the vineyard divided up into eight segments."

"Then what did you do?"

"We went back to the house to drop off the samples and measure the Brix. Wade opened a bottle of '96 late harvest and we took glasses of it with us on a walk up the ridge to the top of the vineyard to watch the sunset. That was about six-thirty. After that I was tired, so I went home. I left around seven or seven-fifteen."

"Where did you go from there?"

"I stopped at the supermarket. The Safeway over by the railroad tracks. Then home. I was home all night after that."

"Did you talk to anyone? Did anybody call or come over?"

"Monty Lenstrom called, I think around nine o'clock. And I sent some e-mail around ten."

Steve took a tiny notepad out of his breast pocket and used the little pencil that came with it to write something down, probably Monty Lenstrom's name. As a wine merchant who sold expensive, hard-to-find wines, Lenstrom circulated to all the better parties and seemed to know everybody up valley, at least well enough to call them customers. Steve probably knew who he was. He sat quietly for a moment with the pencil hovering above the pad. Sunny studied his short, neatly combed blond hair, thinking that it was probably stiff to the touch. He'd have to use a strong gel to freeze it into place and have it last all day like that. His fingernails were perfectly clean, too. She glanced at her own hands, which were comparatively barbaric, her nails shaggy along the edges, the strong tendons too pronounced, the skin scarred from things sharp and hot in the kitchen. Catelina Alvarez, the old Portuguese woman who lived across the street the whole time Sunny was growing up, had small, gnarled hands that could take a live chicken strutting around the backyard and turn it into neat pieces arranged in a baking dish in minutes. Sunny had seen her reach into a pot of boiling water, pull out a potato, and start peeling it with the steam coming off in plumes. Sunny's hands were already more like Catelina's than like Monty Lenstrom's girlfriend's, who had petal-soft skin and long fingers like beautifully shaped twigs; hands best suited to the application of eye makeup.

Steve returned the notepad to his shirt pocket and put his hands together, fingers interlaced, and stared down at them. After what seemed a painfully long silence, he looked up at Sunny and asked, "How would you characterize your relationship with Wade Skord?"

Sunny wondered if that was an official question or a personal one, or merely curiosity. Cops are the best source of gossip in a small town, next to the hairdresser and the DA's office. She said, "We're friends. Have been for years."

"Nothing more?"

"No. Is that part of this?"

Steve looked up at her with a new fierceness in his eyes. "Ms. McCoskey, may I remind you that a man has been killed, shot with a rifle not half a mile from Wade Skord's home. What Wade Skord was doing last night and who he was doing it with are very important pieces of information. People's lives could depend on it."

Wade's life could depend on it, thought Sunny. She said, "We aren't lovers. We never have been. We're friends, and we collaborate in our businesses. I work with him as a consultant in his winemaking, he produces wine for Wildside."

Steve seemed to relax slightly. He said, "Did he seem upset or agitated about anything last night? Did he mention anything that was bothering him?"

"No. In fact, he seemed extremely relaxed. It's been a good growing season; the fruit looks like it will be exceptional, if the weather holds. Assuming nothing goes wrong in the next few days, it will be one of the best harvests in years." Sunny paused. She'd been trying to ignore the obvious subtext of their conversation, but the time had come to face it. "Steve, Wade Skord isn't capable of murder."

"I've never met anyone I thought was, but plenty of murders happen," said Steve. "People are capable of more than you think."

"Not Wade. I've known him for years. He thinks about three things: the vines, the grapes, and the wine. He is completely absorbed in his work."

"And what if something threatened that work?"

Sunny didn't reply and Steve stood to go. After he left, she sat staring at the card he'd given her with his mobile-phone number penciled on the back. "In case you remember something," he'd said. Like what? That Wade planned to shoot Jack Beroni later that night after she left?

Rivka stuck her head in a few minutes later. "What was that all about?" she asked.

Sunny looked up, feeling suddenly on edge. "Long story."

"It wasn't about Jack Beroni, was it?"

Sunny hesitated. Rivka came into the office and plopped down on the couch. She took a bunch of Sauvignon Blanc grapes from a bowl on Sunny's desk and began to eat them, piling the seeds on the corner of an old newspaper lying on the coffee table. After several grapes she said, "Alex called right after you left. He told me about them finding Jack this morning. Everyone's talking about it."

"What did he say?"

"He said Silvano Cruz, the guy who oversees the vineyard, was driving along in his tractor early this morning when he noticed something red running down the steps of the gazebo. Turned out to be blood. He went up there and found Jack sprawled on his back, dead. About this time, Alex pulls into the winery for work, and here comes Silvano running up the road saying Jack's been shot, they have to call the police. Alex said he was white as a sheet. So Silvano goes inside to phone while Alex drives down to the gazebo to stand guard until the police get there. He said there was blood all over the place. He sounded pretty shook up about it. He waited around until the police got there, then helped them tape off the area and lift the body onto the stretcher and everything."

Sunny rubbed her head with her knuckles, making circles at her temples and working her way back to her neck. The day was getting weirder and weirder, and there was every reason to believe it was only going to get worse. She tried to make it all seem real. Jack Beroni was dead. The police clearly considered Wade a suspect, at least for the moment. And Steve Harvey, perennial big softy about town, was coming on like a big-city cop. "Did he say if they have any ideas about who did it?" she asked Rivka.

"Nothing so far. Whoever shot him was careful. They never even came near him, just shot him from way off, probably from the trees along the west side of the vineyard. They didn't find any footprints or anything. They have about a dozen guys out there looking for evidence. They think the killer used a rifle, a powerful one that's effective from a long way away, probably fitted with a night scope. Alex says those guns are incredibly accurate if you know how to shoot them. The killer could have hit Jack from a hundred yards away and ditched the gun in the forest. The only evidence they found, as far as Alex could tell, was the body and the bullet."

"And they could tell exactly what kind of gun was used?"

"Yeah. They could tell by the bullet. They can even match the bullet to a specific gun, if they find it. Don't you watch cop shows on TV?"

"No TV. I'm a recovering addict, remember? I haven't watched TV since they invented the remote."

"Right, I forgot. Anyway, every gun barrel leaves its own particular marks on the bullet when it's fired, like a fingerprint. They're threaded, so the bullet spins and the threads make little scratches on the bullet that they can match up to the gun."

Sunny felt a wave of relief. This was very good news. The police had the bullet. If there was any real suspicion of Wade, which the rational side of her mind seriously doubted, the police could always check the bullet against his gun. She took a deep breath.

Rivka looked at her. "What?"

"Nothing."

"You thought something."

"No, just thinking about that bullet. How somewhere out there in the world there's a gun that matches it."

Sunny looked at the clock above the couch. It was after ten; they'd have to hurry if they were going to be ready to open in an hour. Rivka went back to the kitchen and Sunny picked up the phone and dialed Wade's number. She tapped the office door closed with her foot.

By noon the restaurant buzzed with news of the murder. From her station behind the zinc bar Sunny caught snatches of conversation from the dining room. It seemed as if everyone was talking about Jack Beroni. Each time a waiter or one of the customers encountered someone new, they seemed compelled to establish whether or not the other person had heard the news, and if so, whether every scrap of available information and informed speculation was known. If a reference to *the tragedy, what happened last night,* or *Beroni Vineyards* went unacknowledged, the instigator would say, "You haven't heard?" and then relate in ever increasing detail what had happened.

Sunny plated a row of salads from an enormous aluminum mixing bowl full of dressed baby greens and added a disk of pistachio-crusted goat cheese and a fan of date slivers to each. Like the rest of the town, she couldn't get used to the idea of somebody like Jack being gone all of a sudden. He'd been a fixture in the valley as much as Beroni Vineyards itself. Every party and charitable event had to include an appearance by Jack Beroni in a tuxedo. The man wore a tux more often than most movie stars. Around St. Helena, he was everywhere. She'd see him coming out of the hardware store on Railroad Avenue, having coffee at Bismark's, getting a sandwich at the Oakville Grocery. It wasn't that she knew him well, it was more that he was part of the fauna of the valley, like the quail and the coyotes and the rattlesnakes—creatures she assumed were there and saw occasionally, but who otherwise went about their business well outside the range of her familiarity. "I just can't believe he's dead," she said to Rivka, who was working the grill behind her.

"Not dead," corrected Rivka, "murdered." Before they opened, Rivka had changed into her checked pants and tied a triangle kerchief over her braids. Her ears were generously pierced with tiny silver hoops and posts. On the back of each slender brown biceps was a tattoo of a red and blue swallow, one swooping forward, the other back, which gave the impression of birds circling around her. She stood guard over the grill in her long white apron with tongs poised, watching a collection of husky salmon filets and pork chops sizzle. She repositioned one of the slabs of salmon precisely ninety degrees to the left to complete a neat crosshatch of black grill marks. "I always knew he would mix it up with somebody eventually. He was a troublemaker," said Rivka, putting the accent on *maker*.

"How do you know that? He seemed like an okay guy. Sort of snobby, maybe."

"Just because he's dead doesn't mean I have to start lying about him and saying a lot of phony bullshit. Why do you think so many people hated him? Why did somebody hate him enough to put a bullet through him? Even Alex didn't like him; he said he was a nightmare of a boss."

Sunny was quiet. It seemed disrespectful to talk about Jack that way considering what had happened, even if he had been less than a model citizen.

Rivka said, "I'm just saying that there were plenty of people out there who thought how nice it would feel to put their fingers around that fancy-pants neck of his and give a good squeeze."

"He was just a rich, snobby guy who went to a lot of parties," said Sunny.

Rivka pointed her tongs at her. "Alex says he was a hothead. You couldn't do enough to please him. He was always yelling." She went back to monitoring the grill.

It had been the same all morning. They would work quietly for a while, then return to the shock of Jack's murder, rehashing some new aspect. One of the waiters said there hadn't been a murder in St. Helena in more than four years, nor one involving a man as prominent in the community as Jack Beroni for as long as anybody could remember.

Sunny was having trouble concentrating. She hadn't heard

anyone mention Wade as being involved, but just the talk of murder was unsettling. She was mixing up her third batch of aioli, having ruined two already, when Rivka glanced over at her and asked, "How much of that stuff are you going to make?"

"The usual. Those first two were for practice."

"Right."

In the seven years since cooking school, Sunny had gone from sous-chef at a San Francisco monolith to owner and chef of the tiny, best-kept secret in the Napa Valley. But today she couldn't keep her mind on what she was doing, couldn't even slip into that automatic efficiency that usually took over when she was distracted by ordinary concerns. She watched her hands as if they were someone else's. Without any connection to what she was doing, she assembled plates of roasted duck breast with cranberry chutney, sides of grilled vegetables and Gorgonzola mashed potatoes, and shallow dishes of fettuccine with chanterelles. She dropped dollops of crème fraîche and chives into bowls of butternut squash soup and slipped a wedge of garlic crouton in beside it. She arranged slices of pear tart with vanilla bean ice cream and sent out platters of figs, dates, and tangerines for dessert. When the last espresso had been served and the last check put down, Sunny pulled off her chef's jacket, exhausted.

Rivka said, "Hey, it's Friday. Are we still on for tonight?"

Sunny looked up, stretching her arms. "Yeah. Maybe it will help get things back to normal."

"You want me to bring something?"

"No, I'll get everything from the walk-in. Is Alex coming?"

"He's working late. I'm meeting him after for a drink. What about Monty?"

"He's coming. And Charlie and Wade."

"This from the girl who says she can't get a date. Your house is full of guys every Friday night."

"Yeah, but it's like a Roman senate. Purely platonic." Sunny sat down on the metal stool beside the phone and poured herself a glass of white from an open bottle on the counter. She took a sip to see if it was still okay, then poured a glass for Rivka, who was busy wrapping up cheeses.

"Not so platonic," said Rivka. "I see the way Charlie looks at you. And Wade's been in love with you for about a thousand years."

"That's silly. Wade loves me, but like a friend."

Rivka snorted.

"And Charlie's cute but he's just a whippersnapper," said Sunny. "I couldn't take myself seriously if I was dating somebody twenty-three."

The back door opened and Claire Baker shoved her way in, dragging a hand truck loaded with boxes of produce from Hansen Ranch, the organic farm that supplied most of the fruit, vegetables, and herbs for the restaurant.

"Claire, tell Sunny it's okay to date a younger guy."

Claire shoved the tower of boxes off the hand truck. Petite and athletic-looking, she wore her blond hair pulled back in a shiny ponytail. Her cheeks glowed with the work of hefting boxes and she puffed slightly as she arranged the paperwork on a clipboard and handed it to Sunny. She was dressed in a burgundy fleece pullover and jeans with hiking boots, her usual uniform for making deliveries. A little pink triangle of T-shirt showed at the open neck of the fleece. This sporty look was about as close as Claire ever came to looking like a farmer. She had two kids and she still did her nails and put on a skirt and blouse when she went to the post office. She said, "Who's the guy?"

"There's no guy," said Sunny, perusing the order.

"Charlie Rhodes," said Rivka.

"The pest management guy?"

"He's an entomologist," said Sunny.

"Cute. But young. What is he, twenty-one, twenty-two?" asked Claire.

"Twenty-three," said Sunny.

"Old enough," said Claire, grinning.

Sunny looked in one of the boxes, pulled out a bunch of arugula, and smelled it. She signed the sheet and handed the clipboard back to Claire. "Did that extra celery root make it in there?"

"Ouch, I forgot. You know what, I can drop it off in about an hour. I have to swing back through here anyway. Will you still be around?"

"If I'm not, I'll leave the back door open."

"Perfect."

"It must be great being married," said Rivka to Claire. "You don't have to worry about going out on dates with random guys, and you always have Ben right there at home."

"Yep, I always have Ben right there at home," said Claire with a mischievous smile. She hung the clipboard on the hand truck and wheeled it toward the door, turning to shove her way out and clanging it down the steps behind her.

Rivka raised her eyebrows. "Sounds like somebody needs to get out of the house more often."

Sunny nodded but said nothing.

She was working in her office an hour later when the back door swung open and Ben Baker shouldered his way in, carrying a box of celery root. He was tall and well-built, with the loping gait of the long-limbed, and thick, light-brown hair that curled in big, springy waves across his forehead and around his ears.

"Hey, I thought Claire was going to drop that off," called Sunny without getting up. "I hope it wasn't any trouble."

"No trouble at all," said Ben, setting the box down and poking his head into the office. "It's Baker teamwork in action. Claire's at home trying to figure out a way to stop the deer from eating her herb garden. Last night they ate a whole section of it right down to stubble. I'd hate to be a deer with basil on its breath right now."

"The deer around here will eat anything."

"Too bad they don't eat glassy-winged sharpshooters," he said, walking out the door.

4

At eight o'clock sharp the doorbell rang. From the kitchen, Sunny yelled, "Come in." She heard the front-door bells jangle and a moment later Monty Lenstrom appeared, carrying two bottles of wine and a small paper bag.

"These arrived today from St.-Emilion," he said, lifting the bottles. Sunny was kneading pasta dough at the worktable in the middle of the kitchen. Monty came around so they could exchange a kiss on each cheek. He found the wine opener in a drawer and went to work on one of the bottles. "I hear it's drinking pretty good," he said, winking.

Monty Lenstrom always dressed exactly the same way, regardless of the event. In more than six years of friendship, Sunny had never even seen his legs. He probably didn't own a pair of shorts or a T-shirt. His closet must look like a section of Brooks Brothers, thought Sunny, the one with khakis folded up on shelves and a row of washed denim shirts hanging above it. The other elements of his daily uniform included a TAG Heuer watch, a brown woven leather belt, and matching Timberland loafers. Gold wire-rim glasses sat on top of his nose, sheltering pale eyes. There was a secret about Monty Lenstrom's glasses.

Sunny had discovered it by accident when she was trying to pick out glasses of her own and asked him if she could try his on. He hesitated, then handed them over with a resigned smile. They were plain glass. Monty Lenstrom didn't need glasses at all, he only wore them because he wanted to. It wasn't a fashion statement: He wore them the way some women wear lipstick, as a protective foil between himself and the rest of humanity. It was more than being shy, though that was part of it. Monty's intuitive interaction with his surroundings was olfactory. If most people saw the world, he smelled it. Eye contact was outside his comfort zone.

"What's in the little bag?" asked Sunny.

"Late-harvest blackberries from the patch behind the garage."

"Garage berries. My favorite."

Monty pulled the cork with a satisfying *ponk!* and set the bottle on the counter to air. "What's cookin'?" he said.

"Roast chicken with potatoes and carrots, fettuccine with chanterelles and cream, asparagus, and what's left of a pear tart for dessert."

Sunny's shoulders flexed with effort as she worked the heavy round of pasta dough in her hands, throwing her weight into it. She was stronger than she looked. Years of hefting heavy pots and working ingredients had given her strong, wiry arms. She could feel perspiration moistening her forehead.

Monty poured her a glass of wine and slid it in her direction. "I assume you heard all about Jack Beroni."

"I did. I still can't believe it."

Monty ticked his glass against hers still on the table and sipped. The deep ruby red caught the overhead light and threw off a glow like stained glass. He said, "I can't believe you're making fresh pasta. Have I mentioned lately how much I love you?" He quivered his lip Elvis style.

"That's just the fettuccine talking," said Sunny.

"Maybe, but that doesn't make it any less real, does it?"

"Yes, I think it does."

He leaned toward her, an intense, earnest look on his face. "Listen, the way I see it, we get out of this place. Who ever heard of making any kind of life in a place like this, anyway? It's nothing but grapes, for God's sake. We'd go somewhere nice. Maybe buy a secondhand trailer, a double-wide, or get ourselves a yurt, and set it up outside of town, by a river. I'd sit outside in a lawn chair and watch the sunset while you cooked. You could cook dinner for me every day for the rest of our natural lives. What do you say?"

"Jeez, Monty, that sounds pretty great, all right," said Sunny, breaking into a laugh. "But wouldn't your girlfriend mind?"

"Annabelle? She'd get over it. We're not actually that close."

"You've been living together for three years."

"Three brief, inconsequential years. She's more of a friend. I'm telling you, McCoskey, you're letting a good one get away. This kind of offer won't last forever."

"Duly noted," said Sunny with a smile, thumping the dough against the table and sending up a puff of flour. The fact was, this dinner was more involved than it needed to be. She could have served regular pasta out of a box and thrown together a green salad, but she'd plunged into the activity of cooking right after she got home. She needed a distraction from the day's events. "Speaking of that woman you hardly know, where is Annabelle tonight?"

"Book club." Monty made quotation marks in the air. "What those women do in the name of literature. It gives reading a bad name."

The doorbell rang again and Monty went to open it. Sunny heard him greeting Charlie Rhodes in the living room and soon the two of them came in, Monty scrutinizing the label of the bottle of wine Charlie had brought, and Charlie looking brown and ruddy with sun. Handsome boy, thought Sunny. He was wearing a new T-shirt, a turquoise blue one that still had the folding seams along the top of the sleeves.

Monty took down another glass and poured, holding the wine bottle by the punt and the glass by the foot like a sommelier. Charlie took the glass. He was listening to Monty chatter about tannins and maceration, but his attention turned to the glass long enough to look, smell, and taste at least that first sip. It always interested Sunny to see how a person reacted to a glass of wine or a new food. It was a one-second preview of how they would act when faced with the unpredictable, a snapshot of how they approached experience. Some people were hardly aware they had a glass in their hand, and the wine in it would be gone before they realized they were drinking. Charlie wasn't a connoisseur and didn't pretend to be one, but he was clearly interested enough to want to stop and taste what he was drinking. Meanwhile, Monty was explaining why the rocky soil in St.-Emilion, France, was superior to the rocky soil anywhere else in the world, and why this particular wine displayed its qualities better than most.

Charlie told them how he'd spent the afternoon riding his mountain bike around the Stag's Leap district, checking insect traps. Monty asked about the condition of the vines. Charlie said the harvest was going well; it looked like all of the Chardonnay and Sauvignon Blanc was in already, as well as some of the Pinot Noir, Cabernet Sauvignon, and Zinfandel growing low.

"I haven't had a look lately, but I assume the stuff up in the hills is getting close, too," Charlie said.

The doorbell rang again. This time it was Wade, who walked in looking haggard and unshaven. He's worried, thought Sunny. Still, she could tell by the waft of soap when he kissed her that he'd showered before coming over and had put on his best shirt, a wrinkled gray linen button-down with the sleeves rolled up, a gift from his last girlfriend. He clicked on the light in the oven to see what was roasting, inspected the mushroom sauce simmering on the stove, and stared in awe at the silver pasta crank clamped to the table where Sunny was twisting pasta dough into long strands. "Wow, is it my birthday? You're making all my favorites."

"It's Wade Skord Appreciation Day," said Sunny, smiling. "We've declared a new international holiday. From now on, children will look forward to Wade Day every September, when they get to eat all the noodles, wild mushrooms, and garlic chicken they can hold."

"It's about time," said Wade. "I've been lobbying for Wade Day for years."

Monty Lenstrom handed him a glass of the St.-Emilion. "How's the fruit?"

"Impeccable, as always," said Wade, extracting a bunch of deep-purple grapes from a knotted kerchief and depositing them on the table. "Taste for yourself."

Sunny rinsed her hands and came over. They'd been waiting for exactly the right moment to harvest. Today had been warm and the fruit would have ripened a good deal in just a few hours. At this time of year, what locals called crush, Wade took samples from each quadrant every few hours while the sun was out. He had to be ready. If he let the grapes get too sweet by staying on the vine, there would be too much alcohol in the wine, and if they weren't ripe enough, the wine would lack flavor. Monty plucked a grape and examined it as if it were a diamond, holding it up to the light. Sunny took a handful and squeezed them gently, inhaling the fragrance they released. She crushed one between her thumb and forefinger, scrutinized the color of the skin, juice, and seed, then popped the whole handful into her mouth and chewed carefully, running the juice over her tongue. The rich, fruity sweetness with a hint of plum and cherry was delicious. "They're close," she said, spitting several seeds into her palm. They were still slightly green. When they were completely ripe, the seeds would be nut-brown and oaky-tasting.

"Getting there," said Wade. "Depends on how hot it gets tomorrow. They say it's going to cool off again. If that happens, we'll have to wait."

"Have you thought any more, or any differently I should say, about taking on that extra Zin from Deer Park?" asked Monty.

"I'm not interested. I'm just going to keep it simple for a while. I don't need any new headaches."

"Simple and small," said Monty.

"Small is beautiful," said Wade.

"If you won't expand your Zin production, why not team up with somebody growing Cab and see what you can do with it in a partnership? I'd love to taste a Skord Mountain Cabernet Sauvignon," said Monty.

"I'd still have to hire people, expand the winery. And I'd lose control of the quality. The way I'm doing things right now suits me just fine."

"But imagine if you teamed up with one of the better growers up my way, for example. Somebody on Mount Veeder who really knows what they're doing. They do all the work, you just come in and tell them what you like and what you don't like. The Cabernet up there is getting better every year. That land is starting to talk and it has some very interesting things to say."

Wade shook his head. "I'm too much of a control freak. I couldn't have somebody else making my wine."

Monty had been trying unsuccessfully to get Wade to produce more wine for years. As it was, Skord Mountain Zinfandel was almost always sold out in futures; the entire supply, other than what Wade kept around for friends, was sold a couple of years in advance. Monty had a contract for a good portion of it, but he always said he could sell as much wine as Wade could make, which wasn't much.

Sunny cranked the last of the dough through the pasta machine and folded the noodles into a pot of boiling water.

"You should have seen this guy I had in today," said Monty. "He's opening a restaurant in Chicago and he heard about Skord Zin. I told him if he wanted anything under four hundred dollars a bottle retail, he'd have to go with a recent vintage, and you know what that means."

"His tongue's about to get run over by the Skord Express," said Sunny.

"I told him, 'Here's what you do. You buy a few cases of something recent enough to be affordable and you sit on them. Then in a few years you put them on your list for what they're worth, which will be a lot.' But of course he can't wait, he doesn't know if his restaurant is going to fly or not, so I open last year's release for him to taste."

"And?" said Wade.

"Tasted like an unbathed raccoon got loose in a blackberry patch," said Monty.

"My finest work," said Wade. "If drinking my wine was easy, everyone would do it."

The bells on the front door jangled loudly and Rivka walked in, looking ready for a big date. She'd let her hair down and it fell in a long sweep to the middle of her back, slightly wavy from being braided. She was wearing a dress that showed off the golden skin of her shoulders when she slipped out of her jacket. She looked at Monty and took a deep breath. "Isn't it awful about Jack Beroni?"

"Unbelievable," said Monty. "I'm still in shock."

For some reason Sunny had hoped to avoid this conversation. She would feel much more like talking about Jack Beroni once the ballistics tests on Wade's rifle had cleared him of all suspicion.

"What about Jack Beroni?" said Charlie.

"You haven't heard?" said Rivka. "How could you not have heard?"

Rivka recounted the story, beginning with how Silvano Cruz had found the body. She included all the details she'd collected throughout the day, Alex helping to carry the body to the ambulance, Al and Louisa Beroni's stunned anguish. She paused to push a strand of hair back over her shoulder. "The cops even came to question Sunny."

From the oven, where she had just bent down to stick a fork in the roast chicken, Sunny looked back at the faces staring at her. The smell of garlic and rosemary filled the kitchen. "They did not come to *question* me. Steve Harvey stopped by to find out if I saw anything suspicious last night when I left Wade's house." Phrasing things properly helped keep events in the right perspective; she certainly didn't want things to get any more out of control than they already were.

"What time did you leave?" asked Monty.

"Way before it happened. Around seven," said Sunny.

A cell phone started ringing and Rivka groped in her handbag.

Monty scowled. "Turn it off! This is a no-phone zone!"

"All right, fine," said Rivka, killing it and dropping it back in her bag. "Feeling a bit edgy?"

"I just liked life better before we all had to carry mobile tracking devices."

"Do they have any idea who did it?" Charlie asked Sunny.

"Nothing yet. They have the bullet and the body but no weapon and not much to go on, as far as I can tell." She pulled the heavy crockery dish out of the oven. "Everyone to table, we're on. Monty, take that plate for me? Wade, if you'll bring the pasta."

The large wooden table occupied much of one half of the cozy living room, which was painted a warm shade of golden yellow. Sunny put the chicken down and moved a rusted iron candelabra to the middle of the table, straightened the tall candles, and lit them. The other half of the room held a small couch—formerly the love seat to her mother's living-room set—a leather chair as weathered as an old tree stump, a coffee table made out of industrial ceramic chimney blocks with a sheet of glass on top, and an Art Nouveau–style torchier with a tulip-shaped shade. A painting of pears on a blue plate hung over a small brick fireplace. The guests took their seats on the hodgepodge of wooden chairs. Platters were passed, wine poured, glasses ticked.

Wade loaded his plate with pasta. "How goes the war on bugs?" he said to Charlie, who was carving a leg off the roast chicken.

"It's going pretty well." Charlie speared a potato and a couple sections of carrot. "Nothing so far, at least in the sharpshooter department. No news is good news."

"I missed the last ag board meeting. Are they still planning to poison us when the new leafhopper comes to town?" Wade asked.

"Possibly. I'd say the meeting went pretty well if you're in pesticide sales and application. Profits are likely to be way up. They talked about a full-force mandatory application of carbaryl across the county as soon as there's a sharpshooter on the radar."

"I thought we talked them out of that last time," said Wade.

"The big guys are still pushing for it pretty hard."

"Well, at least one of them won't be pushing for it anymore," said Wade.

"Yeah, I guess not," said Charlie.

"You mean Jack?" asked Rivka.

"He was a big proponent of broadcast pesticide application," said Wade. "Very persuasive in front of the ag board. Beroni and two or three of the other big wineries basically pay their salaries and then some, so the board listens. The program they're pushing would mean door-to-door nerve poison delivery, residential included. They'd spray every yard, garden, farm, and park, in addition to all the vineyards. It's amazing that there hasn't been more of a protest about it. People around here seem to be okay with the idea of having their homes dipped in nerve poison so that the big wineries can stay in business."

"People don't think it's a real threat. I mean, I don't actually believe that the county would try to spray my place," said Monty.

"Believe it. They did it in Sacramento and Fresno already. And it didn't do a damn bit of good, by the way. The bug is as entrenched there as it ever was. Did anybody bring that up at this last meeting?"

"Ben Baker did," said Charlie. "Then the spray lobby pointed out that Fresno and Sacramento didn't get to it in time and that's why it didn't work. It actually strengthened the argument to do it at the very first sign of infestation."

Wade looked incredulous. "That's great. So some guy dressed like an astronaut in a biosuit is going to pull up with a tanker truck of nerve poison, knock on your door, and say, 'Throw a tarp over the dog because your yard is about to be doused.' It amazes me they're even considering it. We're not talking about a threat to the general public here. This is not an outbreak of West Nile Virus. This is a little leafhopper that just happens to spread a disease that just happens to kill grapevines and not much else."

"Even the Beronis won't get that through around here," said Rivka.

"I wish you were right," said Wade. "But don't forget that very big money is at stake. Every wine-related job in the valley is on the line. We've got the bumblebees and the ladybugs on one side and a six-billion-dollar wine industry on the other. I can take a pretty good guess at who is going to win that argument."

They were quiet and Wade went back to his plate, hunching over it and stacking his fork with chicken, pasta, and potatoes.

Charlie spoke. "The big wineries are scared. They saw what happened in Southern California and they know the glassy-winged sharpshooter could be the end of them. I was down in Orange County last week and it's pretty spooky stuff. They treated some of the vines that are still alive down there with white kaolin clay, trying to save them. Frankly, it hasn't worked and it does almost as much damage as Pierce's disease because it impedes photosynthesis and you get a lot of defoliation. But at this stage, it's their only hope." He looked at Wade. "Imagine your entire vineyard covered in white chalk. It looks like a ghost world."

Wade chewed and swallowed. "Better that than carbaryl. That stuff goes everywhere. Drifts half a mile from where they spray it, sinks into the soil and the water, gets taken up in the roots of every bush, tree, and blade of grass. Kills the bees and all the other beneficials. It's bad stuff, I don't care what they say about how it's as safe as chewing gum. That said, Pierce's disease will wipe me off the map. There is probably a place for pesticides in this fight, but not at the first sighting and not the whole valley."

"The county needs to put their energy into inspecting the incoming plants," said Monty. "It seems like the most logical approach is to keep the bug out in the first place. If they can keep the garden suppliers from delivering the sharpshooter right to our door, Charlie's friends up in Davis might have enough time to cook up a solution. The Department of Viticulture and Enology has saved our butts before. Give them time and they'll engineer a vine that's resistant to Pierce's disease or has a sharpshooter repelling gene in it. They're already planning to release a wasp that eats glassies in the meantime, right?"

"It's not quite ready yet," said Charlie, sounding cautious. "You never really know the ramifications of releasing a new predator into an ecosystem. *Gonatocerus triguttatus* didn't seem to cause any problems in Florida and Texas, but the researchers need to take a closer look to be sure. And they're going to need time to test it locally, release it in a controlled area and watch what happens. Plus there's more than one wasp option, so they'll want to look at which one will have the least impact on the environment. There's one kind of parasitic wasp, for example, that paralyzes the sharpshooter, then buries it and lays its eggs on top of it. When the baby wasps hatch, sharpshooter breakfast is waiting for them. That's okay. Then there's the other tiny one, the GT they're using down in Florida and Texas, that's a little guy about the size of a grain of polenta, that lays eggs inside the sharpshooter's eggs. When they hatch, they eat their way out."

"Ugh," said Rivka. "The sharpshooters alone are bad enough. They're so ugly. But I hate wasps."

"Better to have wasp babies eating sharpshooters than sharpshooters eating grapes," said Wade.

"And the viticulture and enology people are going to need years to get anything genetically engineered to market," said Charlie. "That's not really an option for a long time. Like a decade or so."

There was a pause in the conversation as people concentrated on eating and drinking. Sunny kept looking over at Wade to see how he was doing. She was trying to convince herself that there was nothing to worry about, but the look on his face wasn't helping. He was eating, but he seemed worried, and a few times when she looked over he seemed lost in some unpleasant thought. Yet it was perfectly reasonable for the police to question Wade. After all, he was the Beronis' closest neighbor. It was also perfectly reasonable for them to question her, since she was with Wade on the night of the murder. He probably wasn't even a suspect. Probably they were just covering their bases. She pointed her fork at Monty. "Lenstrom, you know everybody who's ever set foot in this valley. Who do you think killed Jack Beroni?"

"Who says it was someone in the valley? It was probably a random psychopath on his way through town," Monty replied.

Sunny shook her head. "No, it's gotta be a local. Who else is even going to find that gazebo way out there in the sticks, let alone in the middle of the night with Jack standing in it. I say it was somebody from the valley, somebody he knew, maybe even somebody he agreed to meet out there in the gazebo. Think about it. Who'd stand to gain from his death?"

It was the question they'd been avoiding all night, or at least some of them had. Now that it was on the table, Monty was taking it seriously, judging by his expression, which resembled that of an oracle priest mulling over a question of state. He put down his knife and fork and ran his fingers over his shaved head thoughtfully. He'd developed the habit of smoothing his fingers over his scalp when he was perplexed, perhaps because he'd recently switched from keeping what was left of his hair very short to shaving it entirely. Rivka poked at a puddle of wax developing under one of the candles.

"Plenty of people disliked Jack," said Monty slowly, as though delivering an impromptu eulogy. "I didn't particularly like him, but of course I didn't hate him, and I certainly never thought of killing him. He was simply not pleasant to know. He was born to privilege, and he used that privilege in the most self-aggrandizing manner. He was Napa royalty, and he was unapologetic and even arrogant about what that entitled him to. He was handsome, intelligent, rich, and poised, but he was not a gentleman, and he didn't even go to the trouble to behave badly enough to be a scandal, which might have been interesting to watch at least. He was intimidating and generally considered to be dishonest. Where his father was shrewd, he was conniving. Where Al was tough, he was mean."

"To the point, please," said Rivka, striking a match and lighting a cigarette.

"The point is, Madam Smoker, that I could make a list of at least twenty people who had good reason to put a few pins in their Jack Beroni voodoo dolls, ranging from insult to injury to underhanded business practices, but I can't imagine any of them killing him."

"That's almost exactly what Steve Harvey said today," said Sunny. "But of course it did happen, so somebody is capable of more than we think they are. I never knew everyone hated him so much in the first place." She motioned to Rivka, who handed over the cigarette. Sunny took one drag. She didn't allow herself whole cigarettes anymore, just one puff now and then after dinner.

"Not hate, more like quietly but persistently loathe," said Monty, "and not everyone."

"What about his sexy girlfriend?" said Rivka.

"Larissa? Why would she want Jack dead?" said Monty.

"From what I've heard, he wasn't exactly faithful to her. And he dated her for five years without asking her to marry him."

"I truly hope that is not justification for murder," said Monty.

"If she was desperately in love with him and he kept yanking her chain," Rivka said, "it could be if it went on long enough. At the wine auction last year, he put his hand on my backside like he owned it. This was while Larissa was standing about ten feet away."

"And?" said Monty, smirking.

"Don't give me trouble, Lenstrom. You know you can't handle me."

"Napa's most eligible bachelor comes on to you and you didn't respond?" said Monty.

"I don't date other women's boyfriends. And he wasn't my type. Too pretty and too sleazy. I like a boy with dirty hands and a clean heart."

"I have the dirty hands at least," said Monty.

"I meant dirty from working outside," said Rivka.

"Oh," said Monty. "The construction worker complex again. It's pervasive. When are you girls going to get over the he-man thing?"

"It just shows that you never really know the whole story about a person," said Charlie. "You think you do, but then there's all this behind-the-back stuff going on."

Rivka gave him a look and stabbed into the roast chicken on her plate, spearing a bite.

Charlie stopped and blushed slightly when he realized the double entendre. "I mean, he seemed honest and straightforward, but maybe he forgot to pay somebody, maybe he got in somebody's way."

"I don't know about that," said Monty. "The Beronis have always been thoroughly legitimate. They maintain plenty of influence up in Sacramento, but they don't have the criminal ties like some of the old families did before the corporate wave came in, back in the eighties. The Beronis make overpriced, mediocre wine and throw big fancy parties and that's about it, as far as I can tell."

"It wouldn't have to be the Mafia," said Charlie. "It could be anything. Drugs, gambling, the wrong kind of friends."

"This is all speculation," said Sunny. "The truth is, we have no idea what happened and probably never will. Somebody shot him and walked away."

Monty spent some time aligning an errant spear of asparagus with the others on his plate. "It's terrible," he said, "but my first thought when I heard about the murder wasn't sympathy for Larissa or Al and Louisa. My first thought, I'm ashamed to admit, was that Beroni Vineyards had lost its heir. Jack was Al and Louisa's only child, and he wasn't married and didn't have any kids. The only other family is Ripley Marlow, and she's a cousin through Al's mother, so she's not even a Beroni. There may be other cousins or distant relations somewhere, but I've never heard of them. I can't even imagine what Beroni is worth, and now there is nobody to inherit it, no one to take over running it when Al retires, which I'm sure he was hoping to do soon."

"You bet," said Wade. "This could be the end of Beroni Vineyards, at least as a family business."

They went on talking about the murder for some time after dinner, compulsively driven to recount where they had been when they heard the news and what their first response had been. It was as if repetition of the details would lead to some understanding, or to a way to make the events more real. When they'd finished eating, Sunny pulled the cork on a slender bottle of Sauternes *Botrytis cinerea* Sémillon, a gift from Monty, and served slivers of the pear tart she'd brought home from the restaurant. The cool, deliciously sweet flavors of the wine almost made them forget their curiosity about Jack Beroni's death.

Later, sitting on the couch, Sunny recognized the signs of being very tired. She felt suddenly slow and heavy, like someone had turned up the pull of gravity. She stared at Charlie Rhodes's wide, tan hands. She thought that after everyone left she would soak in the bathtub and then sleep late into the morning. When she woke up, she would call Steve Harvey, get the results of the ballistics report, feel tremendous relief, and go over to Wade's place to celebrate. After that, as sad an event as it was, Jack Beroni's death would not be her concern anymore and she would forget about it. Life would go back to normal.

She realized she hadn't heard anything that had been said for several minutes. Monty and Wade were talking about who they could recruit to help with the harvest at Skord Mountain, and Rivka was giving a capsule version of the action flick she and Alex had seen the night before. After a while, Rivka and Monty got up to do the dishes, telling Sunny not to even think about trying to help. Wade sat in the big comfortable chair quietly.

Sunny sat up and looked at Charlie. "The county wouldn't really go around spraying people's yards, would they? I mean, there's been talk about it, but they won't actually do it, will they?"

"They might. The question is when and how wide a sweep. You've got to understand that this is a genuine threat to the entire industry. These aren't the blue-green sharpshooters that hang out by the creeks and nibble a leaf now and then. These guys are voracious, highly mobile, and extremely active reproductively. There's an entomologist over at the Department of Food and Agriculture who says that if a glassy-winged sharpshooter was as big as a person, it would drink forty-three hundred gallons of sap a day. I'm sure you could say something equally shocking about their reproductive capacities. Even if they didn't spread Pierce's disease, they'd present a serious problem just based on the damage they do once a certain population is established. Basically the blue-greens suck a whole lot less," he said with a lopsided smile.

The three of them stared at the candles burning, sleepy and lost in their own thoughts. Rivka and Monty emerged from the kitchen with coffee and cups. "I wouldn't be surprised if one of the employees at Beroni did it," said Rivka. "Alex says Jack was a tyrant at work and everybody had it in for him."

"It doesn't look like a work-related meltdown to me," said Monty, sinking into the couch beside Sunny. "The guys who do that always show up midmorning after they've tanked up on four or five quadruple vanilla lattes and go on a public rampage. And they always take themselves out afterward. They don't want to get away with it, they want the drama. They want the guys they hate to know who did it, to see how mad they are. The guy who goes postal wants everyone to see how powerful and revengeful he can be. He wants to be on the evening news."

"This isn't somebody going postal, but it could still be work related. It could be somebody who'd had enough and decided to finally get even," said Sunny.

Rivka poured half an inch of cream in her coffee and drank it fast. She looked at her watch. "I better get going. I'm meeting Alex for a drink."

Monty yawned and Charlie stood up. It wasn't long before Sunny closed the door after all three of them. She went back to the couch, put her feet up on the coffee table, and looked at Wade, the only one left. "Do you want to watch a movie?" she asked.

"Did you get a television?"

"No. I just wondered if you wanted to," she said, smiling at him.

"You are insane."

"What's up? You've been preoccupied all night. Is it this business with Steve Harvey?"

"You could say that." He leaned in and poured himself more coffee, then went to the kitchen and returned with a bottle of bourbon. "This coffee needs a little something. Fix you up?" he asked, raising the bottle.

Sunny shook her head.

Wade settled back into the leather chair. "After you called, I thought about it and decided you were right. The best thing to do was take the bull by the horns and just give them the gun. I figured they'd be back for it before long, anyway."

"Is that what Harry suggested?" asked Sunny.

"I didn't get to talk to Harry. I left him a message but he hasn't called back."

Sunny kept quiet despite the urge to pepper him with questions.

"I got nervous just waiting around," said Wade. "So I went down to the winery to get the gun. I was going to call Steve and ask him if he wanted to pick it up or if I should bring it in."

"And?"

"Well, it wasn't there."

"Your rifle was gone?"

"My rifle was gone."

"Are you sure? Maybe you left it out."

"I'm sure. I looked everywhere, all over inside the winery and in the workshop. I looked everywhere in the house. I've kept that gun in the same place for at least six years. You know where I always put it, behind the fermentation tank in the corner. You wouldn't see it if you didn't know to look behind the tank. Even then, you can't really see it. You have to feel around."

"Maybe you put it back somewhere else this time."

"I may be pushing fifty, but I don't think I've lost it completely yet. I know where I put that gun."

"You're pushing sixty and you don't have to lose it to misplace something. You know how it is. I've found things that I put away in odd places before. It's late, you're tired, distracted by the harvest, maybe you just put it down somewhere and forgot about it. Maybe you even put it somewhere totally different, like in a closet."

"No, I'm always careful. I have a system. I always clean it on the first Monday night of the month. Then I put it back in the case with the safety on, in exactly the same place, a place where I didn't think a thief would find it. I shot that gun last night at nine o'clock. Twice. I put the safety on, zipped it back into the case, and put it where I always keep it. I put the spent casings in the garbage and the extra cartridges back in the box. I always do it exactly the same way. Today when I went to get it, it wasn't there." He scrubbed at his hair until it stood on end. "Sunny, do you know what this means? Well, I guess you and I both know." He tapped a weathered finger on his knee. "Somebody knows where I keep my gun, somebody who has been to my house."

He didn't finish. Sunny was suddenly acutely aware of the picture window in the living room, a massive rectangle of black from the inside, a lighted portrait of her and Wade from the outside. Maybe the killer was watching them right now. "Let's not panic and jump to conclusions," she said.

"I'm not panicking, but the conclusion is fairly obvious."

"Unless you misplaced it."

"Unless I misplaced it, which I didn't."

"I think we should forget about it for tonight. I don't see what we can do about this right now. I know I'm exhausted and I have a feeling you are, too. I think you should stay here. I'll make up the couch and in the morning we'll go over there and find it together in the daylight with our rested eyes. It will be there."

Wade shook his head. "That's kind of you, Sunny, but I'll head home. I've never been afraid of the dark and I'm certainly not going to start now."

Hours after Wade had left, Sunny lay awake in bed. Her old clock radio read 3:13. It was a dingy relic, but she loved to watch the paddles with the numbers on them slap into place. She stared until the tiny card with the four on it flipped over the three in thirteen with a satisfying smack, then she counted slowly to ten six times, feeling the obsessive's kick of pleasure when the five came up and over the four exactly as she finished. She did this until 3:19 and then made herself stop. Wade had put the gun back exactly where he said he did, she knew that. They would not find it mislaid around the house or put away somewhere in the workshop. He might not be fastidious about his appearance or his housekeeping, but when it came to equipment of any sort, he maintained the strictest standards. Wade thrived on ritual and accuracy; that was what drew him to shooting in the first place. Who stole Wade Skord's rifle? How did they know where to find it? Where was it now? Had it been used to kill Jack Beroni, or could there be some other explanation?

She threw off the covers and got up. Out in the kitchen, the floor was cool on her bare feet. The house was pleasantly quiet. She needed to sleep so that she would be clear-headed tomorrow. She would make Catelina's cure. It was designed for a cold, but worked just as well for a restless mind in the middle of the night. She poured half a cup of red wine in a saucepan, sliced an orange and squeezed the juice in, and turned the heat on low. When it was warm, she added a tablespoon of honey and one clove.

Sunny pulled the drapes in the living room across the picture window and bolted the door. When was the last time she had done that? It was just a precaution, she thought, not fear. This house is the safest place in the world. St. Helena is the safest place in the world. She curled up in the leather chair and wrapped her hands around the cup of hot wine.

Someone had removed Wade's rifle from its hiding place; that was all she was ready to accept as fact right now. From there, there were two reasonable possibilities: Either the murderer removed the gun, or someone else did. If the murderer removed it, he or she had one of two possible intentions: either to use the gun to commit the murder—maybe to implicate Wade, maybe just to use a stolen gun—or to make it appear that the gun had been used to commit the murder. If someone other than the murderer had stolen the gun, the timing of the theft could just be a coincidence and have nothing to do with the murder. This scenario she ruled out; it was based on too much coincidence. Then if someone other than the murderer stole the gun, they must have both known about the murder *and* wanted to make Wade appear guilty.

This logical process was not helping Sunny get sleepy.

If the thief was not the killer, the thief must have discovered the murder very soon after it happened and quietly put into place the plan to frame Wade. Unlikely. Or must have been aware of the murderer's intentions and therefore had time to plan to frame Wade. That would mean two people were involved, working together. Possible.

She stared into the cup of wine.

Okay, focus on who would want to make Wade appear guilty. Aside from the desire to do it, the thief would need the knowledge of where the gun was kept. She agreed with Wade that it would not have been found by accident. Whoever took it had watched Wade take it out or put it away. That limited the range of suspects dramatically. Wade had friends, but not dozens of them. He had acquaintances, and certainly hundreds of people had visited the winery to help with harvest, crush, and bottling, but there wouldn't have been any Assault Golf on those occasions. Assault Golf was the only time he used the rifle, and it was strictly a two- to four-person game played only with close friends, as far as she knew. She would check with Wade about that. They needed to review every time he had used that gun with anyone around. She'd help him make a list, but the list would not be long. No, she had to face what was most likely the truth: Whoever stole Wade's gun was probably part of the Skord Mountain extended family, somebody who ate with him, drank his wine, helped harvest grapes, and played Assault Golf after all the others had gone home. It had to be one of ten or so close friends.

Sunny tried to stop thinking. She sipped the hot wine and felt it go all the way down. A wave of relaxation came over her despite her flickering thoughts. She made her way back to bed and promptly fell into a deep, sound sleep.

It took several rings before she understood that the sound was the telephone, and a couple more rings before she realized that she should get up and go answer it. She shuffled out of the darkness of the bedroom into the kitchen, where a strong late-morning sun shone through the window. She picked up the receiver, struggling to pull herself out of the underworld of sleep. It was Wade. She looked at the clock. Close to eleven.

"Sorry to wake you. You're sleeping late."

"Yeah, I guess so."

"Listen, Sun, I'm in town, down at the police station. Steve Harvey and another officer came by this morning with a search warrant for the rifle. When they found out I didn't have it, they arrested me."

Sunny was instantly awake. "Wade, are you in jail?"

"Yeah, I guess you could say that."

"Okay. Okay. Are you okay?"

"I'm fine. I'm worried, and I'm in jail, but I'm fine."

"Okay. This is getting sort of serious. We need to get organized. What can I do?"

She was glad he didn't waste time hedging or apologizing for putting her out. They made a list. Take care of Farber the cat. That was easy enough, he was mostly wild anyway. Bring down a toothbrush and other toiletries. Call Harry and make sure he has everything he needs to get the legal aspects moving. Take a Brix reading from every other section of the vineyard as often as possible, ideally every four hours. Brix was the measurement of the sugar content in the grapes. If it looked like a section was going to get close to twenty-four degrees Brix within a day, Wade wanted her to let him know as soon as possible.

"From what I can tell, it's going to be a little cooler today. If that's the case, we're probably good for another day or two. Assuming I can get out of here on bail, we can harvest on Tuesday or Wednesday."

"I can take care of all that, but we need to focus on what's really important. We need to find that gun," said Sunny.

"This is one hell of a time to be sitting in jail," said Wade irritably. "I've got twenty-eight tons of grapes just about to turn into either wine or raisins, and I'm doing yoga in a six-by-eight cell."

"Wade, are you being funny? This is not funny."

"I'm in denial, Sun. And I am doing yoga. What else am I supposed to do in here?"

"I don't mean to be a downer, but you do realize what this all means."

He was quiet and she was sorry she'd said it. Of course he knew what this meant, he was in jail on suspicion of murder. When he spoke his voice was low and serious. He said, "Sunny, go find that gun and get me the heck out of here." It was more prayer than request.

"Don't worry. I'll find it," she said, and set the receiver back in the cradle. The sun warmed her back as she stood staring at the telephone.

In the shower, it occurred to her that from now on, the police would be more interested in proving that Wade Skord was guilty than that he was innocent. If that gun wasn't simply misplaced, it would be up to her to prove that Wade didn't kill Jack Beroni, and to do that she'd have to find out who did. She stood directly under the shower, letting the warm water hit the top of her head. A disturbing sensation, almost a tickle at the back of her mind, interrupted her thoughts. Was there any possibility, under any circumstances, that Wade had actually done it?

5

Wade's scrawny old arthritic cat, Farber, scampered up a tree and heaved himself stiffly onto the roof of the house when Sunny pulled up. She found the key under a potted rosemary and let herself in. The house was quiet. Only two days earlier it had felt like her second home, now it was filled with troubling, unanswerable questions. She shook dry cat food into a bowl and set it on the deck, then quickly gathered the few personal items Wade had asked her to bring, stuffing them into a day pack she found hanging behind the door. She tossed the pack into the truck and walked down to the winery.

It was a perfect early-fall day, bright and fresh, especially on top of Howell Mountain. Catelina's recipe had certainly worked; she hadn't felt so rested in weeks, and the world looked vibrant and solid again, like when she was a kid. She cut through the yellowed grass to the old barn that Wade had converted into his winemaking facilities. Using one carefully placed finger, she slid the winery door open and slipped inside, noting that she needed to ask Steve Harvey if they had fingerprinted that handle. The air smelled dusty and sweet like any old barn, and at the same time sour and boozy like all wineries. During fermentation the funky smells of yeast and sulfur would be incredibly strong, and afterward, when the new wine had been transferred to barrels for aging, the place would reek like a fraternity house after a big party.

She waited for her eyes to adjust to the lack of light. Barrels were stacked several rows deep against one wall and two eight-foot-tall fermentation tanks stood against the other. She checked the narrow space behind the furthest tank, where Wade's rifle had always been kept. It wasn't there. She went down to the cellar, where the wine aged for a year or two once it was bottled. She poked around the storage room packed with pumps and hoses. She climbed a ladder made of rope and two-by-fours to peer into what used to be the hayloft. The rifle was nowhere. Half an hour later she emerged from the winery, beat the dust off her jeans and sleeves, and headed back to the house empty-handed.

Wade's place was rustic verging on Spartan, more cabin than house, and didn't take long to search, especially for something as big as the .22 Hornet. The gun wasn't anywhere visible, and neither was the box of shells Wade said he kept in the closet, nor the two spent cartridges he'd put in the garbage. Probably the cops took that stuff, thought Sunny. The gun also wasn't in the sparse workshop Wade had built out back. His tools hung neatly from their hooks and the workbench was tidy. The storage room held only the predictable supply of fertilizers, wheelbarrows, defunct wine barrels, cover crop seed, coffee cans full of nails and screws, and salvaged scraps of lumber from various projects. By twelve-thirty she'd given up on finding the Hornet anywhere logical. That left just the illogical places, those millions of unknowable places an object can get to without explanation.

In the workshop, she picked up Wade's collection kit, an old wooden painter's box with a handle on top and labeled cubby-holes for samples. On her way out she stopped to grab a small harvester's knife with a serrated blade shaped like a half-moon, and reached for the old red gardening gloves that always lay on the shelf by the door, but they weren't there. She hunted for them briefly, then headed out into the vineyard, gathering fruit samples from each of the eight sections of the vineyard. When she got back she cleaned the refractometer, sorted and squeezed the juice from the grapes, and measured each sample, holding the device up to the light to take a reading. Light bounced off the sugar molecules in the juice at a different angle than it bounced off the water molecules, producing a fairly accurate reading of sugar content. She pulled a photocopied recording sheet from a stack on the makeshift desk and noted each reading. Most of the grapes were at seventeen degrees Brix, which meant they could be ready to harvest after the next warm day or two, maybe three if it stayed mild, and would probably be overripe by the end of the week. She folded the paper and tucked it in her pocket.

Near the end of town, the St. Helena police station crouched low and flat at the side of the park like a fugitive, its wide eaves warped and drooping at the edges, and the stucco walls streaked with rust. Inside, two hefty women in uniform sorted and stapled paperwork behind a sliding glass window, like receptionists at a doctor's office. Sunny stated her business and waited. Twenty minutes later, a female cop waved her through a doorway and into the visiting room. Wade came in wearing an orange jumpsuit. She felt a surge of tears at the sight of him.

He sat down in a metal folding chair on the other side of a wall of glass. "Hey, sis."

"Hi. I brought your stuff. They said they'd give it to you."

"Great."

"How are you holding up?"

"Okay, all things considered. Did you talk to Harry?"

"Yeah. He's working on everything. He said he won't know if we can get you out on bail until tomorrow or maybe Monday, depending on when you get to see the judge. He said you'll probably have to put up the vineyard."

He nodded and Sunny went on. "I tested the Brix and fed Farber." She took the paper out of her pocket and pressed it against the glass between them.

Wade studied it. "Looks like we might need to harvest on Tuesday or Wednesday. If I can't be there, you might have to make some phone calls for me, see who we can get to help. I guess we can talk about that once we know about the arraignment."

"Right."

After a minute, Wade said, "I guess you didn't find anything."

She shook her head and sighed. "I'm not through looking yet, but I went over the winery, the house, and the workshop pretty carefully. I figure I might as well look around outside, in between the house and the winery. I don't know how it would get there, but you never know, since we don't know how it vanished in the first place. And I forgot to check the Volvo."

"Well, the cops did all that, anyway." Wade looked away, staring at the far wall. "I guess I thought there was a chance that it was right in front of me and I just couldn't see it for some reason. Crazy. I don't know what I thought."

"I'll find something, either the gun or the person who took it. We're going to get you out of here."

Wade met her eyes. "That's what's got me worried, Sunny. This is getting serious. Whoever killed Jack Beroni is still close. They know me, and they know you. This is somebody with enough malice and nerve to kill Jack and send me to jail for it.

They're capable of anything. It's not safe for you to be running around out there. Who knows what might happen if they notice you snooping around? Whoever took my gun and killed Jack is probably watching your every move."

"No, they've gotten away with it; they won't do anything to risk getting caught now. They're just going to blend back into the woodwork and wait it out."

Wade rubbed the pressure points at the bridge of his nose. "I never should have gotten you involved in all this. I'm sorry I did. Now I'm asking you to get out of it and stay out. This isn't your problem anymore."

Sunny leaned in and talked low, almost whispering. "Wade, this is no time to cross our fingers and hope everything is going to be okay. Do you really want your fate in the hands of Steve Harvey? He's a nice guy, but do you really want him deciding whether you spend the rest of your life in jail or not? The fact is, somebody is trying to get away with murder at your expense, and I'm not going to let that happen. I'm not going to do anything crazy. I'm just going to go about my business like always, and along the way I'm going to check into a few things, try to find out what the heck is going on around here. Okay?"

Wade looked at her with the faintest suggestion of a smile. "Okay."

She took a notepad and pen out of her knapsack. "They're going to make me leave in a second, but before I go we have a job to do." She pointed the pen at him. "We don't have time to argue about this." He didn't say anything, so she went on. "I want you to try to remember every person who might have seen that gun or even heard about it. That includes anyone who ever spent enough time in the winery to have seen it by accident."

The glare of the sun blinded her when she stepped outside the doors of the police station. One of the women behind the desk in the reception area had said she would probably find Sergeant Harvey at the taqueria down the street having a late lunch. True to habit, he was sitting alone at a table by the window, eating one of three tacos from a red plastic basket when Sunny came in.

"Hi, Steve."

"Hi, Sunny."

"Can I join you for a minute?"

"You bet. Have a seat."

She slid in across from him in the smooth plastic booth, glancing at his food with a covetous twinge of hunger. Lunch would have to wait. Steve Harvey took another bite of his taco, giving her time.

"I wanted to talk with you about Jack Beroni's death. I was hoping you could tell me a little more about it, about what you found out there."

"That's police business, Sunny. I don't know that I can tell you much, at least not much more than is already being squawked about all over town," he said, turning a concerned face back to his meal. He wore a wristwatch that reminded Sunny of the one her father always wore, a gold Timex with a Twist-O-Flex band.

"Well, specifically, I was wondering if you and your team had fingerprinted the handle on the door to Wade's barn."

"Wade's place isn't a crime scene. We haven't fingerprinted anything over there."

"And what about the bullet that killed Jack Beroni?"

"What about it?"

"Has it been checked for fingerprints?"

Sergeant Harvey chuckled. "It's at the lab, but I wouldn't hold my breath. Even assuming the perpetrator didn't wear gloves, and I think that's not a very safe assumption since we are talking about premeditated murder, there is only a space about an eighth of an inch across where the bullet sticks out of the casing and could pick up a fingerprint. And, to answer your next question, since you've become such an investigator, that almost certainly means not much chance of picking up any DNA, either. The bullet expands on impact and then passes through six inches of blood, bone, tissue, and fabric. It's nice to think the killer's signature would still be on there, but it's just not practical in most cases."

"Still, you might find something."

"Might. But are you sure that's going to help your friend? I assume that's what you're after."

"Wade Skord is innocent. If there are someone else's prints on that bullet and the same person's prints on the barn door, that would prove his innocence."

"Not necessarily, but it would be interesting. And extremely unlikely." Steve Harvey wedged the remainder of taco number one into his mouth.

Sunny said, "You haven't found the gun. You took a pair of gardening gloves from the workshop at Wade's. I assume you'll test those for gun powder residue. You took a box of shells and the two casings out of the garbage can. You have the bullet, and the body. Is that the extent of the physical evidence?"

Steve looked surprised, then smiled. "Not entirely. There's the angle of entry. That tells us that the shooter was standing about a hundred yards away, probably to the southwest, in the trees beyond that artificial lake they have out there by the gazebo. Whoever did it had to be a good shot, to be that decisive at night. And the coroner has confirmed the time of death at around ten or eleven o'clock Thursday night. There's some other stuff, but I think I've told you everything I can. This is a police investigation. I'm not at liberty to share all the details."

"You must have Jack Beroni's cell phone records. Whoever he was supposed to meet probably called him to set it up."

"Yes, we have cell phone records, if we need them. And that's all I'm going to say about that. You understand, don't you, Sunny? I can't go around divulging our case."

Sunny clutched her car keys, thinking. She said, "Somebody is trying to frame Wade Skord for murder."

"Well, if that's the case, they've done a pretty good job of it."

Sunny glanced around the taqueria. Two girls about junior-high age were giggling at a table across the room, an old man was reading a newspaper at the window table on the other side of the door, and the crew behind the counter were standing with their arms folded, talking in Spanish. Otherwise, the place was empty. Sunny lowered her voice. "Wade Skord didn't kill Jack Beroni or anyone else."

"I wish I could agree with you, Sunny, but the facts are standing in the way on this one." He tore a bite out of taco number two and chewed robustly while maintaining eye contact. He had big brown eyes lined with dark brown lashes that emphasized the startled look he wore much of the time, like Bambi in uniform. "Facts are facts, Sunny," he said. He took a hearty pull on the straw stuck in a bottle of Mexican orange soda.

"What facts?"

Steve chewed another enormous bite of taco into submission and worked it into manageable mounds tucked into either cheek, thus freeing up the area in the middle so he could speak. He took his notepad out of his breast pocket, flipping to a page and reading out loud. "Suspect is known to possess a registered firearm of the same make and model as that matching the bullet found at the scene of the crime and determined to be the cause of death. Suspect is known to have fired said firearm in the vicinity of the murder at the approximate time of death. Suspect has had disputes with victim requiring police intervention in the past, including a recent spate of alleged death threats corroborated by multiple witnesses. Suspect was unwilling or unable to surrender his firearm for ballistic testing. Suspect has no verifiable alibi for the time of the murder." He looked up from the notepad. "Plus some other stuff I can't tell you about. It doesn't look too good."

"Just because he lives nearby, owns a gun, and can't prove he didn't do it doesn't mean he's guilty," said Sunny.

"No, but it establishes probable cause. That's enough to get a warrant and make the arrest."

"What good does having Wade in jail do?"

"I can't let a murder suspect run around town just because he's a friend of yours," said Steve. "We will continue to investigate this crime until we get to the bottom of what happened, but for now I need to make sure the suspected perpetrator doesn't fly to Brazil while I'm taking fingerprints off a dilapidated barn door." He sipped from the orange soda, rationing the last of it, and wiped the corners of his mouth with his fingers.

Sunny sat quietly, watching him look out the window and study the assortment of pedestrians who ambled between the big silver trunks of the downtown elms.

"I've been in this business long enough to know that the truth is generally fairly obvious," he said, turning back to face her. "The guy holding the gun is usually the guy who shot the gun. The guy lifting the stolen barbecue into the bed of his pickup truck is usually the guy who stole the barbecue."

Sunny turned the ring on her car keys, considering the situation. Even though what he said made sense, it couldn't be right. There was simply no way Wade Skord had shot Jack Beroni. But she needed some more time and some evidence if she was going to convince Steve Harvey.

He read her thoughts. "Sometimes you think you know your friends, and then you find out that maybe you know a lot less about them than you thought you did. Happens to everybody."

"What's this about Wade threatening Jack?"

Steve consulted his notebook. "Several witnesses have corroborated the story that Wade Skord threatened Jack Beroni with physical injury up to and including death on several occasions, most notably September third at a meeting of the Northern California Vintners Association and Wine Auxiliary. And there's a good deal more than that, Sunny. Skord has a long history—including a criminal history—of abuse and conflict with Jack Beroni."

"That's ridiculous. Wade never threatened to kill Jack Beroni."

"Well, several witnesses of good standing in the community say he did."

Steve finished his meal. He's relaxed, thought Sunny with a sickening feeling in her stomach. He thinks he's got his man. She said, "Did you find anything else at Beroni? Were there footprints, signs of a struggle, anything unusual?"

"Nothing. This was a classic medium-range hit by a trained sharpshooter. We are talking about somebody confident in their ability to hit a target from a good distance at night. Somebody who practiced that kind of marksmanship on a regular basis." He watched her as his words sank in. "The shooter never even got near the target. Just stood in the woods, put the crosshairs on Beroni's chest, and pulled the trigger."

Sunny thought about it, imagining Wade possessed by a demon anger she'd never witnessed in him. She pictured him in an angry conversation with Jack on the phone, maybe drinking. He stormed out of his house, hiked half a mile through the night to the base of Beroni Vineyards, stood at the edge of the woods, and raised the butt of his rifle to his shoulder, releasing the safety. He would steady it, peering through the scope. At first darkness and the shadowy forms of distant trees would fill the viewfinder, then he would find the white of the gazebo, the orange glow of a cigarette, and finally the white field of Jack Beroni's shirtfront. He would hold the gun steady, exhale, correct his aim, and pull the trigger. She shook her head. "A sharpshooter would steal a gun and leave it behind. He certainly wouldn't use his own traceable gun and take it home with him."

"I agree that he would get rid of the gun." He seemed to delight in letting her make Wade look guilty. She felt her face flush with anger. "So he might use his own. Sometimes people do stupid things when they're upset. They get impulsive."

He stood up and went to the counter, coming back with two orange sodas. He handed her one. "Let the professionals handle this, Sunny, okay? You've got two choices. Either your old friend is in big trouble, or else I'm wrong and the bad guy is still out there. Either way, you're going to be a lot better off at home or taking care of business at Wildside. Poking around in a murder investigation, particularly a high-profile operation like this one, is certainly not going to help anybody. I'm getting plenty of pressure from high places, and the last thing I need is the local foodies running around stirring up trouble."

They walked back toward the station past the emerald-green lawn of the park. The tension of their earlier discussion seemed to dissipate in the bright sun.

Sunny drank her soda. "So he died Thursday night around ten o'clock?"

"Thereabouts."

"Shot just once?"

"Once pretty much did the trick," said Steve.

"What was he doing down there, anyway?" asked Sunny.

"I'd like to know," said Steve. "What makes a guy leave a fancy party where he's having a nice time with his girlfriend just so he can drive home and go for a moon walk?"

"You got me," said Sunny. One of Steve's fellow officers crossed the sidewalk up ahead and glanced at them long enough to register the facts, then strode past into the station. "Is Wade going to be able to get out on bail?"

"Probably. We'll find out Monday or Tuesday at the latest," said Steve.

"Tuesday? Can't they decide before then?"

"It's up to the judge." Sergeant Harvey hitched up his pants, retucked his shirt, and resettled his belt and holster for his return to duty. "I want you to stay out of this mess now, Sunny. A murder investigation is nothing to play around with. I'd be pleased as punch if you want to come down and have lunch with me for social reasons, but don't go getting involved with what's none of your business."

Sunny gave him a submissive smile and turned back toward the main drag of town where she'd left the truck.

In the park beside the police station, the large white gazebo was still decorated with semicircles of red, white, and blue bunting for Labor Day. Her eyes sought the white stairs, half expecting to see blood pooled and dripping. Under a nearby tree, a couple of young guys in dirty jeans and flannel shirts were curled on their sides, sleeping. At the other end, a Mexican family had set up a picnic at the wooden table. She passed a series of tourist shops selling expensive Italian pottery, gourmet ice cream, and coffee-table books full of glossy photographs of the wine country. At the corner, she passed a row of newspaper kiosks. The headline on the *St. Helena Star* caught her eye. SHARPSHOOTER WAITING IN THE WINGS, it shouted in thirty-six-point type. She bent down for a closer look, expecting the lead to describe the cold-blooded assassination of Jack Beroni. Instead she learned that the glassy-winged sharpshooter had moved one step closer to the valley.

6

Rivka's blue beach cruiser was chained to the Neighborhood Watch sign in front of Sunny's house. Rivka was sitting on the front stoop in a pair of ratty jeans, eating a Popsicle. Her lips and tongue were stained an unnatural shade of pink.

"I was hoping you'd be back soon. I brought lunch." She lifted up a shopping bag next to her.

"Thank God. I'm starved. I didn't know you were coming over or I would have called before I left," said Sunny.

"It was an impulse. Last night after I got home I started worrying. This morning I couldn't reach you or Wade on the phone, so I thought I'd come over and put my mind at ease."

Sunny watched her, waited for her to explain.

"The whole Jack Beroni thing. You and Wade seemed quiet last night. And then this morning when I called over there he wasn't around, and then you weren't around. And last night he said the cops had come by yesterday asking questions about the murder. Then I started thinking about how he's always shooting his gun up there, and I started worrying that maybe the cops would wonder if that was a strange coincidence, especially with him living so nearby and being sort of, you know, unsociable."

She looked up at Sunny's face. "They arrested him, didn't they?"

"This morning." She sat down next to Rivka on the stoop. They stared at the jumble of lemon verbena, lavender, jasmine, and local weeds run amok in the front yard. A climbing rose covered in pale yellow blossoms grew thickly over the redwood archway facing the sidewalk.

"Your yard needs watering," said Rivka. "Not to mention some pretty major weed-control action."

"I'll get right on that," said Sunny. "Do I smell barbecue?"

"Yep. Rude Shelley's."

"Still warm?"

"Maybe."

The phone was ringing when Sunny opened the door. She picked up the cordless and Monty Lenstrom said, "Sunny? What's going on? Is Wade in jail?"

"Monty?"

"People at the shop are going around saying that Wade was arrested this morning for Jack Beroni's murder. Is that true?"

"For the moment."

"What do you mean, for the moment? Are you okay?"

"Me? I'm fine."

"When did you find out?"

"A couple of hours ago."

"Listen, Sunny, are you sure you're okay?"

"I'm fine. Wade's the one in jail."

"I know, but it must be a pretty big shock for you. You two are pretty close."

"Monty, he didn't do it." Sunny made a face at Rivka, who was pulling white takeout cartons out of the bag and arranging them on the counter.

"Are you sure?"

"Yes, absolutely sure."

"He's been violent in the past."

"Jesus, Monty. Like when?"

"Like last year at the Meadowood Croquet Classic. One of the croquet pros was talking to Ellie and Wade just walked up, handed her his glass, and decked the guy. He almost lost a tooth."

Sunny cradled the phone against her shoulder and took out plates and silverware while she talked. "That was totally different. That guy was a known weasel. That croquet pro was the one who was taking Ellie out to dinner at French Laundry all the time and sending her flowers the day after she and Wade separated. Anybody who will wine and dine a guy's wife before they've decided whether or not to break up for sure deserves to be punched."

"I don't know, you weren't there. Wade was out of control. He has a nasty temper, and he expresses his anger in physical ways."

"Monty, what exactly do you want?"

"I just wanted to know if there's anything I can do to help."

"This is help? You'll have a lynch mob after him by sunset."

"All right, fine. I'm sorry. Just let me know if I can do anything."

"Okay."

"Talk to you."

"Yeah."

She hung up the phone with a look of disbelief on her face. "Monty thinks Wade did it."

"He doesn't really think so. He's just scared."

"He was giving me his 'I've been in therapy my whole life, so I'm practically an expert in human psychology' voice. He said Wade *expresses his anger in physical ways*." She used air quotes around the offending phrase.

Rivka looked skeptical. Sunny braced her hands on the counter. "Okay, be honest. Do you think he did it?"

Rivka considered the question for several long seconds. "I'm not sure. I don't know him as well as you do. But I'd say it's unlikely."

Sunny opened a carton of potato salad and divided it up between two plates. She picked up a barbecued rib covered in sauce from another carton and pointed it at Rivka. "We're going to go visit Silvano Cruz. Right after I give some quality attention to Rude Shelley's spicy ribs."

Rivka found the address in the phone book. Silvano Cruz's house turned out to be a few miles outside of town, right next to where her yoga instructor held weekend classes in the backyard during the summer. Out on Main Street, the tourists were out in force, soaking up the crush season and keeping the traffic moving at a crawl. Sunny took side roads as far as she could, then cut over where Main turned into Highway 29. The afternoon light shone on the hills to the east as the truck plunged into the shadowy tunnel formed by ancient elms lining both sides of the road. When they emerged, Greystone, the granite edifice that was home to the Culinary Institute of America, appeared on their left. On the right were rows and rows of vines, recently unburdened of fruit and on the verge of turning shades of red and gold for autumn. A few miles later, Sunny turned left down a narrow dirt road. A meadow of dry yellow grass and gray weed stalks opened to the left, then the dense oak woods resumed. Further on they passed the yoga instructor's house, surrounded by neatly manicured trees. Soon after that, they came to a mailbox labeled *La Familia Cruz* in slanted gold and black letters.

Sunny pulled into the driveway and turned off the truck. She thought about chickening out, but it was too late, a woman was peering at them through the drapes in the living room. The woman opened the front door, looking puzzled but not displeased to have surprise visitors. Her shiny black hair was cut in a bob just below her ears and she wore a tidy glaze of pale lip gloss. She was about thirty-seven, maybe thirty-eight years old and was dressed in stonewashed jeans, a pink cotton blouse, and white running shoes. Clean, pretty, feminine enough but mostly efficient and practical. Her face looked slightly familiar, probably from the restaurant. “My name is Sonya McCoskey,” said Sunny, “and this is Rivka Chavez. Are you Mrs. Cruz?”

The woman smiled warmly. “Yes, I’m Julia. You have the restaurant in town. I remember meeting you there once, very briefly.” Behind her, a slender girl of about nine tiptoed close enough to see who was at the door, then ducked back into another room. Sunny heard a man ask who was at the door, and the little girl said, “Some strangers.”

“I thought you looked familiar. You’ve been in for lunch,” said Sunny.

“A couple of times. I’d come in more, but I don’t have time for sit-down lunches very often.”

Sunny smiled. Why didn’t anybody have time for sit-down lunches? Why couldn’t Californians learn something from the Mediterranean cultures? They’d all live longer, happier lives if they took a little time to relax in the middle of the day; then they could work until ten if they wanted. It was a pet peeve of Sunny’s. She put the thought aside. “I’m sorry to drop in on you like this. I was wondering if I could talk with Silvano for a moment.”

Julia stared.

"It's about Jack Beroni."

"I see." Julia Cruz disappeared down a hallway and a few minutes later a stocky Hispanic man in his late forties came to the door in a plaid Western-style work shirt with short sleeves and Wrangler jeans riding low on a sturdy frame. Silvano Cruz had a wide brown face with heavy cheeks and a pleasant smile. He shook her hand and Rivka's when they introduced themselves. "What can I do for you girls?"

Sunny hesitated. "I was wondering if I could ask you a few questions about what happened yesterday. About Jack Beroni."

Silvano's face darkened and his smile disappeared. "A bad business, very sad," he said. "Why don't you come on in. We can talk in my study."

Silvano's study looked like a fifties-era den, complete with burgundy leather chairs, a big oak desk, and a matching oak cabinet with glass doors, stocked with highball glasses and bottles of bourbon and scotch. A leather-bound set of *Encyclopaedia Britannica* filled the bookcase along one wall, and another held viticultural texts and agricultural manuals whose titles were liberally sprinkled with acronyms—*UCCE & DPR Guide to Row Crop Pest Management* and *Viticultural Preparedness: Recommendations from the CDFA NNPP Task Force.* He motioned them into the leather chairs and sat down behind the desk. "You want something to drink? Soda? Beer?" He held up the bottle of beer he was drinking as an example. They declined.

Sunny said, "I was hoping you would tell us about yesterday morning. I understand you were the one who found Jack."

Silvano nodded. He looked anything but pleased to be having this discussion. "I found him, in the morning, first thing."

Sunny waited but he didn't go on. "The police seem to think that Wade Skord killed him."

"Wade Skord, as in Skord Mountain Vineyard?"

"Yes."

Silvano raised his eyebrows. He seemed to be waiting for Sunny to elaborate. She said, "I think they're wrong. I've known Wade for years and I flat out don't think he had anything to do with it. I thought I'd try to figure out what's going on, at least find out what there is to know."

"And you figured you'd start with me."

"Yes."

"I'll tell you what I know, but I don't think it will have much bearing on Wade Skord's predicament. I've told the police everything that happened already."

"Well, you never know," said Sunny.

Silvano pursed his lips. He told them about driving by in the tractor and seeing the dark marks on the stairs, and having a hunch right away what it was. "Blood looks different, you can just tell." He said Jack was sprawled on his back on the floor of the gazebo with nothing around him to indicate what he'd been doing there, other than the remains of a cigarette he had apparently been smoking when he was killed. The cops said he'd been dead quite a while by the time he was found, maybe six or seven hours.

Silvano hardened his expression and pointed to his chest. "There was a hole in the front of his shirt, right over his heart, about as big around as my little finger." He held up his finger for them to see. "The back was a different story. The exit wound was about as big around as a silver dollar, maybe bigger. I don't suppose you know much about rifles or do any hunting?"

Sunny shook her head no.

"Well, it's not pretty. Those kind of bullets, hollow points, expand on impact, so they go in small and come out big, sometimes real big, depending on whether or not they hit anything real solid, like bone. They are designed to kill. It's what you'd use on something you wanted to make sure was dead but didn't intend to put on the wall. I'd say he died right off the bat. Even if it missed his heart, he would have bled to death very quickly with that kind of hole in him." Silvano studied Sunny and Rivka, checking to see how they were handling this kind of information. "He was dressed up, wearing a tuxedo. They found his wallet on him full of cash, credit cards, the works, and he was still wearing a watch worth more than my car, so it wasn't a robbery, but then nobody thought it would be. Whoever killed him never even came near him. They shot him from way off in the woods. I don't think the cops found anything nearby in the way of footprints and such. Untraceable. I don't know what they have on Skord, but whatever it is, I don't think they found it at the scene of the crime."

Sunny waited quietly to be sure he had said all he planned to say.

Rivka fidgeted.

When Sunny was sure he was through, she said, "You saw his face?"

"Sure."

"What did it look like?"

"Look like?"

"The expression. I mean, did he look upset?"

"Well, I don't know, mostly he looked dead." Silvano took a slug from his beer. "Very white and very dead. And annoyed. If I had to describe his expression, I guess I'd say he looked shocked and annoyed."

"Did the police find anything else on him besides his wallet and watch?" asked Sunny.

"Cell phone, car keys, lighter, smokes, that kind of stuff. What you would imagine. I didn't hang around too long watching. I had work to do." He nodded to himself as if that was the end of that. He seemed to have contributed all he was interested in sharing. Sunny waited. He drank from the beer again.

She said, "What was Jack like? I mean, as a person. You must have known him. Did you like him? Did you like working with him?"

"You didn't know him?"

"I saw him at parties now and then, and I'd see him around town, but I wouldn't say I knew him personally."

Silvano leaned back and put his feet up on the desk. He was wearing Birkenstocks with woolly socks. That would be Julia's doing, thought Sunny; something more comfortable than boots to wear on the weekends and in the evenings. He didn't strike her as a man who would buy himself a pair of highbrow German sandals.

He brooded over his beer for a moment and then said, "Al Beroni, Jack's father, is a good, respectable man, and Louisa, his mother, is as sweet as they come, but Jack was a different story. He was a real son of a bitch, pardon my French."

Sunny noticed Rivka blink and shift in her seat. Silvano frowned. "Maybe I should be more diplomatic."

"Not at all," said Sunny. "We want to know the truth. Tell me about a time when he acted like, like a son of a bitch."

Silvano smiled sheepishly. He looked from her to Rivka and back again. "I told all of this to Steve Harvey already. I drive up, I see the blood, I see Jack, I test that he's dead, I run up to the winery and call for help. That's it for me. If you want to know more about this stuff, I'd suggest you go talk to Ernesto Campaglia."

"Ernesto? What does he know about it?" Sunny glanced at Rivka, who didn't seem to have any reaction to the name, or at least wasn't showing any. Ernesto Campaglia was the father of Alex Campaglia, the guy she'd been dating for the past several weeks.

"Probably nothing, just a long shot. Nesto is the winemaker at Beroni, supervises the entire production from harvest to blending, been doing it his whole life."

"What would he know about Jack's death?" asked Sunny.

Silvano took his feet down and leaned toward them. "Listen, I never had any problem with old Skord. He keeps to himself, but there's nothing wrong with that. And you can't blame him for knocking horns with Jack now and then." He leaned back again and pulled on his beer, mulling over his words. "Let's just say that Nesto and Jack were never on friendly terms."

"Did they have a fight?" asked Sunny.

Silvano looked pleased that she had guessed, giving him the freedom to elaborate. "They had some words. On Thursday morning, Jack came by the winery. He was pretty steamed up because he'd told Nesto he wanted to start harvesting on Wednesday and be finished by Friday or Saturday, but it wasn't happening because Nesto didn't agree. Nesto wanted to wait until the weekend, said the grapes weren't ready. They argued about it for a while and then Nesto said as long as he was winemaker at Beroni Vineyards, he would damn well decide when to bring in the grapes. Jack said if that was the case, then he had just decided for the last time. Then he stormed off. Nesto didn't show it much, but he was upset."

"And Jack was killed that night," said Rivka.

"I'll tell you, there's a lot of water under the bridge between those two families. There's always some kind of a catfight going on up there."

"Between the Beronis and the Campaglias?"

Silvano nodded.

"And what about you? Did you get along with Jack?" asked Sunny.

"I kept out of his way. Luckily, he didn't pretend to know anything about my business. Anybody who can lift a glass might convince himself he's a wine expert, but you can't fake viticulture. Either your vines produce the right amount of grapes at the right time in the right condition, or they don't. That whole crew—Nesto, Jack, Al—keeps their distance from me. I just take care of the vines and stay out of the dramatics."

"And that's the way you like it," said Sunny.

"That's the way I like it," said Silvano with a smile. He stood and showed them out. At the door he said, "One more thing. You might ask Nesto where his son Gabe was Thursday night."

They bounced back down the dirt road to the highway. "What do you think he meant with all that stuff about Alex's family?" asked Rivka.

"I don't know. I was hoping you did."

"I met his father. He seemed like a nice guy. I don't know Gabe that well. And I don't know anything about any problem with the Beronis. If they don't like each other, why would the entire Campaglia family work at the winery? Alex's mom even comes in to cook for their tastings. And they all live in staff housing on the vineyard."

"It's worth checking into."

"Great. We'll get Wade out of jail and then they'll arrest someone in Alex's family."

Sunny nosed into the weekend traffic. As they inched along she took in the view of the mountains to the east. Beyond the first ridge, nestled in the hills that surrounded Howell Mountain,

Wade Skord's vineyard was waiting for her. "Do you have plans for the afternoon?"

"Nothing specific," Rivka said.

"Would you mind going over to Wade's place and testing the Brix? You know how to do it, right? You just take a sample from each section and write down the results on one of the charts in the workshop. The sections are numbered on metal stakes. You could just fill it out and leave it there. I'll swing by later tonight and take it to Wade first thing in the morning."

"Meanwhile, you're going to go see Nesto," said Rivka.

"I was thinking about it."

"I'd like to come along."

"And when Alex finds out you've been questioning his father about whether or not he killed his boss, you'll say . . . ?"

Rivka wrinkled her nose. "Right. Could be awkward. I'll be out taking crop samples at Wade's."

Sunny rolled down her window and surfed her hand through the warm air.

Rivka said, "Do you suppose I've been making out with the killer's son?"

"I don't think so. And probably not the killer's brother, either. But it's nice to know you're making out."

Nesto Campaglia's home, a pretty Edwardian, sat on the west end of a large parcel of Beroni vineyard situated several miles to the northwest of the winery and main house. The smoothly packed dirt driveway wrapped around a giant oak tree that was surrounded by a puddle of sparse lawn. Another square of lawn lay between the driveway and the screened-in front porch. Overgrown hydrangea bushes, loaded with blooms, grew on either side of the door. Their petals had faded to shades of lime, eggshell, pale blue, rust, and lavender, which Sunny thought were prettier than the uniform periwinkle they were in spring. The house itself looked well maintained and was freshly painted squash-yellow, with trim the color of oregano leaves and paprika. An aging BMW coupe, a well-worn station wagon with faux-wood side panels, and a homemade trailer for hauling firewood were parked around the side under a sixties-era carport.

Sunny pulled to the side of the driveway and turned off the engine. Her steps crunched on the pebbly dirt as she walked up to the door. White wicker chairs and potted plants sat on the porch. She rang the bell. No answer. She listened. The day was perfectly quiet. She could hear faint sounds of activity from the backyard, a door opening and closing, someone talking softly as though to a cat or a dog. She followed a narrow path that led around the side of the house, past a supersized lilac bush, and called out, "Hello? Anyone home?"

"Out back!" came the gruff reply.

Sunny walked around the back of the house in time to see a man she supposed to be Nesto Campaglia emerge from a green metal garden shed, the kind advertised with other farm and garden equipment on billboards in Napa. He pulled off his work gloves and tucked them in his back pocket, frowning as he scrutinized Sunny up and down.

"Mr. Campaglia?" she said.

He nodded.

"I'm sorry to interrupt you." She glanced into the shed out of habit and was surprised to see an impressive array of pesticides, fungicides, herbicides, defoliants, and poisons lining the shelves. The rest of the space was filled with garden implements and a riding lawnmower. Nesto followed her glance to the wall of poisons.

"We attract plenty of pests around here. Luckily, there's no shortage of ways to get rid of them." Behind him a thriving garden spread out over a half-acre or more. "The tomato worms are the ones that really tick me off. Nothing's too bad for them. When I find them, I put them out in the driveway for the birds to peck," he said with a nod in the direction of the road.

Nesto wore the loose trousers and cardigan sweater of a man approaching seventy. His eyes were bright and his handshake was strong and steady when Sunny introduced herself. His gray hair was cut short in a dense nap. Bushy salt-and-pepper eyebrows overshadowed his dark eyes. He had a dignified, intelligent, stern look to him. She guessed there was a stint in the military somewhere in his past. "Sonya McCoskey," he said. "You own the restaurant where my son's girlfriend cooks."

So Rivka was Alex's girlfriend now. That was fast, thought Sunny. She smiled. "Rivka's been working with me for about two years."

"My son Alex seems to think a lot of her. I'm not sure about that nose ring, not to mention those birds tattooed on her arms. I'm old-fashioned, but it seems a bit daring for a young lady."

"I guess they were all out of anchors," said Sunny.

He chuckled at that. "I guess so. What brings you out here?"

"Mr. Campaglia, I'm interested in finding out a couple of things about Jack Beroni."

"You're not helping the police, are you?"

"Not exactly. I'm trying to help a friend." She hesitated. "I was wondering what Jack's relationship with the rest of the Beroni crew was like. I mean, did the employees like him?"

"Like him? Hell no, I wouldn't say that any of the crew liked him. Too big for his damn britches, not that he deserved to be killed for it. I've known him his whole life. For a while, it looked like he was going to grow into a fine young man, and he might have yet if he hadn't run into trouble. He wasn't very old in the grand scheme of things, and his only real fault was arrogance. Spoiled rotten. That was his dad's fault, mostly. Sometimes a person will wear through that given enough time. Unfortunately, he didn't."

"You must have worked closely with him. Did the two of you get along?"

"Ah, I think I see what you're getting at. Better to just come out and ask. Yes, Jack and I had a fight on Thursday. It's no secret, there were plenty of people around and it was good and loud, and it wasn't the first time, either. Jack liked to come up with ideas for improving the way we do things at Beroni. The trouble is, he's never spent more than twenty-five minutes in the vineyard at one time, let alone the winery. He wanted us to harvest and I told him that there was only one good time to harvest and I would be the judge of when that was. I have no idea why this was suddenly so important to him, unless he was trying to show off to his father about being in charge." He looked over his glasses at Sunny. She guessed he was taking a reading of how much she understood about the nuances of father-son relationships. He went on, "I told the police all about this, and about meeting with Al afterward. I was hopping mad and I went to Al to tell him that the next time his son threatened me, I would quit and take my boys with me. We've had plenty of offers to set up shop on our own. This valley knows who makes the wine at Beroni Vineyards."

"What time was that when you talked to Al?"

"About five, I'd say."

"And what was his response?"

"He told me he would take care of it, talk to Jack." Nesto smiled at some private thought, nodding to himself. "Al and I go way back. He's been like an older brother to me. There's just four years between us. He's always looked after me, and now my boys."

"Then what did you do? I mean after you talked with Al."

"I went home."

"And you stayed there all night?"

"I did." He thought for a moment. "Who is this friend you're trying to help?"

"Wade Skord."

Nesto stared off at the row of blue mountains edging the view to the west, taking in this information. The day was getting late and Sunny could tell that Nesto was thinking he'd better get back to work before the light died on him. He said, "Skord didn't like Jack any better than anyone else who had to deal with him on a regular basis. There was that fight they had about that drainage line a few years ago, and just the other day they got into it at the Vintners Association meeting. Skord said outright that he'd shoot Jack or anybody else if they came near his property without his permission. I assumed he was speaking figuratively, of course." He looked over his glasses at Sunny again, probably wondering if she'd heard that story yet.

That must have been what Steve Harvey was talking about, she thought. "What was the context of that remark?" asked Sunny, keeping her face neutral.

"They were talking about the glassy-winged sharpshooter. Jack was insisting, on behalf of the larger growers, that the board members support him in his recommendation to blanket the area with a ground application of carbaryl or even an airdrop of chlorpyritos. Skord and a number of others were against it, even though they couldn't offer a better solution."

While Sunny listened, she decided that he was right. It was better to just come out and ask. "Mr. Campaglia, where was your son Gabe on Thursday night?"

"Gabe?" He hesitated, his eyes widening.

He's going to lie, thought Sunny. Or he's going to tell me to mind my own business.

"He was here at the house with us. With me and his mother, Mary."

"Until when?"

"Oh, midnight or so."

"I'm surprised he would stay that late. I'd imagine you get up pretty early."

"We do, but we were watching a movie."

"Which one?" She looked at Nesto, silently confirming that she was calling his bluff.

"I'm not sure. I didn't see the beginning," he stammered. "To be honest, I didn't pay that much attention to it. I had other things on my mind."

Sunny glanced at her watch. Close to five. "I don't want to keep you from your gardening," she said, "but I do have one more question." As a matter of fact, she had three more questions, but two of them would have to wait. For the moment, there was no point in asking why he'd never left Beroni. His reasons were no doubt psychological—fear or loyalty, and neither explanation was likely to provide her with more facts about Jack's murder. She was also tempted to ask his opinion on who would inherit Beroni Vineyards now that Jack was dead, but with both Louisa and Al alive and in good health, it was anybody's guess. Al could divorce Louisa or outlive her, remarry, and start a new family. Stranger things had happened. She ran her hand through her bangs and squinted at Nesto. "Can you think of any reason Jack's girlfriend might have wanted him dead?"

"His girlfriend? I don't know that he had what I would call a girlfriend."

"What about Larissa?"

"Whenever there was a fancy banquet to attend or a cocktail party to go to, Larissa Richards would get dressed up and stand next to him, but I don't think there was much else there." He paused, mulling over the next bit of information that came to mind, deciding what to say about it. Sunny held her breath. Nesto fixed her with his over-the-glasses stare. "This part I didn't tell the police, though I guess I'd better, now that I think of it. I didn't think it was anybody's business when they came by before, but who knows, maybe it's important. Jack was seeing somebody else, somebody other than Larissa. Larissa has long red hair. This other woman was blond. I saw them walking under the trees out behind his place a couple of times. You feel like no one can see you back there because you can't see anybody, but from the vineyard on the adjacent slope, it's a straight shot. If you're standing up there, like I often am, you can hardly avoid seeing somebody on the other hill."

"Do you know who it was?"

"No, but he was certainly a good deal more affectionate with her than he ever was with Larissa. I never saw him take Larissa Richards in his arms the way he would this woman. Frankly, I worried about him. There was a sadness to it. I can't explain, but you could see it. Forbidden love, if you ask me."

Sunny thanked him and walked back out toward the truck. Nesto followed. When they were crossing the front yard, a white Toyota truck with the Beroni logo stenciled on the side roared past, sending up a cloud of dust behind it. The driver raised a hand in an expressionless salute as he sped by, which Nesto half-heartedly returned.

"Was that Gabe?" she asked.

Nesto nodded and walked back toward the garden.

PART TWO

Nights of the Vine

7

Bothe State Park was full of rattlers this time of year and dusk was their favorite time of day to stretch out across the trail, looking for warmth. Even so, Sunny was going for a hike. She pulled off and parked the truck, skipping the day-use fee since the ranger was nowhere to be seen. She needed to think, and this was a good place to do it. She started down the trail toward the redwoods, listening to the buzz and tick of evening insects. Up ahead a good-sized hawk cruised low, hunting the same field mice that kept the rattlesnakes in business.

She was no closer to figuring out who stole Wade's rifle, let alone who murdered Jack Beroni, but she was sure that Nesto was lying about something—either where he was on the night of the murder or where Gabe was or maybe both. For his part, Silvano Cruz had been entirely too forthright about his suspicions to be taken at face value. Why would he want to send Sunny chasing after Nesto and Gabe Campaglia? Did he genuinely suspect them? Or did he have some other reason to imply that the Campaglias may have been involved?

A sliding movement caught Sunny's eye and she jumped back, sucking in her breath. A couple of feet ahead, a gopher snake cruised across the trail, vanishing back into the dry weeds on the other side without a sound. He'd better watch out for that hawk. Several times while out hiking or driving she had seen a hawk dive and come up with the long, curving J of a snake hanging from its talons. It was the kind of sight, dramatic and unusual and a little scary, that would keep popping back into her head for months. Another image was a swarming nest of ladybugs she'd seen one misty fall day deep in the woods by the coast. They'd bubbled up and overflowed from a rotten stump by the millions, like lava spilling onto the forest floor of damp leaves.

Sunny took in a slow, deep breath, savoring the layers of weedy sweetness coming off the sunbaked earth. As she walked, she went over the list of people she and Wade had put together at the jail. It was not as long a list as she had hoped. In fact, she could only hope they had overlooked the guilty party, because it read like the guest list for a get-together of their dearest friends. Dozens of people had helped out with harvest and crush at Skord Mountain over the years, but the vast majority were acquaintances who never even set foot in the winery. Friends of friends, visiting enology and viticulture students, wine aficionados, and chefs and sommeliers with a taste for the basics would show up at three or four in the morning for duty. It was a grueling drill. They'd take a wooden crate, trudge out into the vineyard, fill the crate with grapes, lug it back to the lean-to where the crusher-destemmer was set up, grab another empty crate, and head back into the vineyard. It was exhausting, back-wrenching work, and they generally staggered home and collapsed after a late lunch, often with a bottle of Skord Mountain Zin riding shotgun.

But none of those people would have seen the Hornet or played Assault Golf. In fact, Wade almost always played alone.

It was an eccentric loner's ritual in defiant celebration of freedom, or at least that was Sunny's theory. Freedom was the most obvious benefit of a solitary rural life. He might suffer loneliness at times, but at least he could do whatever he wanted, when he wanted. She suspected that Ellie may have disapproved of Wade's target practice. What better demonstration and enjoyment of his complete personal freedom than a round of Assault Golf before bed? The half-dozen times Sunny had joined him, she'd felt an exhilarating power over the night. Monty Lenstrom had shot with them several times as well, and a friend of Wade's, a vintner named Josh Freelander, had played a couple of times. Wade couldn't think of any other person who had shot his gun. Napa Valley's residents were divided into those who thought shooting for sport was an acceptable way to spend a Saturday afternoon and those who considered it the vice of ruffians. Like smoking and drinking French wine, it was best left unmentioned, unless the company were known initiates.

There had been, nevertheless, one notably excessive dinner party that ended with a game of after-hours Assault Golf. Half of the group had stayed at the house talking and drinking wine while Wade, Sunny, and four others had bundled up and walked down to the winery, ostensibly to work off the weight of dinner. They'd stood by while Wade reached behind the fermentation tank for the gun. The group was made up exclusively of close friends and included Rivka, Monty, Charlie Rhodes, and Josh Freelander. Josh had since moved to Washington State to manage a new winery.

Those who stayed behind might have stood on the deck and seen Wade and the others return from the winery with the gun, and in theory could have searched the structure until they found it. The group at the house was made up of Monty's girlfriend, Annabelle; Josh's wife, Susan; Claire and Ben Baker; Sandy Furrier, a professor of linguistics at Sonoma State and Wade's nearest neighbor other than the Beronis; and Soren, who waited tables at Wildside three days a week. Sunny ran through the list in her head several times, picturing each face and thinking of what Charlie had said, that there was always "behind-the-back stuff" you didn't know about a person. What didn't she know about Charlie? Could there be anything significant that she didn't already know about dear Rivka or Monty? And for that matter, what about Wade? Clearly, someone she knew well and trusted implicitly was not what they seemed. They were dangerous.

The setting sun warmed her arms and she glanced around at the trees covering the hillsides. Their steady acceptance of the elements, their permanence and predictability, acted on Sunny's frazzled nerves like a balm. Up ahead, the trail dipped into a shady grove of coast redwoods made shadier by the waning sun. This, plus the empty spot in her belly where a glass of Cabernet Sauvignon and a mushroom crepe ought to have been, caused her to turn back toward the car. Making her way up the hill, she wondered again what it was that Nesto Campaglia was trying to hide. And what, if anything, was going on between the Beronis and the Campaglias. She thought of Gabe Campaglia's expressionless face, the stony straight-ahead look as he drove by, his father's halfhearted wave. Whatever it was that Nesto was trying to hide, Gabe would know what it was, and he might be surly enough not to bother indulging his father's cover-up. She decided she would go see him first thing in the morning.

It was dark by the time Sunny got home. She opened a bottle of Vieux Télégraphe and let its contents chug into a wide-bellied glass while the phone messages played. Harry, Wade's lawyer, called to say that they had an appointment to see the judge on Monday morning. Assuming the judge set a reasonable bail, he'd have Wade out of there by noon. That was the good news. Rivka phoned to say that most of the fruit on Skord Mountain had hit 20 degrees Brix, which was dangerously close to a full load of sugar. They would need to harvest Monday or Tuesday unless the weather cooled.

She sautéed a handful of mushrooms in butter, a splash of cream, and a hit of white wine, then whipped up a minibatch of crepe batter and shredded some Jarlsberg. The problem with sleeping through half the day, aside from sleeping away half the day, was that she wouldn't be ready to go to bed until midnight. It was just as well, since she still needed to go over to Wade's place to check on a few things. It could wait until the morning, except there were already too many things to be done tomorrow. She took her dinner to the table. The day's mail held nothing of particular interest, so she unfolded the Saturday *Napa Register* while she ate. The headline on the top of the front page shouted, JACK BERONI, 36, SHOT DEAD, and featured a photograph of the victim in his signature tuxedo, looking undeniably dashing in a menacing, swarthy sort of way. The article outlined the facts of the murder but offered nothing she hadn't already heard.

By seven-thirty Sunny had finished eating and put the dishes in the sink. She pulled on a sweater, grabbed her jacket, and headed out the door before she could think of a reason not to go. Outside, a three-quarter harvest moon had come up big and white and bright as a lantern, with Venus sparkling just below it. It was a remarkable night. With that moon shining down, it wasn't dark out so much as a strange kind of daylight stripped of color, a black-and-white world. Sunny looked up, feeling the strong light bathe her face. On the ground, her shadow was as dark as in the daytime.

The drive to Wade's didn't take long on the empty roads. Fifty yards from his house she turned off the headlights, cut the engine, and coasted up next to Wade's old beige Volvo hatchback. Other than the truck's engine ticking, it was completely silent. Normally, when Wade was home, he turned on the light outside above the door. Now the house stood dark against the night landscape. She grabbed a flashlight from behind the seat of the truck and went over to check the Volvo first, though she wasn't quite sure what she was looking for. Something out of the ordinary. Something so close that Wade wouldn't see it. She clicked the flashlight on, then off again. She could see more easily by moonlight. The gun wasn't in the car, assuming it wasn't bolted to the underside of the chassis. There were gum wrappers and change in the ashtray, and the usual maps and dried up pens in the glove compartment. She flipped down the driver's-side visor. Nothing.

On the deck, she tipped the potted rosemary up, hoping that Rivka had remembered to put the key back, and was relieved to find it was there. A dense thud at her side announced that Farber had given up his lonely vigil on the roof. He threw himself against her legs and made a hiccup noise that sounded like he said, "Ike!"

Sunny took care of her chores quickly: She fed the cat, deposited the mail on the kitchen table, listened to the phone messages. There was one message from Ellie, saying she'd heard what had happened and asking if she could do anything to help. Another was from a customer requesting to be added to the Skord Mountain mailing list, an entity that Sunny happened to know existed only on Wade's list of things he would like to do if he were the sort of person who had time to do that kind of thing. Other permanent items on Wade's to-do list were *learn to speak Spanish, build seaworthy canoe,* and *live in Burgundy for one year (become fluent in French, study cooperage).*

She examined the notepad beside the phone, looked in the refrigerator, and used barbecue tongs to prod the contents of the trash cans in the kitchen, office, and bathroom. Stinky sardine tins, orange peels, and coffee grounds in the kitchen, junk mail in the office, tissue in the bathroom. If there was any doubt that her activities had crossed the line from helpful inquiry to invasive search, they were put to rest when she pulled back the sheets and groped under them, expecting to find . . . what? Something, anything, to show that his life had taken a turn, or else that it hadn't and all was perfectly well, perfectly normal. Wade subscribed to three magazines: the *Zinfandel Growers Association Monthly, National Geographic,* and *Wooden Boat.* Well-thumbed issues of each were layered on his nightstand. She checked the pockets of the dirty jeans in the hamper and the jackets hanging on hooks in the hallway.

In the office, she sat at his desk. She examined the papers scattered over it and opened the drawers, then started his computer. At the password prompt she tried *skordwine* without success, then *skordmountain, ellie, farber, zinlover, wadelicious,* and finally *skordelicious. Skordelicious* hit the jackpot and the system started to boot. When it was up, she opened and began to peruse his e-mail, a breach of trust even in their profoundly permissive friendship, even given the circumstances. He was engaged in a witty flirtation with a Parisienne who had visited in the spring with her husband, a cookbook editor with one of France's better publishing houses. He'd also been corresponding with Josh Freelander, but their exchanges consisted of the usual forwarded jokes and shoptalk.

Sunny opened his Web browser and perused the history folders. He'd been to various farm supply sites, CNN.com, Land's End, Amazon, the home page for Zinfandel Advocates and Producers, and a few travel sites where he'd searched for flights to Costa Rica and looked at a bargain trip to Hawaii and a golf vacation in Sedona. His computer files were equally innocuous. In fact, she couldn't find anything anywhere in the house to indicate anything other than a modest life lived as usual. There was nothing to hint at a demented secret loathing of Jack Beroni, a grand plot against his wealthy neighbors, or the sort of conflict that could produce an enemy willing to frame him for murder. There was nothing suggesting that Wade led a double life or had hidden blood lust, dementia, paranoia, or criminal ties.

She dropped Farber outside, locked up the house, and stopped in at the workshop for Rivka's notes on the afternoon Brix readings. Farber chugged along after her, and she stopped to scratch his fur. What would Wade say if he knew what she had just spent the last forty-five minutes doing? He might tell himself she was trying to help him, but he would know somewhere down deep, just as she did, that she'd needed to confirm in her own mind that he was innocent.

On her way back from the workshop, she sat on the stairs to the deck, taking Farber onto her lap for a good scruffing. The night was remarkably bright and peaceful. It would have been even brighter on Thursday, when the moon was nearly full. If it had been a night this wondrous, wouldn't she have noticed? Maybe not. She'd driven to Wade's in the daylight, and on the drive home the rising moon would have been behind her.

She tried to figure how difficult it would have been for someone to take Wade's gun from the winery and walk to the base of Beroni Vineyards. Could it be done without being seen? That would mean without using a flashlight, but a flashlight wouldn't have been necessary on a night like this.

Sunny disrupted Farber's kneading and purring and put him aside. He stared at her with an appalled look of indignation. She walked out past the truck. The winery stood gray and solemn at the bottom of the hill, clearly visible, the woods crowding up behind it. As far as she could tell, a person could reach Beroni Vineyards by hiking through the forest to the east of Skord's vineyard, heading northeast up over the ridge, then continuing on over the next rise. The bottom of that furthest hill would most likely run into the southwestern edge of the Beroni estate, facing the artificial lake. From there, the gazebo ought to be in plain view. She looked at her watch. Ten minutes past nine.

The weeds behind the winery quickly covered her socks with pinpricks and burrs. Ticks, thought Sunny, even if I don't get lost or eaten by coyotes, I'm going to be covered in disease-bearing ticks, not to mention poison oak. She zipped up her jacket against the imagined onslaught of ticks and pushed her way through the live oak and manzanita underbrush that grew between the Douglas firs, digger pines, and oaks. And rattlesnakes, thought Sunny. I am going to step on a rattlesnake, who will then bite me and thrash around, hooked into my flesh by its sharp fangs. But it won't matter because I will die of a heart attack at the sight of it. Branches scraped past her face and clawed at her hair. Be reasonable, she thought. The snakes are nicely tucked away in their dens sleeping by now, and other than mountain lions, there was not much else to fear out here. Really, what are the chances of being mauled by a wild animal? These things don't happen. But then, how often do people go scraping through the underbrush at night? Best not to think about it. She thought of Wade instead, when he said, "I've never been afraid of the dark and I'm not about to start now." There was nothing in the landscape by night that wasn't there by day. She could see perfectly well, even in the dense brush, and the night was calm and pretty. She shoved ahead.

The narrow, densely forested draw made walking difficult, and she often had to duck or squeeze between the narrow trunks of the tightly packed vegetation. After fifteen minutes of struggling through the cloying, prickly underbrush, claustrophobia began to settle in her mind. She plunged deeper into the brush, knowing it would be just as hard to work her way out as in, even assuming she kept a straight course. With no landmarks to help her keep her bearings, she navigated by selecting a tree as far up ahead as she could see and making her way straight toward it. Once there, she chose another, and so on.

Ten minutes later, the ground began to rise and the brush and trees thinned. After a steep climb and scramble over loose rock that had the annoying tendency to give way as soon as she put her weight on it, the top of the ridge arrived suddenly, cleanly forested with mature Douglas firs evenly spaced, and offering a moonlit view of Wade's house, the vineyard, and the winery, all neatly arranged below her like a storybook drawing. To the south, a sea of hillocks ran toward the valley, every third or fourth dotted with a ranchette's light or two, and further to the south, the lights of Napa spread out. To the northeast, a series of wooded rises hid the Beroni estate. Sunny studied the shape of the hills between her and Beroni, imagining how their contours would look when she got closer and her perspective shifted. She picked out unique-looking trees and bald spots and placed them in relation to one another in a map in her head.

Then she looked around at what she could see of the ridge she was standing on, noting the shape of the tallest trees. Getting lost could add hours to her night hike. She comforted herself with the thought that in the worst case, if she became utterly lost, she could always follow the moon to the west, where she would strike vineyard or road eventually.

The east side of the ridge plunged quickly back into tall chaparral, obscuring any landmarks. It would have been much faster to skip all this bushwhacking, thought Sunny, and walk straight across the vineyard, but that would be risky, if the goal was to stay out of sight, especially on a moonlit night like Thursday. The killer would not have taken the risk. Underfoot, a thick layer of fallen live oak leaves and pine needles cushioned each step and left few prints. It seemed doubtful that any sign of the killer's journey would remain. Near the bottom of the ravine, the live oaks, manzanita, bay, and digger pines closed in more tightly, and she worked to squeeze between them. It was also darker down there, with only eight or ten feet of visibility. As she groped through a particularly dense thicket of underbrush, she thought she saw something scuttle away to the right. She froze, searching the darkness and listening. There were sounds that might have been a bird flicking up dry leaves in a search for insects, or a lizard's movements. She felt suddenly far from home, farther than she actually was. She pushed on, eager to get to the top of the next rise. From there, she would be able to see the lake and the gazebo below. Sharp branches scraped her hands and face as she forced her way through the brush. When she slipped, her foot catching on a dead branch, she thought for a moment the branches would catch her, but they gave way under her weight and she fell, her hands hitting the rocky soil hard and branches tearing into her side. She scrambled to her feet, but could feel the sting of a cut or puncture on the back of her arm, and her palms burned, scored with abrasions. The hot sensation of angry tears welled up and her throat tightened.

"Shit!"

She examined her hands and poked her fingers through the tear in her jacket by her armpit, groping the wound underneath. "Shit," she said more softly at the pain in her leg. Her knee was bruised, but there was no serious damage, she thought. When her heart settled down, she walked on. It was not much further to the base of the hill, and as the terrain grew steeper, she was more easily able to find openings between the trees. After a few minutes of trudging uphill and clambering over scree, she was at the top. As it turned out, the top was covered with brush and forest and didn't offer the overview of Beroni she had hoped for. Still, it seemed certain that the lake would be near the bottom on the other side.

She went on more slowly, giving herself more time to negotiate the way. The trees seemed to go on forever, and she began to consider the possibility that she had strayed off course and was headed into the dark open stretch of hills to the south, having missed Beroni Vineyards altogether. There was no choice but to keep going until at last, after what seemed too long and too far to be right, she caught a glimpse of something shiny through the trees. A moment later, she suddenly broke into open, flat space. She stood still, staring at the lake. Her watch read ten-fifteen. The hike had taken an hour. It proved that it would have been possible, and even easy, for the killer to wait until Wade had put his rifle back after shooting it, then slip in, retrieve it, hike to Beroni unseen, and kill Jack. Unfortunately, it also proved how easy it would have been for Wade to do so.

A fringe of cattails crowded one end of the lake, and at the other, the lawn rolled up to the base of the vineyard. In the middle of the lawn, shiny white in the moonlight, was the gazebo. At the top of the hill opposite, above the vineyard, was the Beroni mansion with its Victorian tower. Palm trees lined the driveway, which circled in front of the house and then dropped down toward the lake, sending off a narrow shoot of pavement before winding back to the main road. This narrower road led to the winery, tucked among the trees to the east. There was no pavement beyond that, just the dirt tracks that ran beside and between the sections of the vineyard. Behind the main house were other buildings, including, she assumed, Jack's house, which she'd heard described as a six-bedroom, three-bath "cottage" built by one of his ancestors a century before.

Sunny stepped back into the woods a few paces, letting the shadow of the trees shield her from view without obscuring her line of sight, the way the murderer would have. Steve Harvey had said that the shooter was standing about a hundred yards away to the southwest. That would be close to where she was now. Sunny imagined watching Jack Beroni emerge from the compound behind the mansion and stroll down the hill on the paved road. He would be plainly visible, even obvious, with the white shirtfront of his tuxedo reflecting the moonlight. At the winery, he would veer off the road and take the path down to the gazebo, where he would stand on the steps, admiring the lake. Soon he would be bored, annoyed to be having this appointment in the first place, and now doubly annoyed to be kept waiting. He'd take a cigarette from the case in his breast pocket and smoke while he waited. She could almost see him standing there now, one hand on the railing. Killing him would be easy, not even a difficult shot for a decent marksman, or woman, especially with the help of a night-vision scope such as the one Wade's gun was equipped with. She glanced around as though the rifle would still be there, leaning against a tree, right where the killer had left it.

It seemed like a good time to go have a closer look at the scene of the crime. Sunny skirted the lake and walked across the lawn, enjoying its springy feel underfoot. Suddenly the night felt open and easy, the ominous feeling of the forest had vanished. She stopped just short of the gazebo. They'd cleaned the blood from the steps, but the stain was still visible on the smooth white paint, even by moonlight. Up close, she could see where the long, slender puddles had formed on the stairs and a wide pool had spread out from the body. She shivered and stepped carefully inside the gazebo. One of the posts had a nick out of it, and she wondered if the bullet had struck there after passing through the victim's body. She reached out to touch the spot, stopped, listened, and was just about to turn around, instinct having told her to look before she had the conscious thought to do so, when a hand touched her shoulder and she screamed.

"Jesus H. Christ!" she yelled.

A man jumped back.

Sunny stared, not breathing. It took a moment to recognize Gabe Campaglia. "Shit. Sorry," she said. "I'm sorry. You scared me. What the heck are you doing creeping around here at night?"

He grimaced. "Me? I work here. What in the hell are you doing creeping around at night? Who are you, anyway? I'm not the one trespassing, among other things."

"Sonya," she said, gasping for breath. "I'm Sonya. I just wanted to have a look at where Jack was killed."

"At night?"

"I didn't want to bother Al and Louisa. I had some questions about the crime scene."

She could see him try to place her. She said, "I saw you drive by late this afternoon, while I was talking to your father."

"Who are you again?"

"My name is Sonya McCoskey. I'm looking into Jack's murder on behalf of a friend."

"Are you a cop?"

"No."

"You're a private investigator."

"No."

"I don't like this. You're coming with me and we're going to call the cops. They can figure out what you're doing here."

"What are you going to tell them about what you were doing here?" she asked. "You were on your way home when your father and I saw you. Why did you come back?" She studied his face. He had a very slight twitch in his left eye, on the bottom. It must be irritating, thought Sunny, wondering if it did that all the time, or just when he was nervous, like now.

He said, "I needed to check a few things."

"Such as?"

"I can't imagine why that would be any of your business. Why were you talking to my father?"

"I told you. I'm looking into the murder on behalf of a friend. I wanted to see if your father could tell me anything."

"Like what?"

"Like why the Campaglias and the Beronis hate each other." She watched him. His eyelid quivered with a tiny spasm. He looked angry. "I'm a friend of your brother's girlfriend, Rivka. She works for me at Wildside."

"Wildside is your place?"

"Yes."

"You're Sunny?"

"Yes."

"Listen, Sonya Sunny McCoskey, you shouldn't run around out here with a murderer on the loose. You never know who you'll run into."

"Then you don't think he did it, either?"

"Who?"

"Wade Skord. They arrested him for murder earlier today."

She couldn't read his expression. It seemed as if he hadn't heard about the arrest, but beyond that she couldn't tell what he was thinking. She took a deep breath. "Would you be willing to meet me for coffee tomorrow? There are some things, small things, that I'd like to ask you about, but this doesn't seem like the best place."

"Like what?"

"Just a few questions. It'll only take a couple of minutes."

He stared at her. "I'm heading out early in the morning. I'll be gone by seven. If you want to come by the house before then, go ahead. I don't know what you think I'm going to tell you, especially since I don't know a damn thing about Jack Beroni's murder, but you're welcome to waste your time asking if you want." He looked down, then back at her face. "You're bleeding."

So she was. A spray of tiny droplets and one larger splash marked the floor of the gazebo. She held up her left hand, where there looked to be a fairly deep gash at the base of her palm.

"What happened to you?"

"I stumbled. It's no big deal."

"Let's hope they don't come back for more DNA samples," he

said, giving her a look that might have been malicious or merely teasing.

Sunny put her hand lightly against her right arm to stop the bleeding.

"I have a hunch you already know where I live," he said.

"I think so. Further down the road after your dad's place."

Gabe turned away and walked back up toward the winery. Sunny's heart beat in her ears and throbbed in her hand. She felt the night getting cold. She waited until she heard him drive off, then walked quickly up to the driveway and jogged down it to the main road, then down the road to the turnoff that led to Wade's place. Gabe's sudden appearance had made her skittish, so when Farber yowled at her she started with a jerk, every muscle tense. Feeling foolish, but unwilling to stop herself, she checked the back of the truck for boogeymen and even lifted up the tarp folded in the corner before she got in and drove home.

In the house, she went straight to the bathroom, where she poured hydrogen peroxide on her hands and on the two-inch scrape she'd discovered on her upper arm and watched them bubble, then she covered them with bandages. At last she crawled into bed, bruised and exhausted. Thoughts flickered through her mind as she quickly fell into a deep sleep. Poor Farber alone up on the hill with the coyotes howling. Wade lying on a hard bed in a jail cell, trying to stay warm under a thin wool blanket. Jack Beroni's body laid out on an icy table in the darkness of the basement morgue in Santa Rosa. And somewhere nearby, maybe even in a home where she had eaten dinner and opened bottles of wine, the murderer was warm in bed.

8

The alarm went off at five. This was no way for a Sunday morning to begin, thought Sunny, staggering to the shower. Sunday mornings were supposed to be about sleeping late, eating waffles, and watching cartoons, not grilling possible murder suspects at the crack of dawn.

Yesterday had exhausted the limited levels of tomboy testosterone swimming in her veins, and today the feminine impulse had bubbled to the surface with a vengeance. She wanted a long bath, a massage with lavender oil, a warm and puffy bathrobe to lounge in, and something sweet like chocolate to sip. Instead she smoothed her hair with gel, tipped her lashes with a tiny stroke of mascara, and fastened her favorite necklace in place. After selecting a snug butter-yellow sweater with three-quarter sleeves and a dusty blue knit skirt with a slit just this side of sexy on one side, she slipped into a pair of mules. Luckily the slit in her skirt was on the left and the nasty black-and-blue bruise on her knee was on the right. There was no point in playing up the rough girl with Gabe Campaglia; she had a hunch she'd get much further with the soft approach.

In the kitchen, she boiled half a carton of eggs with a tablespoon of vinegar while the coffee brewed. There was no telling what kind of food they served at the jail, but whatever it was, home cooking, even out of a paper bag, was bound to be an improvement. She made up two sack lunches with egg salad sandwiches on sourdough bread with arugula and pickled onion, chocolate chip cookies, sliced apples and Cheddar cheese, and a Thermos of coffee spiked with red wine. By six-fifteen, the truck was idling while she used a kitchen towel to wipe the dew from the outside mirrors and rear window.

The drab white cottage where Gabe Campaglia lived sat under an ancient oak tree. The yard, nothing more than bare dirt and a few patches of weeds, was littered with the year's enthusiastic production of acorns. Similar structures, built to house vineyard workers during the wine boom that preceded Prohibition, dotted the landscape up and down the valley. They could be charming or squalid, depending on their upkeep; this one was just barely hanging on to the middle ground, with peeling paint and sagging front steps. Gabe Campaglia came to the door as she walked up.

"You're up bright and early," he said, orange juice in hand.

"I wanted to be sure to catch you," said Sunny.

"Let's see that hand."

"It's fine. It wasn't that deep." She held out her palms, one of which was covered with a big square bandage.

He studied the scrapes and peeked under the bandage. "Looks like you took a real winger."

"Yep."

There was a pause while she waited for him to invite her in. He took a sip of juice. "You might as well come in, I guess."

"Thanks."

Gabe's house revealed a profound disregard for aesthetics. The front door opened onto a small living room furnished with a wood and plaid fabric couch of a style Sunny recognized from country dive bars and laid-back coffee shops in university towns.

Its arms were threadbare and the cushions beaten into submission by decades of use. Behind the couch was a set of free weights that took up much of the room, and tucked in one corner was an old television set with rabbit ears on top. An upended white plastic five-gallon bucket served as a TV stand. There was a plastic lawn chair with a hunting vest draped over it next to the TV, and a thrift-store coffee table stuck in front of the couch. Resting on top of the coffee table was a rifle. Judging by the metallic, tingly, electric smell of gun oil, he'd just finished cleaning it. Sunny found the smell tantalizing, like the seductive gas fumes that used to rise up at the pump before accordion nozzles came on the scene. She used to linger in the room when her father cleaned his guns on rainy days. Wade's house sometimes had that smell, too.

Gabe walked into the kitchen area and waved her toward a miserable little chair set up by the Formica table. The table, at least, had aged well, decoratively speaking, and its Art Deco chrome was still shiny. A dented metal lunch box sat open on the counter. In front of it was a sandwich wrapped in waxed paper, an orange, and a plastic baggie full of cookies like the ones Rivka liked to make. Toast sprang from a toaster and Gabe began to smear butter on it. The kettle whistled.

"Here, let me do that," said Sunny, taking over the butter and jam.

"You want tea? Juice?" asked Gabe.

"Tea? Sure," said Sunny.

Gabe fiddled with the cellophane wrapping on a new box of Lipton's tea, then cracked open a carton of milk and set it on the table. The jam was new, too. Soon an unopened box of sugar was added to the setting and they sat down. Sunny said, "You don't normally have tea and toast for breakfast, do you?"

"Not usually. I didn't think you'd like what I normally eat."

"What's that?"

"Leftover rice with lentil soup."

She picked up a mostly empty bottle of Tabasco on the table. "With this?"

He nodded.

"A homespun variation on classic North African cuisine. Do you want me to cook you an egg?"

"There aren't any. Besides, I need to get going."

Sunny doctored her tea with milk and sugar and took a sip. "What were you really doing out there last night?" she said.

"Why don't you answer that one first."

"I was testing a theory. Trying to see if a person could walk to the lake from Wade Skord's house without leaving the forest. A person can."

"I could have told you that. No need to go out throwing yourself on the rocks at night."

She glanced into the living room. "Isn't that gun the same as the one used to kill Jack?"

"It's similar, but that doesn't mean anything, in case you're thinking it was me who took him out. Anybody who hunts deer or has gophers owns a rifle, and that's just about everybody around here."

"And last night?" asked Sunny.

"I was doing the same thing as you. Snooping around. Curious."

She sipped her tea. "What happened between your dad and Jack last Thursday?"

"The usual crap. Beroni throwing his weight around."

She waited, but he didn't go on. "What about Al Beroni? What is he like?"

"Nice enough guy. Fairly clueless. Rides around in his LeBaron and stays out of the way."

"And what about Jack? What did he do all day, I mean generally? Your father said he didn't spend much time at the winery."

Gabe snorted. "Nope, he didn't."

"So what did he do with his time?"

"How should I know?"

"I just thought you might have an idea." She stirred her tea. "And Thursday night?"

"What about it?"

"Where were you?"

"I think you know the answer to that already."

"I'm not sure I do."

He sipped his tea, his flat expression making it clear he wasn't going to say anything else. She was getting frustrated, and she could tell he was enjoying it. She decided to try a new topic. "Did Jack have a girlfriend?"

"Sure."

"What's she like?"

"A knockout. Tall, long red hair, plenty of attitude. A real high-society bitch."

"Is that Larissa Richards?"

"That's her."

Sunny thought for a moment. "Why does your father think Jack has another girlfriend who's blond?"

Gabe smiled. "Even the royalty can't get away with anything around here. The blonde was just the latest side dish. Probably somebody's wife."

"She's married?"

"I assumed so. She seemed to want to keep her visits a secret."

"How could you tell?"

Gabe smiled again. "Over at the winery, there's a spot down at the base of the driveway where you can pull off and park. It's part of an old logging road; you can't see it much from the pavement. You can follow the old road on foot up to the back of the house. It pops out by the old stables where Jack's place is. I saw her pulling out of that spot once, and another time I saw her car parked there. Every once in a while I walk down there for lunch. You can get to a nice spot by the creek that way."

Now they were getting somewhere. He was having as much fun giving out information as he had been keeping it back.

"What kind of car?"

"One of those old Land Cruisers. Maybe an '84 or an '86. I think it was tan or pale yellow. Could have been off-white."

"Do you know who this woman is?"

"No idea. I only saw her that once, just the back of her head. I saw blond hair and that's about it."

They sipped their tea. Gabe bounced his knee, probably getting anxious about the time.

"One more question?" she asked.

He shrugged.

"Why did you hate Jack Beroni?"

He looked up, surprised. He set down his cup, pushed back his chair, and stood, indicating with a sweep of his hand that it was time for her to leave. At the door she stopped and looked up at him. What was it about him that made her want to push and shove? He stared at her, one tanned and callused hand on the door frame.

Gabe sucked in a breath and knocked on the door frame twice. "I guess I was just born to hate him."

It was still early and visiting hours at the jail didn't start for three more hours. The library, where Sunny was hoping to do a little research, wouldn't be open for two. There was plenty of time for a trip up to Wade's place to check on the grapes.

Outside Wade's workshop, Sunny stepped into his old rubber boots and headed out into the vineyard, being careful not to get her good clothes dirty. Particularly in the chill of a new morning, the grapes tasted delicious. Cool and sweet, they hung down in perfect clusters from the leafy green vines lined up across the hillside, an exhilarating sight. She took her time collecting samples of the fruit, with Farber tagging along behind her. After testing the Brix and packaging up some samples for Wade to taste, she stretched out on one of the chairs on the deck and let the sun heat up her face and arms.

Back in town, it was still too early to go to the library. She pulled into a parking spot in front of Bismark's and went inside to kill half an hour. A smattering of locals sat singly at tables, reading the Sunday papers and looking pleased with themselves for getting up at a reasonable hour and for having the time and freedom to go to a café and relax over a cup of coffee. Before she even sat down, Sunny saw that the front page of the local paper was devoted almost entirely to Wade's arrest, and included the picture the staff photographer had taken of him last year when they did a profile of Skord Mountain for the weekly column devoted to the wine business. She slipped the front-page section off the paper and folded it up. She'd decide later whether to show it to Wade.

At nine she walked over to the public library, where vineyard grew right up to the parking lot. A special building housed extensive archives devoted to the local history of the wine business, going back all the way to the Franciscan padres who planted mission grapes for making sacramental wine for Mass in the early 1700s. There was plenty in the library computer system about Beroni Vineyards. She found and perused several books, but they all addressed Beroni as it was today, mostly with slick color photography of the grapevines and the winery, looking regal in its ivy covering. Silvano Cruz had talked as if there was a long-standing rivalry between the two families, and what Gabe had said about being born to hate Jack also implied history. Whatever there was between the Campaglias and the Beronis, it was bound to predate both Gabe and his father. Searching under *Campaglia,* she hit pay dirt. There were two entries, both of which looked promising. One was a history of the early days of winemaking that included a chapter called "The First Wave: Early Pioneers from Agoston Haraszthy to E. Augustus Campaglia." The other was an audiotape listed as part of an oral history made by the St. Helena Historical Society in the mid-seventies. The synopsis of one of the histories, told by a man identified as Patrick Munzio of Rutherford, included the entry "Stella Campaglia and the Cortona Winery."

She checked the book first. A single paragraph devoted to E. Augustus Campaglia described him as an Italian-born merchant who had emigrated to the United States as a teenager and made a small fortune selling provisions to the would-be miners streaming into San Francisco after gold was discovered in the Sierra foothills in 1849. In 1879 he decided to retire to the Napa Valley countryside with his young wife and try another venture, winemaking. He bought three hundred acres of land in the hills above St. Helena and built a Victorian mansion on the prettiest rise, a fitting home for his new bride. Following the advice of Gustave Niebaum, who had just purchased Inglenook, he planted his acreage to Cabernet Sauvignon, Zinfandel, and Pinot

Noir, and punched a vast cave into the rocky hillside for making and storing wine. A photograph on the page opposite showed the newly built mansion with Augustus and Stella Campaglia standing in front of it. The caption read, "E. Augustus and Stella Campaglia, Cortona Winery, 1881." Augustus stared out from under wild, bushy eyebrows, looking fierce with determination, every bit the self-made man. Willowy Stella stood close to him, her arm hooked through his and her head dipped in uncertainty, or tenderness, or perhaps only avoiding the glare of the sun. Scrawny fledgling palms had just been planted to either side of the house in a half-moon following the new dirt driveway. They hadn't added the front porch yet and many of the outbuildings were still to come, but it was unmistakably Beroni Vineyards.

The librarian brought over the tape player Sunny had requested. The machine was the size of a shoe box. Sunny found a place at a table and plugged in the headphones, loaded the tape, and punched PLAY. The interviewer, sounding like she was in another room, said, "First of all, why don't you tell us your name and something about yourself?"

"My name . . . is Patrick Munzio." He breathed heavily. "I was born in Sicily, but I don't remember it. I grew up here, in St. Helena. I've lived here my whole life."

"How long is that?" asked the distant interviewer.

"Eighty-four years. I'll be eighty-five come January."

His voice sagged and rasped as he described the Napa Valley of his childhood, the store where they would pick up goods ordered from the Sears catalog, the dust kicked up in massive clouds on the old dirt roads in summertime. Sunny fast-forwarded for a count of ten, then listened again. "There were orchards all up and down the valley back then. Prune trees, mostly, but also olive, almond, apple, pear. In the spring, the trees would be covered with blossoms. They smelled wonderful. You could stand in an orchard and feel the petals falling in the breeze like rain. The petals would be like a white carpet under the trees. They tore out the trees to put in the grapevines." She punched fast-forward again, glancing at the synopsis. She listened again. In the background, the interviewer's voice said, "What year was that?"

"Oh, I was a boy. Must have been 1895, 1896, 1897. All in there. We used to run around like wild things all through those orchards, and when they were gone, through the vineyards, too."

She advanced again, then hit PLAY. The interviewer's voice said, "—lived on the Beroni Vineyards Estate?"

The old man coughed and cleared this throat. "Back then we still called it Cortona. The Cortona Winery. My father went on calling it Cortona his whole life, and he worked there for ten more years after Old Man Beroni changed the name. He never thought Beroni should have had the vineyard in the first place."

"Why was that?" asked the interviewer.

"I don't know exactly. People didn't talk to children about grown-up matters in those days. It was none of our business. We never heard much about what was going on. But I would find out. I was interested in everything having to do with wineries when I was a kid. Well, my whole life, I suppose. I think I got the impression that my father didn't trust Old Man Beroni. He always liked Stella Campaglia, and he felt sorry for her after her husband died. Stella and Augustus were the ones who started Cortona. My father said Stella didn't know how to run a winery, and after her husband died, Beroni came around to help keep the operation going. The next thing you know, Beroni owned the place and moved Stella and the boys to the housing for the hired hands, which was a house like the one we lived in, nothing fancy, and moved his own family into the Cortona mansion. My father resented that. He said on a number of occasions that it wasn't right to move a widow and her children out of her home. He always said Beroni was a swindler who took advantage of a young widow who didn't know any better. When I was older, my mother would send me up to see Mrs. Campaglia—that was Stella Campaglia—with a fresh pie or a basket of bread or a bag of vegetables from the garden. I knew her sons pretty well. I was a good deal younger than they were and I looked up to them quite a bit. I'd hang around the winery and try to help out, tapping down the must with a big stick during fermentation or taking a turn at cranking the old press. Those old crank presses were work. The Campaglia boys were running that whole operation even then—the winery, the vineyard, the cellar, everything. I figure they couldn't have been more than sixteen, eighteen years old at that time."

Sunny rewound the tape and returned the setup to the librarian, then made a photocopy of the photograph of Augustus and Stella Campaglia. Outside, she sat down on a concrete bench facing a gurgling fountain and called Monty Lenstrom on her mobile.

"Sun."

"Monty."

"What's up?"

"What do you know about the history of Beroni Vineyards?"

"Not much, just the usual dross. Established at the end of the 1800s, owned and operated continuously by the Beroni family, legacy of decent Cabernet Sauvignons and above average Pinot Noirs, recent tendency to cash in on a recognized name by releasing grotesque quantities of mediocre Merlot sold for about double what they're actually worth by any reasonable standards."

"Who would know more?"

"Like about what, the winery?"

"Mostly about the Beroni family."

"I guess Ripley Marlow might."

"She's related, right?"

"Al's cousin."

"Listen, Monty, how would you like to go pay her a visit? Like, for example, this morning."

"This is about Wade, isn't it? Sunny, why are you getting all mixed up in this stuff?"

"I'm not mixed up in anything."

"You can't go around grilling Jack's extended family. Ripley is a very gracious person, but I think it's a bit much to assault her on Sunday morning, especially when she is probably upset about Jack and not in the mood for company."

"But it's important. I'm sure she would like to know who killed Jack as much as I would."

"It's insanity. You've lost your mind."

"Just call her and be ready. I'll pick you up in an hour."

She slipped the phone into its pocket in her bag and headed for the police station, which was only about four blocks away. St. Helena had put on its best Mayberry face for a glistening Sunday morning, and the tourists in their ironed khakis and cotton blouses had come out in force, strolling past the quaint shops looking for ways to spend their money. Sunny marched up the street, making a list of points she needed to cover with Wade.

He looked tired when he came out of the holding area and shuffled into the metal chair across from her. The dark print of a sleepless night showed under each eye.

"You holding up okay?"

"I'll be fine. Harry says he's hoping to spring me tomorrow morning."

"Have him call me when you know anything, okay?"

"I will."

"I brought you lunch, and samples of berries from all eight sections. They're all labeled. And I made you a Thermos of coffee, but they won't let you have it. I guess they're afraid you'll use it to bust your way out of here." He shook his head and she smiled. "Rivka measured Brix yesterday around five and I took another reading first thing this morning." She dug the papers out of her bag and held them up to the glass for him to see. He leaned in and studied them.

"Good. That's great, Sunny. Thanks for taking care of all this stuff."

"No problem. Do you want me to come to the arraignment tomorrow?"

Wade sighed and roughed up his hair. "No, you go take care of your restaurant. You have plenty to do without watching me sit around in an orange jumpsuit. I'll call you when it's over. Is Farber still kicking?"

"I think he's more or less living on the roof. He came down this morning and followed me out into the vineyard."

"The roof's a good safe place for him, away from the coyotes. He's a smart cat." He looked at her, holding her eyes in a steady gaze. "He knows how to stay out of trouble."

"He may be the only one," said Sunny.

"I hope not," said Wade. "You're in a hurry to get somewhere. What's going on?"

"Oh, nothing. Just lots to do today. We have a new menu at the restaurant tomorrow, so I need to get in there and make sure I've got all the kinks ironed out. We're doing coq au vin, which I haven't cooked in about three years."

Wade said, “Uh-huh,” emphasizing the second syllable, which meant he didn’t buy it.

She sighed. “What do you know about the Campaglia family?”

“You mean Nesto?”

“I mean the whole family.”

“Well, he has two boys. I think they work with him there at the vineyard.”

“No, I mean what do you know about the Campaglias and Beroni Vineyards?”

“Beyond the fact that they work there, nothing. I know Nesto has been winemaker at Beroni Vineyards for as long as I’ve been around.”

“So you’ve never heard of any old rivalry or bad blood between the two families?”

“I know that Nesto and Jack knocked heads on occasion. That’s not that surprising considering that Nesto has been running the winery forever and Jack struts around like he owns the place, which he does, so that probably just makes it worse.”

“Right.” She looked at her watch. “You need anything before I take off?”

“Not a thing. What’s this all about?”

“Just curious.”

Wade scowled. “You made coq au vin not three weeks ago.”

“That was a different kind. Parisian. This one is Provençal.”

“I see. You are a terrible liar, McCoskey.”

She pinched her lower lip. “I need to work on that. Don’t worry, I’ll be careful.”

He frowned. “Careful isn’t enough. Don’t go getting yourself killed.”

They stood up and she trailed her fingers across the glass after him, then left the visiting room. There was just enough time to make it to Monty’s house by eleven-thirty. She stormed down Highway 29, taking a few risks to pass on the two-lane road headed for the Oakville grade. The truck chugged up Mount Veeder, laboring in the steepest section around a tight turn. Sunny downshifted, revving the engine to get the RPMs up on the old engine. Up ahead to the left, Monty's turnoff came into view. As she pulled into the driveway, Monty opened the front door and came out with his jacket in hand. He hefted himself into the cab of the truck and slammed the door.

"For God's sake, when are you going to buy a new car?" he said.

"Never. I'm shocked you would even suggest such a thing."

"I'm sorry, but I guess the turn of the new millennium made me think you might consider an upgrade."

"The Ranger has twentieth-century-retro appeal. I thought you loved the seventies."

"It's completely embarrassing. I love the twenties, but I don't want to drive a Model T. Do you mind if I sink down as we go through the populated areas?"

"This from the man who suggested we go live in a yurt by the river."

"I'm sorry, you must be thinking of someone else." He looked her up and down. "You look nice. Showing some leg and everything. You have a date later or is this for me?"

"Spare me."

"Showing some nasty-looking bruise, too. And what happened to your hand?"

"Where are we going?"

Monty directed her back across the valley to the Silverado Trail. They headed up into the mountains on the other side, climbing switchbacks and catching slices of the view through gaps in the trees. Monty pointed to a turnoff that took them through a fieldstone gateway and up a blacktopped drive lined with olive trees. The trees were loaded with small green fruit getting ready to turn. Sunny calculated the yield out of habit as she drove, counting the trees and estimating the tonnage. There was enough fruit for a substantial to overwhelming supply of olives even for a restaurant, or a modest supply of olive oil. They parked in a paved oval lot tucked off to the side of the road and hopped out. Sunny fished in her knapsack for the photocopy from the library and folded it up, tucking it into the sleeve of her sweater.

Ripley Marlow's home was the picture of modern, understated elegance. A combination of white adobe, slate, and dark wood, it gracefully spread out at the top of the hill, its double front doors richly varnished. Sunny smoothed her skirt and tugged at her sweater, feeling relieved that she wasn't wearing her usual jeans and T-shirt. Monty rang the bell. The sound of heels clicking on wood floors grew steadily louder and a moment later the door opened.

As a fixture of Napa Valley high society, Ripley Marlow had spent years opening her door to guests. Her face showed the easy poise of social skills burnished to a luster by decades of practice. She was probably close to seventy years old, and her face was lovely, with almost no makeup. Her silver hair was combed back and loosely gathered at the nape of her neck, and she wore small, tasteful gold earrings. She was dressed in a chocolate-brown sweater knit of very fine wool and herringbone trousers with wide legs and cuffs. Everything about her bespoke taste, from the simple gold wristwatch to the alligator belt and matching mules. She embraced Monty and held a thin hand out to Sunny.

She stood back and looked at them. "What a lovely surprise, Monty. I'm so glad you called. I can't remember the last time you came to the house."

"It was July, for your wonderful midsummer party."

"Wasn't that a fine evening! I always enjoy my midsummer dinner." Ripley smiled warmly at him.

"I'm sorry about Jack," said Monty. "It must have been a great shock."

"Yes, it was. I was supposed to have lunch with him just the day before he died. We always had luncheon together on the third Wednesday of the month, you know. He canceled that morning so he could fly to Los Angeles for business, so I didn't get to see him. And of course now I never will. It hardly seems real."

She gave them a resigned half-smile and led them through a tile entryway to a sunken living room as big as a football field. Sunny caught a glimpse of kitchen through a far-off archway, enough to tell her it was as big as Wildside's and full of immaculate stainless-steel appliances.The living room faced a wall of windows overlooking a narrow pool dropped into the stone patio in back. Beyond the pool lay the green expanse of the valley. Sunny sat down on the white couch facing the fireplace with its slab of what she guessed was mahogany for a mantel.

"Sonya, come sit on this side or you will miss the view," said Ripley. "Will you two join me in a glass of wine? I know Monty will. It's only just noon, but it is Sunday, after all. We should be allowed." She smiled broadly at Sunny. "Monty, you've seen the view a hundred times. You come help me and let Sonya enjoy it for a moment."

They returned a few minutes later with a bottle of Grgich Hills Fumé Blanc and a tray of grapes, sliced pears, crackers, and two kinds of soft white cheese veined with blue and green. Sunny began to wish her visit didn't involve a lot of nosy questions. She hadn't thought until now that Ripley might be deeply saddened by Jack's death.

"To a fine autumn day," said Ripley. They touched glasses and drank. The Grgich Hills Fumé Blanc was one of Sunny's favorites, though a Pinot Noir might have made a nicer complement to the cheeses, especially if there were walnuts. She sipped the cool wine. Ironically, the only thing better than a glass of Fumé Blanc was a handful of the Sauvignon Blanc grapes themselves. She'd tasted them once on a visit during harvest. At the time it had seemed a tragedy to crush them so they could rot into wine, but of course the berries last only a day or two and the wine captures the flavor for years. She had always meant to ask for a cutting so she could plant it in her yard. The grapes she'd grow might not taste exactly the same, might not be so delicate and fragrant, since they wouldn't be pruned and stressed the same way, not to mention they'd be growing in a different microclimate, but it was worth a try if they were willing to give her a cutting—a practice some wineries considered a sacrilege, like sending one's child to live with the neighbors.

Monty popped a slice of pear in his mouth and loaded a cracker with cheese.

Ripley leaned back into the couch and looked perfectly at ease. "Now, I know you aren't here just to visit. What can I do for you?" she said.

"I'm interested in the history of the Beroni and Campaglia families," Sunny said. She paused, considering her approach. "It's not just a passing interest. If you read the paper this morning, you know that Wade Skord, the vintner whose place is adjacent to Beroni Vineyards, was arrested for Jack's murder yesterday. I've known Wade for years and I don't think he did it. I do believe that there may be a lead to the actual killer somewhere in the histories of the two families."

"Wade Skord. I didn't read the paper today, but I do remembering meeting Mr. Skord, at the wine auction a couple of years ago. If I am thinking of the right person, I remember that he struck me as a man who has weathered a difficult life, which, unfortunately, had robbed him of the finer nuances of manners. To be perfectly honest, I found him coarse, but he did not strike me as dangerous. Not a murderer, if I had to guess. More of a maverick. They've never been my type." She winked at Sunny.

Monty tipped a slab of cheese onto another cracker. "Wade's finer nuances were stunted long before he experienced any difficulties. But I don't think he did it, either," he said.

"I also doubt ancient history is a factor," said Ripley. "If the Campaglias were going to kill for control of Beroni Vineyards, they would have done so a long time ago."

"I found this at the library this morning," said Sunny. She slipped the photocopy out of her sleeve and unfolded it, smoothing away the body heat before handing it to Ripley.

"Sunny always has something up her sleeve," said Monty, smirking.

While Ripley examined the grainy reproduction, Sunny recounted what she had heard on the tape at the library about Augustus Campaglia dying, Stella Campaglia not knowing anything about business, and "Old Man" Beroni buying the vineyard from her. Ripley looked at the picture for a long time.

Sunny said, "It seems odd that I've never heard these stories about Beroni Vineyards. We know the stories of all the other prominent wineries, who owned them and all the changes they went through, and what's more, this one has exactly the elements of tragedy to it that make it perfect for gossip. You would think it would have become part of the Beroni lore."

"Hardly," said Ripley. "Great-grandfather Beroni lived into his early nineties, and he would never have allowed anyone to speak of such private matters. It was strictly forbidden to discuss family matters, not among the family and certainly not outside it. He was a gruff, stern old man. I remember him up in that house when I was a child and he was still running things. He'd sit in his chair on the porch and watch everything that went on at the vineyard. We were all terrified of him.

"To be honest, I don't know exactly what did happen between him and Stella Campaglia, and I don't think anyone alive does, or ever will, for that matter. It is true that what is now Beroni Vineyards was once owned—was established by—the Campaglias. It was called the Cortona Winery after the town in Tuscany where Augustus Campaglia had emigrated from. After Augustus died, Great-grandfather Beroni bought the winery and changed the name. Stella Campaglia, Augustus's wife, was still a relatively young woman then, and her boys would have been children of nine or ten years old. She was dead long before I was born. I always heard that she went somewhat mad after her husband died. Her two boys stayed on, working for Great-grandfather Beroni. I think the younger of the two eventually joined the service. In any case, he went away and never came back. The older boy—that would be Ernie Campaglia's grandfather—was a very sweet man called Aggie, who everyone adored. I remember him. He would take us swimming, and I remember he once took us to get ice creams in town. A sweet, gentle man. He died when I was about five."

Ripley massaged her hands, immersed in the summer days of her memory. Her rings caught Sunny's attention. They sparkled with gold and diamonds, each probably marking a significant moment in a successful life of privilege: confirmation, engagement, marriage, anniversary. Her hands where veined with age, but still showed an inherent beauty.

"I spent summers at Beroni Vineyards throughout my childhood. Al's mother was my mother's sister, so Al and I are cousins. We are more or less the same age. Then there was little Ernie Campaglia—everyone calls him Nesto now—who was a few years younger. We were a gang, running around over there. We had a ball. Swimming, horseback riding, hiking. It was a paradise for children." She sighed and looked at Sunny and Monty to see if there was anything in their experience that would enable them to imagine it. "In any case, all that is irrelevant to recent events. If there was anything sinister about Great-grandfather's methods of acquiring Beroni Vineyards, they are safely vanished into the void of history."

"So Al and Nesto got along as children?" asked Sunny.

"Oh, yes. They were fast friends. Al is three or four years older, as I said, and he was completely devoted to Ernie. They were inseparable. Al always looked after Ernie. They grew apart as they got older, mostly because their responsibilities separated them, but I think they have always remained fond of each other. Al's father was very traditional. He brought Al up to be a cultured, educated member of the ruling class, while Ernie plunged into the nuts and bolts of the winemaking business. When he was about ten years old, Al was sent away to school. I don't think Ernie even finished junior high. Ernie loved being at the winery from a very young age. He was fascinated by the transformation of grapes into wine."

"So Al's and Nesto's children weren't raised together," said Sunny.

"No. You have to understand how the business changed over the years," said Ripley. "Beroni Vineyards today is ten times the size it was when I was a child. The gulf between the two families widened a great deal between my generation and my children's. By the time Jack came around, the Beronis had become a very wealthy, very international family. Ernie's kids went to public school in Calistoga and had summer jobs helping out at the winery. Jack went to boarding school in Switzerland until high school and spent summers yachting on the bay."

Sunny reached for a cluster of grapes. "And what about now? Do you know of anyone who might have wanted Jack dead?"

Ripley smiled sadly and reclined against the soft white couch, her glass of wine misted over with coolness and sparkling yellow. She sighed. "My dear, so many people might have wanted Jack dead."

Sunny waited, giving Ripley's sadness time to be felt. She wanted to ask who? And why? But the look on Ripley's face prevented her. She thought of her own cousin, whom she'd spent summers playing with and who had just had a baby girl. How would it feel to watch that child grow into a young woman, only to meet a fate like Jack's? She put her glass down. The wine in the middle of the day, without much to eat, was making her head soft. She said, "What about Jack's girlfriend, Larissa Richards? Do you know her?"

"Yes, I know her quite well."

"What did you think of her relationship with Jack?"

Ripley paused, then said, "Larissa is a lovely girl from a very good British family, but the fact that she has chosen to live here, thousands of miles from that family, says as much as I could about her background. I think that she and Jack were, in some ways, far too much alike to be really good for each other." She paused in a way that made Sunny think that she must have smoked at one time. It was the place in a conversation where she would have lit a cigarette before going on, and for a second, she looked distracted, her hand fluttering nervously, as though resisting a pang of chemical lust. It was gone just as quickly, replaced by her practiced composure. She fixed Sunny's eyes with her own. "Jack and Larissa were both predators. In a relationship, it is better if someone is the prey."

Sunny felt a chill at the remark. She decided to play one last card. She said, "Mrs. Marlow, who inherits Beroni Vineyards now that Jack is dead?"

Ripley smiled. "I haven't the faintest idea."

Once they were driving, Monty asked if it was worth the trouble of going out there.

"I don't know," said Sunny. "It was nice to meet her at least. There's a good spot up ahead for lunch. You want to stop?"

She passed it, made a U-turn, and doubled back, pulling off at an overlook. She grabbed the sack lunch, a bottle of water, and the Thermos from behind the seat and let the tailgate down for them to sit on. Below, the land sloped away steeply, offering a view almost as spectacular as the one from Ripley Marlow's living room. Sunny divided the egg salad sandwich in two and poured water into the Thermos cup for Monty, keeping the liner cup for herself, then set out the sliced apples and Cheddar cheese. It felt good to be outside in the fresh air.

"Thank God," said Monty, squinting through his little gold glasses. "I wanted to lunge at that tray of food, but it didn't seem polite. It was torture just staring and pecking at it."

Every now and then a car went past. When they'd finished the sandwich, Sunny poured coffee and got out the chocolate chip cookies. One of the new Volkswagen Beetles went by, flashing license plates that read WINEBUG.

"That's very cute," said Sunny. "Almost too cute."

"Or menacing. It depends how you read it. You can get the wine bug, that's good. But if you have wine bugs, that's bad. Phylloxera. The glassy-winged sharpshooter."

"I think they mean they are driving the wine bug."

"Right. Gotcha."

"I don't know what makes people get vanity plates, anyway. The only one I ever saw that I really liked was 'Aztec Lover,' with a heart for the 'love' part. I didn't see the driver, but I assume it was a guy who looked like the drawings on those calendars they hand out at Mexican restaurants at Christmas. You know, standing on top of the mountain holding the Indian maiden." Sunny stood up to illustrate what she meant.

"It could have been an anthropologist."

"No, the car was all muscle. Like a Trans Am or something."

"I saw 'Wine Guy' the other night. In fact, I was nearly run down by Wine Guy on my way home. I was about to turn into my driveway when Mr. Guy comes flying around the corner going about a thousand miles an hour. I saw the plates because I looked to see if he was going to wipe out on the turn. He made it, but not without taking some rubber off the tires. He hit the brakes so hard they squealed."

"Was it a silver Jaguar?"

"Yeah, I think so. How'd you know?"

"When was that exactly?"

"Um, Tuesday? No, Wednesday night. I was coming back from dinner at Delfina with the wine buyer from Bistro Five."

"In the city?"

"Yeah. I can hardly ever get him to come up here. I always have to drive all the way to San Francisco."

"So it was late."

"About twelve-thirty, maybe quarter to one."

"You're sure it was Wednesday night?"

"Of course."

"Did you see the driver?"

"I don't remember. I don't think I saw him that clearly. He was wearing a suit and tie, I remember that."

"But you didn't recognize him?"

"Sunny, stop. You're making me nervous. What's this all about?"

"Monty, don't you know that the silver Jag with 'Wine Guy' plates is Jack Beroni's car? I thought everybody knew that."

"Well, not me. As far as I could tell, he was just a maniac driving way too fast on a steep, winding road late at night in front of my house. That was enough for me."

"What could he have been doing up there so late at night, and why would he be in such a hurry?" Sunny wondered aloud.

"I have no idea. Maybe he was visiting somebody."

"Like who?"

"How should I know? The man knew everybody."

"Don't you find it interesting that he was on top of Mount Veeder late at night, driving in some sort of erratic, hyper-adrenalized state on the night before he was murdered?"

"I would, except that he didn't know it was the night before he was going to be murdered. I'm pretty sure it wasn't on his calendar. 'Go to gazebo, be killed.' To him it was just another night. And it's not exactly unusual to drive a fancy car fast on a curvy road. That's what Jaguars are for."

"That's true. Still, it seems odd to me. Especially since he'd canceled his lunch with Ripley that morning so he could fly to Los Angeles for business. That makes for a long day. Wouldn't he be tired?"

"Maybe, but he could afford to sleep in the next day. He didn't exactly have a day job."

They finished their coffee in silence and Sunny drove Monty home. She had the urge to drive further up Mount Veeder to check out who Jack might have been visiting, then decided it could wait. Right now she needed time to think.

9

At Highway 29 she hesitated, then turned south. With luck she'd make it down valley before the Sunday afternoon traffic heading back to San Francisco transformed the road into a parking lot with a view.

Twenty minutes later she pulled into one of a dozen identical shopping complexes in Napa and parked under a scrawny shopping mall tree in front of the gym. Joining the gym had been Rivka's idea. She'd argued that the pounding beat of rave music and the smoothie bar with the curvy Italian chairs would more than make up for the drive down to Napa. Not so, as it turned out, but what did was the Olympic-sized pool. Inside the gym, the air was warm and wet. Sunny changed into her swimsuit, headed for the deck, and dove in, skimming across the top of the water in a shallow dive. The cool rippling of the water passing over her body obliterated all thoughts of Jack Beroni and Wade Skord. Soon she was listening to the white noise of each stroke plunging into the water and was alone, suspended in a colorless, almost odorless world of nothingness. She counted each stroke, enjoying the numbers as they came, one after the other, orderly and predictable shapes like well-behaved students in uniform. At thirty-two, she flipped and felt for the wall to push off, enjoying the pulse of satisfaction when it was there. Half an hour later, she pulled herself out of the water, as if emerging from a sound sleep.

Back out at the truck, the seat felt wonderfully warm from the sun. She sat staring at the brown wood and plastic signage of the shopping mall for a moment, letting the heat soak in. As in all pod malls, the shops radiated out from the parking lot instead of the reverse. It suddenly seemed interesting that the resources of the place were lavished on the cars, which had acres of space, while the shops themselves were shunted to the side: puny, dark, and mostly deserted. Here in the semirural zone, parking reigned supreme. Whatever it is you want to do, whether pick up a few groceries or gun down an acquaintance, chances were extremely good that you would need to drive most of the way there and then you would need to park your car. Skord Mountain, as much as Beroni Vineyards, was isolated. To get there from almost anywhere would be a significant journey on foot. Sunny turned the key and started the truck.

About a quarter of a mile shy of the Beroni Vineyards archway, Sunny noticed twin ruts that led off the road through trees that entwined overhead, camouflaging the spot so that one might easily drive by without ever noticing the primitive road, as she had for years, until just now. She drove on until there was a wide spot on the shoulder. She left the truck shoved as far to the side as she dared without getting stuck, then walked back. The ruts were definitely some kind of road. A deep layer of fallen leaves and pine needles had smoothed over the tracks, which looked like they had been used fairly recently. In places, there were tire scars or depressions in the thick bed of leaves. The old road led around a corner and opened onto a small, perfectly sheltered meadow with an obvious place to pull off and leave a car on the right and an equally obvious grassy spot for Gabe Campaglia to eat his lunch facing the creek to the left. Decades earlier, it had probably been the landing where the logging crew had stacked up decks of logs before they were hauled away to the mill. On the right, near a sagging old embankment, were signs that a car had been parked there recently. There were twin depressions in the moist, grassy ground, and at one end, where the grass was thinner, a couple of inches of tire tread had showed in the bare soil. Someone had scored over them with a stick.

Sunny walked up the road. The forest ticked in the hot sun. Once the rains started, this might be a good place to hunt chanterelles. It would be worth checking after the first storm.

The road became harder to follow as she walked along. No one had driven this far up in many years and the tree trunks were closing in, making it difficult to find the way. Sunny took her bearings to avoid getting lost, and to determine where the road should be. She noted the creek at the bottom of the ravine to the left, the steep hillside to her right, the main road behind her to the west, rising around the hillside. She thought the trail would eventually come out on top of the hillside, behind the elegant driveway that led to the Beroni estate. She was just lamenting that she hadn't brought a bottle of water or a compass when her cell phone rang, startling her in the quiet. The tiny screen read, *Incoming call: Wildside.* She answered it and Rivka said, "You aren't going to believe this."

"What? Do I want to believe it?"

"The thief has struck again."

She frowned. "What do you mean?"

"I mean the candied orange rinds are gone."

"Oh," said Sunny, trying not to sound relieved. "That's terrible."

"I spent hours making them. They were perfect. I just came in here to finish dipping them in chocolate and they're gone."

"Maybe somebody moved them," said Sunny.

"No, I found the container in the walk-in, right where I left it. It was empty. The cookies are gone, too. There were enough for Monday and Tuesday, and now they're gone."

"Strange. I don't think anybody could eat a whole batch of candied orange peels without being sick. Is anything else missing?"

"I don't think so. Last week it was the shortbread."

"I remember. Don't worry about making more today, we can get by without them for a day or so if we have to. Just lock up and I'll talk with everybody tomorrow and see if I can get to the bottom of it."

"Okay. I'm going home. If Heather took them for one of her stupid parties, I'll kill her."

Sunny tucked the mobile back in her pocket. She'd been yanked out of the solitude of her surroundings while she was on the phone; now the quiet rushed back in. She hiked more quickly, eager to find the end of the old logging road. Tomorrow they started a new menu at the restaurant and that always slowed things down. She'd tried leaving the menu the same for a month, but it got tired with the same regulars coming in all the time, so she went back to changing it every two weeks. It was also easier to stay on top of what local ingredients were really fresh that way. The new menu combined with her cut and bruised hands and interrogating the staff promised to make for a challenging Monday morning. Who would steal two pounds of candied orange peels? She stepped carefully, taking care not to fall again. Her hands hurt with a dull ache whenever she thought about them, and the last thing she wanted to do was fall again.

The old road went up over a gentle rise, revealing the winding paths and late-summer flowers of Louisa Beroni's rose garden across a shallow valley. The garden was designed for strolling, and there were stone benches set up here and there and a lawn in the middle. Beyond the rose garden, portions of several structures were visible through the trees, including the round tower and cupola that topped the Beroni mansion. Sunny stood catching her breath. One of the other structures must be Jack Beroni's cottage. She imagined the blond woman parking her car in the clearing and walking up this old road. Jack would meet her on the way and they would walk together, maybe even sit in the rose garden before going on to his place. From what Nesto had said, it was love as much as afternoon delight.

She turned and walked quickly back to the truck. There was one other person who might be able to tell her who this mysterious blond woman was, and maybe offer a few other insights as well. She decided to drive out to Wade's to use the phone book and the bathroom, get a drink, and maybe make a list of questions to ask Larissa Richards, assuming she would agree to meet. While she was there she could check on the berries, feed Farber, and satisfy her curiosity once and for all. Something had been nagging at her since yesterday afternoon. She'd looked for that gun, and looked carefully. Still, she couldn't shake the desire to search the winery one more time.

At Wade's, she found the phone book in the office and flipped through the white pages. There she was, "Richards, L." Sunny picked up the phone and dialed, then suddenly hung up. It certainly wouldn't be a good thing for her to see the call ID'd as Wade Skord. She reached for her mobile but remembered there was no cell reception at Wade's. She jotted down the number and went to work feeding Jasper and examining the vineyard. When she was done she headed for the winery.

It was turning dusk and she left the big sliding barn door open, letting the last of the daylight in, and switched on the single winery light. A bare bulb hanging from a rafter emitted a weary yellow glow. Wade rarely worked after dark, so he hadn't bothered installing much in the way of artificial lights. Behind her, Farber slithered in and began casing the winery shadows. Sunny stared at the barrels and tanks, the gloom of the rafters above, and the passages leading to the storage room and cave, and felt the bleakness. She could always tell when she was tired, because whatever she was doing suddenly became hopelessly overwhelming. She couldn't force herself to go over the entire winery again now. She'd check behind the racks down in the cave and have another good look around the fermentation tanks, then call it done.

The cool, musty smell of the wine cave heartened her, though she didn't find anything out of the ordinary behind the racks. As far as she could see, which was admittedly not very far in the soft light, there was nothing but dust and a few stray labels. Back in the main room, she stared at the fermentation tanks. Regretting her little yellow sweater, she reached behind the oak tank as far as she could, hugging the rough wood tank and groping along the wall with one outstretched hand. She reached the two-by-four stud that Wade always leaned the rifle against easily. She'd been thinking that the gun could have slipped beyond that and fallen out of reach. She groped further, squeezing in between the tank and the wall. Her fingertips grazed the next two-by-four without any sign of the gun. She followed the stud down as far as she could, inching toward the cement floor, then backed out, sat on the dirty floor in her good blue skirt, and leaned in sideways, feeling along the wall and then patting the floor as far as she could reach. She exhaled and squeezed another inch further into the gap, running her hand back and forth over the floor, hoping against all logic to touch the fabric of the gun case. There was nothing.

Outside, the sun was beginning to drop behind the mountains to the west and the crickets had started whirring. Sunny called to Farber and tugged the door closed after him, trying to touch the handle as little as possible, in case the police ever decided to dust it for fingerprints. She brushed off her skirt and looked down. So much for her favorite sweater. It was snagged in several places and smudged all over with thick dust. Her skirt had fared better, but not by much. Farber hurled himself against her shins while she stood, then wound in between her legs, making it impossible to walk. She bent over to sweep him up and noticed something white in the weeds. It looked like a business card. She put Farber down and picked it up. Printed in shiny, raised black letters were the words *Michael Rieder, Esq., Corporation Law.*

Sunny sat down in the grass and stared at it. The card looked crisp and white. It hadn't rained in months, but there was dew on the grass every morning. A card would get warped and stained if it lay there for very long. Sunny's heart beat quickly. How could a business card have arrived here, just outside the winery door at Skord Mountain? It might have fallen out of Wade's pocket, of course, but Wade had used the same lawyer for years, and Sunny couldn't think of any reason he would need one who specialized in corporate law. Wade didn't like corporate anything, let alone attorneys. It could have been dropped by a visitor, except that it was a notably quiet time of year at the winery with harvest on the way. Wade hadn't had any visitors as far as she knew in at least a week. There was the smallest of chances that she was wrong about that, and an equally slim chance that Rivka had dropped it when she stopped by. She looked up at the winery door with its metal handle and the tall grass and weeds growing to the right, where she'd found the card. The flesh on her arms raised with goosebumps. Suddenly it made perfect sense. She still didn't know who had dropped it, but she could see how it had happened as though in a movie. The card had landed exactly where she would have expected to find it. She walked up to the truck, slipped the card into her wallet, and drove out to the main road.

When she had four bars of cell reception again, she pulled off and dialed Larissa Richards's phone number, still not sure what she would say. Larissa picked up. With that first hello, her voice conveyed the disdain that can be an unfortunate byproduct of good breeding. Sunny stammered, her nerve faltering. What business did she have bothering a woman whose boyfriend had just been killed? This is not about being polite, she reminded herself, this is about helping Wade. Sunny explained her business, how Wade Skord had been arrested and she was looking into a way to prove his innocence.

"The police think he did it," said Larissa. "I don't see why I should subvert their efforts."

"I'm not asking you to do anything subversive, just answer a couple of quick questions. It will only take a few minutes, and you can tell the police everything we talk about. In fact, you've probably told them everything I want to know already."

Larissa reluctantly agreed, which was more than Sunny had hoped for. She followed the directions she'd jotted in her day planner while they were on the phone, wishing there was time to stop at home to change. There wasn't; the dirty, snagged sweater and the skirt with the dusty print on the butt would have to do, even for high society. She couldn't risk keeping Larissa waiting and have her decide to run off for some reason.

The house was a Spanish-style mansion complete with white adobe archways and climbing bougainvillea. Larissa answered the door herself. In her wool crepe trousers and thin purple sweater, she looked tall and almost too thin. She was probably around thirty-five and had the ingredients of beauty with her high cheekbones, pouty lips, and strong eyebrows, without, at least for the moment, actually being pretty. She was smoking a cigarette and looked like she'd been crying; her pale skin was lightly reddened and her lipstick had been rubbed off, probably from blowing her nose. She led the way outside to the patio. "Sit," she said, and gestured to a chair at a glass table. Sunny obeyed. The metal chair was icy cold. Larissa sat down opposite her. "Now, what is it you wanted to ask me?" she said in a crisp English accent.

Sunny hesitated. Behind her hostess, an effusive green lawn faced a pool as blue and inviting as the sea. An enormous avocado tree stood twenty or thirty feet tall, towering over one end of the backyard. It was covered with large, glossy leaves.

"Well, to start with," Sunny said, "do you know what Jack might have been doing on Mount Veeder last Wednesday night, late?"

Larissa made a sour face. "I have no idea. I did not keep Jack's daily calendar."

"Does he have friends who live up there?"

"I don't know, but I wouldn't be surprised. Lots of people live on Mount Veeder."

Sunny shifted in the cold chair. It was getting dark; soon it would be too cold to sit outside comfortably. The patio was an interesting choice of venue for a meeting at this time of day, no doubt designed to ensure a speedy consultation. She said, "Did you know he flew to Los Angeles at the last minute that morning for business?"

"No, but that wouldn't have been unusual. Jack traveled a good deal, often at the last minute, and he didn't exactly make a habit of keeping me informed. We saw each other maybe once or twice a week. I have—I had—no way of monitoring his whereabouts at all times when we were apart, nor did I have any particular interest in doing so." There was more than a hint of bitterness in her words.

"When Jack died, he was wearing a tuxedo. The two of you had been together that night, hadn't you?"

"Yes, he was here at the house. I always put on a formal cocktail party to celebrate crush. There were sixty or seventy people here when Jack left. I'll never do it again now. Now it will always be the night when Jack was shot."

"Why did he leave?"

"His cell phone rang and then he said he had to leave for an urgent meeting." She looked at Sunny with exasperation. "He did not say who he was going to meet or where or anything else about it. The police have been over this a dozen times."

"Did you expect him to come back?"

She smiled bitterly. "I learned a long time ago not to expect anything from Jack Beroni. It was better that way." She stubbed out the cigarette in a glass ashtray on the table and extracted the pack from the pocket of a jacket draped over the chair beside her. She tapped out another and put the pack on the table, angling it at Sunny. Sunny shook her head. Larissa struck a match and went on, holding the tiny flame at the ready. "Jack had a particular loathing of expectations. Wasn't his style."

Sunny waited while she drew on the cigarette. "Is that why you never got married?"

She exhaled a stream of smoke. "Oh, but we did, just not legally. I was reminiscing about that just before you telephoned. We were married on a sailboat in the Marquesas years ago. By a displaced Jamaican priest we'd picked up in Tahiti. Defrocked, of course." Larissa held a thin, pale hand up for Sunny to see. A diamond ring of the sort found in piñatas and candy machines sat on her ring finger. When Sunny looked up, she almost thought Larissa would cry. The next instant, the steely mask came back over her face. "That was years ago. We were terribly, terribly in love, like kids. Or at least one of us was. I was very young." She smoked, studying Sunny. "How much have they told you? Not much, I'd wager. The phone call Jack received here at the party, for example, did you know it was made from the phone booth outside the Dusty Vine?"

Sunny tried not to look surprised. "When exactly was that?"

"About ten o'clock."

The Dusty Vine was a little honkytonk bar a few miles from Wade's place where the locals drank beer and played pool. "I assume nobody saw who it was?"

"Not as far as I know, but I'm sure they'll find someone. If they can get hold of someone who will say it was your friend, they've got him." Larissa pulled on the cigarette and exhaled, smiling. A middle-aged maid in a black-and-white uniform walked by the sliding glass door to the patio, lingering at the opening. Her black hair was pulled back tightly in a bun. Larissa turned to Sunny. "Would you like something to drink?"

Sunny declined. Larissa shook her head and the woman went away.

Sunny said, "Had Jack ever met anyone at the gazebo before? It seems odd."

"Not that I know of."

"Why wouldn't he meet the person at his home?"

Larissa shrugged with a resigned smile.

Sunny said, "I'm sure the police have asked already, but did Jack have any enemies? Anybody who was angry at him? Failed business deal? Argument? Maybe there was a recent event that might have upset someone?"

"I'm sure plenty of people wanted to kill Jack at one point or another. He was powerful, and he had enemies. All powerful people have enemies. Jack made it worse by cultivating them."

"Anyone in particular?" asked Sunny.

"No, no one in particular," said Larissa. "I thought for a while it might have been that old idiot Nesto Campaglia, but he doesn't have the nerve."

"Nesto? Why?"

"Boss's son versus boss's right-hand man. The usual rivalry."

"There has to be something. Was Jack into anything new? New business, hobby, sport? Recent trip somewhere unusual?"

Larissa shook her head.

"Anything unusual at all about the days or weeks before his murder? Anything at all perplexing about his behavior?"

"Nothing. As far as I could tell, Jack was as he has always been. Elusive, opaque, secretive."

Sunny studied her. She seemed to be seething with bitterness and sorrow. People sometimes reacted that way when a loved one dies. She'd seen it in her family when her uncle passed away. The people close to him were overcome with grief, with the exception of his wife, who was raging with anger at him for leaving. Sunny took a deep breath. "You and Jack were together for several years. How would you describe your relationship?"

Larissa stared at her calmly and smoked. Her green eyes were like turquoise stones. Jack would have stared into those eyes on so many occasions, thought Sunny. This face with the white skin and the gemlike eyes was the one he knew best and loved least, if Sunny guessed right.

Sunny said, "I mean, did you see other people?"

Larissa gave her the bitter smile again. "Jack was a serial polygamist. He was always seeing other women. He couldn't help it. He fancied himself a connoisseur, I suppose."

"Do you know who he was seeing recently?"

Larissa stood up and paced the patio—imported slate, from the look of it—and plucked at the dead leaves on a nearby lilac bush with short, fierce little motions. Her red hair picked up the last of the evening sunlight beautifully. At last she said, "I don't really know. I had my suspicions. I thought that he might be trying to rekindle an old high-school romance. It's crazy, but that's what I thought. He was talking a lot about his high-school days, very idealistically. Whenever Jack fell in love, he would idealize the woman's life. If he was sleeping with a ballerina, suddenly the most glorious art form in existence would be dance, and he'd talk about it all the time. If she was a florist, it would be all about ikebana. He'd buy a dozen books on flower arranging and stay up all night reading about the natural history of the tulip. He couldn't help himself. I think this time it was a sort of early midlife crisis, an attempt to return to the warmth and security of his adolescence. He wanted to reclaim his innocence."

"His high-school girlfriend is still here?"

"I think so." Larissa turned and stared at Sunny. Judging by her disapproving look, Sunny surmised she was expected to leave now. She stood and they walked back through the house to the front door. Sunny thanked her for her time. On a whim she threw out one last question: "Who is Michael Rieder?"

"Mike? He's Jack's attorney."

10

The last of a whipped orange-and-gold sunset dissipated as Sunny drove toward Gabe Campaglia's place. He was about the same age as Jack, which meant they would have gone to high school together. There was no point in going to a private school in St. Helena, when the local high school looked like an Ivy League spa and had a better reputation for academic excellence than most colleges. Gabe would probably know who Jack's sweetheart had been.

It took close to an hour to get up the valley to Gabe's house, and by the time she arrived at his place, she was feeling the heaviness of the long day. It was almost a relief to see that the cottage was dark and Gabe's truck was nowhere in sight. She turned around and headed home.

There were plenty of cars on the highway—the usual wine country assortment of farm trucks and midrange family cars belonging to the locals, the European sedans of visitors, and the occasional racy sports car of the successful vintner. She wasn't sure when she first noticed a particular set of headlights behind her. It was more that she became gradually aware of them, perhaps because they stayed constant while all the others sped past, fell behind, or turned off. For miles, one set of headlights was always one or two vehicles back. When she hit town, she turned down Adams Street, then took a left on Adelaide. As she made the turn, she saw the flicker of another car's headlights turning onto Adams behind her. She slowed, then stopped and waited for the car to pass by on Adams, feeling slightly paranoid. She was surprised when it didn't go by. They could only have parked or turned down one of the other two streets between Adelaide and the highway, neither of which supported many houses. Either it's nothing, she thought, or I'm being followed. She made a slow U-turn and parked in front of her place. She couldn't see anything other than elm trees and a few lights on inside each of the houses. She thought of walking up to Adams and checking to see if anybody was sitting in any of the cars parked along the street. Then she thought how she was letting her mind work on her, feeding her unsubstantiated fears. Tomorrow would start very early; now she needed to get some sleep.

Inside, she locked the door just in case and closed all the curtains. She mixed some granola and plain yogurt for a rare stand-up dinner and headed for the bedroom. The window stood open and she walked over to close it, then changed her mind. The night air this time of year was too nice to shut out just because she felt spooked. She changed into sweats and a T-shirt, took a quick peek under the bed out of old habit, and crawled between the sheets, falling immediately asleep.

Two hours later she opened her eyes suddenly. Her muscles were tensed and she had the definite feeling that a sound had woken her. She lay still, her heart pounding, listening. She heard only the creak of the house settling, the occasional scuff of dry leaves moving under some ripple of breeze, a tiny creature scurrying in the backyard. She told herself she was letting her mind obsess over Jack's murder. She was letting fear shake her. She rolled over and wiggled until she was comfortable, determined to go back to sleep. Her left hand hurt. It was throbbing and felt hot. She turned onto her other side, conscious of where she put her hand and the throbbing. Her arm ached as well. She listened again, straining to pick up a footfall or the scrape of a door opening. On the third rotation in bed, her mind began to turn over a growing collection of questions. Who had dropped Michael Rieder's business card? Could Larissa have hired someone to kill Jack? Why did Jack Beroni stay with Larissa? Who will inherit Beroni Vineyards when Al and Louisa die?

It was no use, she couldn't sleep. She opened her eyes. Quarter to twelve. She stretched out flat on her back, then got out of bed and changed into jeans and an old sweater. If she couldn't sleep, at least she would do something productive. Sunny attempted to convince herself that sleeping at night was an essentially arbitrary tradition and that it was merely the rut of habit and closed-minded thinking that kept late-night baking from being the norm. It really was the nicest time of day to bake; perfectly quiet, plenty of elbowroom in the kitchen. To prove her point, she decided to go down to the restaurant and work on replacements for Rivka's missing cookies, maybe even simmer up a batch of candied orange peels. It was better than tossing and turning in bed and trying not to think about things. Baking, with all the gooey and powdery textures and the warm smells, had always been the best way to unwind when something was bothering her. When she got home she would be so tired, she would sleep like a baby, at least for a few hours until it was time to go back to work. Best not to think of everything that had happened. The thing to do was focus on the cookies.

The jangle of the front-door bells as she left the house broke the silence of the sleepy block and started a chain reaction of dogs barking. Sunny crept out through the front yard to the truck and shut the door softly. There was no avoiding the roar of the engine, which to her sounded loud enough to wake every creature for miles. She flipped on the headlights and froze a pair of raccoons skittering across the pavement. They stared into the high beams with guilty faces, then hotfooted it into the shrubs between two houses. Sunny drove out to the highway. Not long after she'd turned south toward Wildside, a pair of headlights appeared in the distance behind her, the only other car on the road. Its sudden appearance was odd, because that stretch of highway was perfectly straight for a couple of miles in either direction and there had been no cars in sight when she pulled out. It must have come from a side road, like she had, without her noticing.

At the narrow, bumpy road leading to Wildside, Sunny turned off, crossed the railroad tracks, and drove slowly toward the parking lot, keeping tabs as much as possible on the highway. She stopped and killed the lights, watching the highway in her rearview mirror. No cars passed. She pulled into the lot and cut the engine, rolled down the window, and listened, watching through the trees for the glow of lights on the highway. A car passed in the opposite direction. After a while, she got out and walked up to where she could see the road directly. There were no headlights. The crimson taillights of the car that had just passed receded toward Mount St. Helena, but the other car had vanished. She walked back and let herself into the restaurant. She switched on the lights.

Even with its stainless-steel racks and the industrial rubber mats on the floor, the kitchen looked inviting. How could the car have vanished? *Vanished,* she thought, chastising herself, is an overly dramatic description. The car had simply turned off the highway, or pulled to the side and turned off its lights, or turned around and gone in the other direction. There was nothing sinister about any of that. How often had cars followed and then disappeared before without her notice? She was nervous and her imagination was running ahead, unimpeded by good sense. It was even possible, assuming the worst, that the car had never been there in the first place and she was losing her mind. The hallucinations of a crazed insomniac baker. Of course, there was one other possibility: Someone was following her.

She took three balls of chilled hazelnut dough out of the walk-in and left them on the counter, then reached for the wire citrus bowl from a shelf and selected eight oranges as bright as Wade's correctional institution jumpsuit. At the sink, she scrubbed the wax off their skins. Someone had followed her home. At least she'd had that feeling, even if she hadn't actually seen the car itself, only lights. If someone really was following her just now, that meant they had been waiting and watching her house. Somebody was losing sleep making sure they knew where she was day and night. It could be Steve Harvey or some other cop keeping tabs on her. She quartered the oranges and peeled away the fruit, then put the rinds on to simmer in a skillet of water and started making a replacement batch of cookie dough. The smell of oranges filled the room.

Rubber gloves protected her injured hand from the acid of the oranges but did nothing to make mixing stiff dough less painful. Each time she turned the heavy dough, the spoon cut into her palm where she'd fallen. There was a power mixer a few feet away, beckoning. She always struggled with the belief—difficult to verify absolutely—that the electric mixer robbed dough of a certain nameless quality. She stopped to strain the orange rinds, cover them with cold water again, and put them on to simmer a second time. She turned the cookie dough a few more times, the wooden spoon forced painfully against her palm, and then brusquely dumped the mixture into the electric mixer's trough and hit the switch. The contraption roared to life, producing smooth and even dough in less than a minute. Too smooth and too even, thought Sunny. It was boring dough, lacking the complexity of idiosyncrasy. On top of it, or perhaps more to the point, the sound had raised the hair on her neck. That sound just gave anyone creeping about outside the opportunity to move around without being heard, even open a door or a window. That sound had just made her all the more vulnerable. The cooling unit on the walk-in clicked on, blanketing the room in low noise that would surely drown out any stalker's footsteps. Baking was not proving to be restful.

Sunny found an open bottle of Bandol red up front and poured herself a generous glass, thinking, Get a grip, McCoskey, it is ridiculous to let yourself get all spooked. You are a grown woman armed with a cook's razor-sharp cutlery and an arsenal of modern industrial kitchen appliances. And so is anyone else in this building, countered her subconscious. She went back to the kitchen and shaped the new cookie dough into three neat balls, wrapped them in cellophane, and stored them in the walk-in, being careful not to startle herself by catching sight of her reflection as she passed by the windows.

She grabbed the chilled dough off the counter and dusted a board and rolling pin with flour. She was letting her imagination take over. No one was following her; no one was watching her. She rolled the dough flat, ignoring the pain in her hand, and began to cut autumn-leaf shapes with a butter knife. Sunny was very good at cutting autumn-leaf shapes, and normally this would be her favorite part of any day at work. She looked at the clock and went to take the orange peels off the stove to cool, then continued rolling and cutting. Assuming that there was only one guilty party responsible for Jack's murder, then the events of Thursday night were relatively easy to guess. At around ten o'clock, the killer stops at the Dusty Vine and uses the pay phone out in the parking lot to make a call to Jack Beroni's mobile. Jack answers and hears something compelling enough to take him away from his girlfriend's party in the middle of the evening to a secret meeting in a dark and secluded place. A few minutes later, he leaves the party and drives home, probably directly. He walks down to the gazebo and waits, growing impatient, even annoyed. He lights a cigarette. Meanwhile, the killer has stashed her—or his—car on the old logging road neatly hidden from view. She tucks a pair of gloves in her pocket and walks to Wade's place. When she arrives at the winery door, she pulls out her gloves and puts them on, not noticing that she has dislodged a business card she was recently given. Knowing at least vaguely where to look, she finds Wade's gun, takes it along with the case, and makes her way overland to the lake at the base of Beroni Vineyards. She waits. With the moon shining, the night is almost too bright for her purposes. She spots Jack walking down the hill, his white shirt picking up the moonlight like neon. She can even see the light hit his polished shoes. She waits, watching. When she is ready, she lifts the rifle to her shoulder and settles her eye to the scope, sliding the crosshairs over the scene until they come to rest on his heart. She knows better than to second-guess a shot. She exhales, steadies her aim, and pulls the trigger.

What comes next is the hard part. She drops the gun, leaving it, the spent cartridge, and the canvas case behind. There is absolutely no reason to risk having the murder weapon found in her possession. She goes back to her car, hoping no one has heard the shot, or if they have, that they assume it is Wade playing Assault Golf. With all those hills and valleys to bounce the report around, no one would be able to say where the shot came from, anyway. But Steve Harvey said that the gun was not there. He and his team had looked hard enough to be certain it wasn't there. Still, it didn't make sense for the murderer to remove the weapon. Maybe she simply ditched it nearby and the police missed it. Sunny had just been over that landscape, and a coyote with a metal detector could miss a gun out there. Between the brush, the down leaves, and the steep terrain, it would be easy to hide.

Sunny thought she had a good idea of how Jack was murdered and still no idea why or by whom. What made her think she could figure it out, anyway? Whoever shot Jack is going to get away with it. And it is entirely possible that a jury will convict Wade Skord. She had to figure out who did it.

She slid a tray of leaf cookies into the oven. The person who killed Jack was almost certainly the person who called him that night at Larissa's party. It had to be someone he knew and wanted to see, even go out of his way to meet urgently and clandestinely. Judging by Larissa's description of Jack, that would almost certainly indicate a woman, perhaps the mysterious blond girlfriend from high school. And yet Gabe had already outed Jack's rendezvous technique. If it had been a simple booty call, surely they would have met at his house, using the old logging road. Whoever he expected to meet, she was a good shot and familiar with Wade, his gun, his property, and the Beroni place. She'd had some kind of contact with Jack's lawyer. And she'd planned far enough ahead not to leave any fingerprints. She also would have needed to bring her own bullet.

There were still one or two more slender threads that might lead somewhere. Sunny would go see Michael Rieder in the morning, ask him who had he given his business card to in the last week or so, and what had he and Jack been talking about lately. It was a long shot, but it was worth trying since she didn't have much else to go on. And she needed to find out who Jack's high-school sweetheart was. That shouldn't be too hard; he went to school with plenty of people. Come to think of it, she had a few questions for Steve Harvey as well, and she needed to turn over that business card as evidence. She had a funny feeling it wouldn't mean much to Sergeant Harvey. She could already see the indulgent look on his face, like, "That's probably been lying around for a month." Still, you never know. Maybe somehow it would help Wade's case.

She pulled the first tray of cookies out and slid another in, then went up front for another glass of wine. On the way back she heard a sound like a shoe scuffing against stone outside the window, and when she looked up she caught a glimpse of a face pulling away from the window. Her heart pounded. She put the wine down and went to her bag, found her cell phone, and checked the signal and battery. She turned the lock on the back door and slipped into the dining room to check the front door. When she came back into the kitchen, she took a ten-inch knife from the rack, placed it on the counter beside her, and stood still, listening and waiting.

Wildside, for all its virtues, was not a secure building. Fortresslike security had never been a priority. The windows were low and accessible, with antique closures designed to discourage a breeze, not a crowbar. Even the bolt on the main door was screwed into soft wood. One good shove would pull it away.

The back door actually sported a hook latch, like the one on the screen door at her grandmother's house. The handle locked, but that was not much security.

She pulled the second tray of golden brown cookies out of the oven and put the orange peels into their final sugary boil. She looked at her watch. Ten minutes after two. Suddenly the insanity of what she was doing struck home. Why was she baking cookies and boiling orange peels at this hour of the morning? Had she lost her mind? She thought of what Wade would say in a phony West Texas drawl when he was pretending not to be scared. "A coward dies a thousand deaths, a brave man dies but once."

She speed-dialed Rivka on her cell. Rivka's phone rang four times, taking what seemed like an eternity between each ring, then the voice mail picked up. Sunny hung up. Normally she would phone Wade at a time like this. She could call Steve Harvey, but he'd give her a speech about staying out of police business. Charlie? She thought for a moment and then hit the number for Monty, who answered in a groggy voice.

"Hello?" he said.

"Monty," whispered Sunny.

"Sunny? What time is it?"

"Late. Or early, depending. Listen, could you just stay on the line with me for a couple of minutes?"

"What's the matter? What's going on?" Sunny heard Annabelle in the background, asking who was on the phone. Monty said, "It's Sunny. Something's wrong."

"Nothing's wrong. I'm at the restaurant and I thought I saw someone creeping around outside."

"You what? I'm calling the police."

"No, don't! They'll make a big fuss. Just stay on the line while I get out of here."

"I'm coming down. I'll be there in seven minutes."

"You don't have to do that. I'm just going to close up and get out of here. I'm going to put the phone in my pocket so you can listen. If you hear a thud or a shriek and the line goes dead, would you send somebody over here?"

"Right. Will do."

Sunny turned off the orange peels, looked at the cookies sitting out on their trays with regret, made sure all the lights were on inside and out, and then threw open the back door. She ran hunched over like a Green Beret to the truck, just in case whoever was out there was a shooter. She managed to slide the key into the ignition, roll up the window, lock the door, start the engine, and hit reverse in one fast, smooth motion. She put it in first and hit the gas. Crunching and throwing gravel, the truck bounded out of the parking lot. A few bounces and a slight fish-tail and Sunny was on the road.

She found the cell phone in her pocket. "You still there?"

"Way to burn rubber!" said Monty.

"You could hear that?"

"You bet. Listen, say 'I'm fine' if you're okay and 'I'm okay' if you need help."

"I'm fine."

"How do I know there's no one holding you at gunpoint, telling you to say that?"

"Monty, there is no one holding me at gunpoint. I'm okay now."

"What—is that code or really?"

"Monty, enough cloak-and-dagger! I'm safe. Thanks for talking me in."

"Okay. Call me when you are inside your house."

"I will."

"Don't forget, or there will be a SWAT team breaking down your door in about ten minutes."

"I won't forget. Thanks, Monty. Um, you and Annabelle won't . . ."

"Tell anyone? No, we won't. I'm getting you sleeping pills for Christmas, McCoskey."

"Thanks."

II

Sunny got out of bed automatically and staggered to the front door, wondering who was knocking at six-thirty in the morning. She peeked through the hole and opened the door. Charlie Rhodes stood on the stoop looking fresh as a new daisy in sport sandals and outdoorsy shorts. His silky brown hair stuck up in front and he had an exhilarated smile on his face, as though he'd just ridden down a big hill on his bike. The collar of an olive-green microfiber shirt showed under a slate-blue pullover made out of some trademarked descendant of fleece designed to wick away or ward off everything from excess personal moisture to rain, sleet, and dead of night.

Sunny stood in the old gray sweatshirt and baggy drawstring pants she'd gone to sleep in and ran her hands over her hair, smoothing her bangs to one side and tucking the loose ends behind her ear. She ran her hand over her face and rubbed discreetly at what must be a crust of drool near the corner of her mouth. Any chance she might have had at a romance with Charlie Rhodes was in serious jeopardy. She frowned at the navy-blue sky behind him and said, in what turned out to be a froggy voice, "When I said let's have coffee at six-thirty, I'm pretty sure I meant let's have coffee at nine-thirty."

"Huh, I guess I missed that part. You want me to come back later?"

"No, no. I just want to complain about it. Get in here, the draft is freezing my toes."

"Are you okay?"

"Mm. Dandy. Why?"

"You seem tired and, uh, grouchy."

"Tired. That makes sense. The grouchy part should wear off in a sec. Don't be alarmed."

She padded into the kitchen with Charlie trailing behind her and put water on for coffee, loaded glossy black-brown beans into the grinder, gritted her teeth against the coming noise, and pushed the button. The roar of grinding assaulted her tender sleep-deprived ears. It was a painful introduction to the day, but unavoidable, and at least it would soon be counterbalanced by the smell and taste of fresh coffee. She took a pair of clunky ceramic mugs down from the cabinet and handed one to Charlie. They stood staring at the teakettle and blue flame, mugs held like sepulchers in front of them. Sunny struggled to stay in the conscious world. Charlie had woken her in the middle of a dream and she kept tumbling back into it. She was at Skord Mountain, walking in the vineyard. The vines were lush with green leaves and heavy with plump fruit, the way they were now. As she walked through them, pushing their reaching arms aside, they began to wither and crumble under her touch until all around her the vines were brown and dead. She looked around in alarm and saw that the entire vineyard was dying. Soon all the leaves and berries had shriveled and fallen off, and the vines themselves were desiccated and brittle. She started to run back to the house to tell Wade, and as she ran, the vineyard turned from brown to ghostly white. When she looked back from the porch, the hillside was an ashen white graveyard of dead vines and stakes sticking up like markers in a wide cemetery. She recited the dream to Charlie.

"It's the kaolin clay. I told you about that on Friday night at dinner," said Charlie. "Down in Temecula, they sprayed the vineyards with clay to keep the sharpshooters from getting to them, but it didn't work. They just ended up with acres of dead vineyard painted white."

"I remember," said Sunny, staring dully into space. "That must be it."

"There's news on the sharpshooter front, as a matter of fact."

She glanced up at him. "Good news?"

"Well, I guess I'd have to say it's bad news. They found one late Friday afternoon."

"You mean inside the valley?"

"It was in one of the yellow sticky traps up on Mount Veeder. In an olive grove near the vineyard at the Maya Culpa Vineyard."

"The Maya Culpa. That's up by Monty's house. And Hansen Ranch. Don't tell me they're going to spray up there."

"Not yet. There's an emergency meeting this morning to decide what to do about it."

"But it's a possibility?"

"Absolutely."

"Oh my God, they can't do that. That's where most of Wildside's produce comes from. And they'll put Hansen Ranch completely out of business."

"It's not decided yet. And it might not be the end of Hansen Ranch. They passed a law that says in case of emergency, organic produce can be sprayed and still be called organic."

"Oh, that's comforting. So now *organic* is a euphemism for *pesticide-flavored*. Does this situation really qualify as an emergency? One bug?"

"We'll see. I'm going to suggest we have a good look around before we do anything. It might actually be a single rogue specimen, just some lone sharpie off on his own, way out ahead of the pack. Frankly, it's not likely, but it's worth taking the time to be sure. Unfortunately, the Conservation Corps intern who identified the specimen on Friday didn't tell anybody about it until yesterday, or we might have started checking out the area over the weekend."

The kettle piped and Sunny poured boiling water into a French press and stirred the grounds. While it brewed, she stood on a chair and rummaged in the cabinet over the refrigerator. She took down an unopened bottle of drinkable Merlot, nothing fancy.

"That's just terrible news," she said. "I was really hoping they would be able to keep it out of the valley for a few more months by being super vigilant at the inspection stations. I assume the Maya Culpa people are freaking out."

"I don't think they know yet," said Charlie. "I tried to reach them last night, but I kept getting the machine and I didn't want to leave that kind of information in a message." He held up his fist by his ear as if he were holding a telephone. "'Hey, just wanted to let you know that your vineyard is probably infested with sharpies and about to die of Pierce's disease. Even if it's not, we'll be by to bomb it tomorrow or the next day.' I'll try to reach them again this morning. They're going to want to be at the meeting."

Sunny hunched over the coffeepot and pressed the filter down slowly with both hands. "I'd like to be there, too. If they spray Hansen Ranch, it will have a direct impact on Wildside. I can't serve food that's been treated with carbaryl even if Sacramento says it's organic. We've built our reputation on genuinely organic food and wine."

"Right," said Charlie. "That makes sense. You're more than welcome to attend. In fact, everyone is welcome. It's a public meeting. Has to be because they're talking about putting together a countywide mandatory initiative."

"You mean spraying land from here to Calistoga whether we like it or not."

"Well, yeah. Probably more localized than that."

Sunny cranked the corkscrew down and squeezed the bottle of Merlot between her thighs. The cork made a throaty *ponk!* when she pulled it out, a sound that always cheered her up. She unscrewed the cork and laid it neatly beside the bottle, then poured them coffee and added a splash of red wine to hers. She held the bottle over his cup. "Do you like it this way?"

"I'll skip. I generally try not to start drinking until lunch."

"It's not drinking. It's just a splash for flavor. Robert Mondavi does it."

"So does the pope, but that doesn't make me Catholic."

She grinned. "No need to get sassy about it. If you don't want to be cool like me and Robert, that's fine. Suit yourself."

They went out the kitchen door to the patio and settled into a couple of splintery old redwood deck chairs Sunny kept out there for just this sort of occasion. Come to think of it, it was just the sort of occasion she'd been hoping for: namely, Charlie Rhodes putting his feet up in her house, or at least on her patio. She smiled to herself. It was still cold, but the first of the morning light promised another beautiful day. Even sitting down she had that dizzy feeling insomniacs know so well. Pinpoint lights danced in the periphery of her vision. Sleep deprivation was unpleasant, but being an altered state, it had some enjoyable aspects to offer, assuming you didn't need to get anything done that day. She pulled her legs up under her and huddled over her coffee.

"So when and where is this meeting taking place?"

"Eight o'clock. At the new courthouse. The room number will be posted on the bulletin board as you walk in."

They sipped quietly.

Charlie said, "It should be interesting. Jack Beroni has been the strong arm of the pro-spray contingent for a while now. With him gone, it's hard to say how the debate is going to go."

"The big wineries must have had more than Jack representing them."

"Yeah, they send a cadre of suits to most of these things. But Jack was leading them. He had the most clout because he's a Beroni, and he was charismatic. People listened to him. They'll still have plenty of representation without him, but it's not going to be as credible or persuasive. This could be a real battle for the big wineries. They're big employers, so some people may support them to protect their jobs. I expect the organic contingent to come out in force, and a lot of the public is going to be behind them. The down-valley residents don't want their yards sprayed with chemicals just so the corporate wine baron on the hill can make more money. It's going to be a tough sell."

"Were you there when Wade and Jack got into it recently at some meeting?"

"You mean when he said he would shoot anybody who got near his land without his permission? Yeah, I was there. I've been going to the Vintners Association meetings for a while now."

"I was hoping the account I heard was exaggerated, but I guess not."

"He popped off pretty good, but I don't think anybody thought he was speaking literally. At least I didn't. It was just something you say. You know, 'I'll kill the bastards!'"

"Well, it certainly hasn't helped his case."

"No, I guess it wouldn't. It's just his luck that Jack had to really go and get himself shot. I've definitely seen worse behavior, especially at the ag board meetings. I saw a guy throw a chair at a county supervisor once. It was like watching the Incredible Hulk with everything happening in slow motion." He held up his arm as though warding off a flying chair and demonstrated a slow-motion grimace of shock and horror. "Everybody gets all bent out of shape at these meetings. Their businesses are at stake. What one guy needs to stay in business forces another guy out of business."

"It's crazy when you think about it. All this fuss over grapes. They're just little globes of water and sugar."

"Yep, and money is just little rectangles of paper," said Charlie.

Sunny scrubbed her eyes and succumbed to a forceful yawn. Charlie tugged on her little toe. "What's your story? You seem wiped out. Late night?"

"Very. I couldn't sleep, so I went down to the restaurant and did way too much baking and then scared myself silly thinking the boogeyman was going to get me. Finally I came home and passed out, but by then it was about three in the morning."

"I didn't know you had the boogeyman at Wildside."

"Normally we don't, but last night I could have sworn someone was following me."

"Are you serious?"

"Oh, I don't know. Probably it was nothing."

"It's not nothing if you thought somebody was following you. Did you see somebody?"

"No, not really. Actually, I'm sure it was my imagination, but I thought I saw a face at the window of the restaurant. But I was tired and it was late, so it probably wasn't really there. I hope."

Charlie gave her a look. "I can't believe you went to work in the middle of the night in the first place. What about reading a book or taking a warm bath?"

"It's easier to understand if you run your own restaurant. Manic compulsive disorder is part of the job description."

Charlie nodded slowly, studying her face. He looked at his watch, a plastic and Velcro job that looked like something GI Joe would wear. He tipped back the last of his coffee. "I better get going. I'll see you at the meeting. Eight o'clock."

"Right. I'll be there."

Sunny walked behind him to the door, seizing the opportunity to ogle his calves, which were nicely shaped, with a strong swath of tendon running up each side. She watched him climb into a white pickup truck with the gold Napa County insignia on the door. She waved as he drove away, then went back into the kitchen for more coffee.

She was late for work.

When Sunny pulled up at the restaurant at a quarter to eight, Rivka's car was already there. Sunny got out and scanned the gravel parking lot, hunting some unknown sign that would reveal whether or not a stranger had trespassed the night before. The sharpshooter wanted poster was still there, staple-gunned to the fence that ran along the property line. Somebody had penned a handlebar mustache on the bug's mug shot. Sunny walked toward the entrance to the restaurant and then turned off on the little trail that led around the side. She stopped at the window where she thought she'd seen a face. She felt certain it had been a man. There didn't look to be any fingerprints on the window, nor in the fine layer of silt covering the ledge of the window frame. She crouched down. Beneath the window, in the soft soil beside a bushy growth of lemon verbena, was a large, deep, complete footprint of some kind of work boot, about a men's size ten, if she had to guess.

Inside, Rivka had the music cranked up while she prepped for lunch. Sunny turned it down on her way in.

"Hey, R.C., I have to make some calls in the office. Mind if we don't rock out for a sec?"

"No problem. Happy Monday. Hey, it looks like the orange peel fairy came last night."

"Wow, really? That's great."

"And the cookie fairy. But she left all the lights on and everything sitting out. Very unusual behavior for a kitchen fairy." Rivka looked at Sunny.

"I'll explain later."

Sunny went into the office. She closed the door behind her, then moved a heavy stack of mail off the chair and sat down. *Note to self: Must open mail sometime this decade.* She grabbed a notepad and penciled out a list of questions, then picked up the phone. She put the phone back down and looked around the desk for Steve Harvey's business card with no luck. She dug in her knapsack. Finally she called the police station. After a few transfers and a wrong number, she reached him on his mobile.

"Sergeant Harvey speaking."

"Hi, Steve. It's Sonya McCoskey calling."

"Sunny. I hope this is a social call."

"What other kind is there? I'm just phoning to say how nice it was to run into you the other day."

"Isn't that nice. Why do I feel like we're about to run into each other again?"

"That's very insightful. As a matter of fact, I was wondering if you were free for a quick coffee this morning. We could meet at Bismark's."

"What's this about?"

"I'd rather tell you in person, if that's okay. How soon could you be there?"

"I could be there in, oh, ten minutes."

"I'll see you there."

She hung up the phone and grabbed her car keys. In the kitchen, Rivka was chopping enormous mounds of parsley and cornichons into fine bits for salsa verde, Provençal style. There was almost nothing more delicious with grilled vegetables and roasted meat than Rivka's salsa verde.

"Riv, I have to step out for a bit, but I'll be back as soon as I can. Do you know what we have on the books today?"

"Thirty-eight."

"That's not too bad. We should be fine, assuming I can get back before nine-thirty or so. Maybe ten."

Rivka kept chopping. "Yep, we'll be fine. No worries."

"Ciao, bella."

"Hasta pronto."

Sunny eased the truck into a diagonal parking spot across the street from Bismark's. Inside, she ordered a glass of orange juice, a cinnamon croissant, and an everything bagel with cream cheese, basil, and tomato. There had been a serious downturn in caloric intake during the past two days and her belly spooned in from her ribs. She could feel the custodians in charge of metabolism breaking up the furniture and pulling the siding off the walls, trying to keep the internal furnace stoked up. It was like a scene out of *Dr. Zhivago* in there. While she stood waiting for the bagel to come up, she wolfed down the croissant. She was ready for a full-course meal at the next opportunity, but who could tell when that would be. A girl with wrists like batons and black eyeliner caked along the inside edges of her eyelids slid the warm bagel across to her without smiling or speaking. Sunny perched it on top of her orange juice, grabbed a pre-read section of the newspaper out of a basket on the floor, and selected a table in the corner, far from the stream of people coming in for coffee-to-go. She had read the advice column, the comics, and a movie review by the time Steve Harvey walked in. He scanned the room, acknowledging the people he recognized with a lift of the chin. He came over without getting coffee.

"Morning, Sunny."

"Morning, Steve. Can I get you a cup of the dark stuff?"

He sat down across from her. "No, thanks. I'm all juiced up already."

She took a bite of the bagel and reluctantly returned it to its nest of waxy white paper. She wiped her mouth, trying to think how to begin. Steve looked impatient. Better ante up fast. "I was out at Wade's house yesterday and I found something that might interest you."

"What's that?"

"This." She put Michael Rieder's business card on the table.

"A business card?"

"I found it in the grass off to the right side of the winery door. Do you know who Mike Rieder is?"

"No. Should I?"

"He's Jack Beroni's attorney." She watched him. "Whoever stole Wade's gun dropped Mike Rieder's business card in the process."

He turned the card over in his hands, examining it. "That's only one explanation, and it happens to be one of the more far-fetched. Wade probably dropped it himself."

"I don't think so. I can't think of any reason Wade would have it."

He gave her a skeptical look.

"Steve, you and I both know that somebody is trying to frame Wade Skord."

He slipped the card into his breast pocket in an official-looking capacity. "Thank you, Sunny. I'll see that it is put into evidence."

She tried to look casual while she checked off questions on a list in her head. "Have you heard anything back from the autopsy?"

"Just what we expected. Cause of death: gunshot wound to the chest. Approximate time of death: between eleven and eleven-thirty Thursday night."

"What about Wade's gloves? Did they come back positive for gunpowder residue?"

Steve smiled and shook his head. "Negative."

"I thought so. He doesn't wear gloves when he shoots."

"I wouldn't have expected him to."

"Then why test them?"

"Because if I were going to use someone else's gun, I would wear gloves. I might even wear that individual's own gloves, for continuity and because they happened to be lying around. I could use them and put them back and no one would ever know, whereas if I use my own, I have to dispose of them or risk somebody finding them full of gunshot residue. It was just a little theory of mine that didn't pan out."

"So you're not sure he did it."

"I'm interested in what actually happened. It's my job to investigate every reasonable possibility."

"Did you find any fingerprints in the winery?"

"That's confidential information."

Sunny sighed. That meant they hadn't looked yet. She thought so. There hadn't been any powder on anything. "And what about the gun? Has it turned up?"

Steve seemed to consider whether or not to answer the question. He glanced at the counter, probably reconsidering a cup of coffee. Finally he said, "Nothing's turned up so far."

"You looked in the woods below the lake?"

"Yep. We combed the area thoroughly."

"All the way back to Wade's winery?"

"No, not that far, it's not realistic. But we made a broad sweep of the area."

"How about the spent shell? Did you find that?"

"Nope."

"Wade kept his gun in a canvas case. The case is missing as well. Did you find that?"

"No, but that's interesting."

"And what about the lake? Has anybody looked for the gun in the lake?"

"In the lake? No, I can't say we have."

"Don't you think it's a good idea? It's a great place to throw a gun when you're done with it."

"How many cups of coffee have you had this morning?"

"Just two. I'm just trying to cover everything before your walkie-talkie goes off and you race out of here."

He sighed. "I wish you wouldn't get mixed up in this, Sunny. For one thing, finding Wade Skord's gun near the scene of the crime is only going to further incriminate him."

"I'm like you, Steve. I just want to know what happened. I know that when we find out the truth about what really happened Thursday night, Wade Skord will be cleared of any part of it." She sat up and tilted her head, jerking it abruptly at the exact angle that made the bones in her neck crack loudly. Steve started at the gesture. She reminded herself not to do that in public. If she took time to go to yoga, she wouldn't need to crack her neck in the first place. She said, "That phone call that took Jack Beroni away from Larissa Richards's party Thursday night, it was made from the pay phone outside the Dusty Vine, is that right?"

Sergeant Harvey frowned, encouraging the vertical line that Sunny had noticed developing between his eyebrows. In a few years it would be permanent. "You know I can't discuss the details of a criminal case with you, Sunny. This has gone way too far already."

"Is that a yes?"

"It's a 'No comment.'"

That was a yes in her book. She gave him a smile she hoped would soften him up. "Okay, just one more question." He opened his hands in a gesture that said, "Go ahead. It's not like I can stop you." He wasn't making this easy, but he wasn't making it impossible, either. She took a breath and exhaled. "With Jack Beroni dead, who inherits Beroni Vineyards when Al and Louisa pass on?"

Steve shook his head. "You are in way over your head, Sunny. This is not any of your business, and you're only going to stir up more trouble for Wade."

"It's Gabe and Alex Campaglia, isn't it?"

Steve shook his head in some combination of annoyance, disbelief, and amusement. He looked away and bit his lower lip, sucking air through his teeth in squeaky little bursts like mouse sounds.

"It's true," she said, unable to keep the amazement out of her voice.

He gave her a stern look. "McCoskey, you are treading on thin ice. I think you've pushed your luck just about far enough. I think it's time for you to go do your job and let me do mine. I don't want you running around, sticking your nose into things, when we've got a killer on the loose, and I'm sure you don't want me cooking in your restaurant."

She gaped. "I thought you said the killer was in jail."

He stammered, "You know what I mean. This is police business. If you keep this up, I'll be tempted to cite you for interfering with a police investigation." He stood up and shoved the chair away a bit more forcefully than necessary.

"Steve?"

"Yap. What?"

"Have you or one of your people been tailing me?"

He looked surprised. "No, of course not. Why do you ask?"

"Oh, no reason."

He paused, looking at her, then walked out the door and up the street to his patrol car.

The hearing was well under way when Sunny poked her head around the door of Room 16 of the county courthouse. She slipped in and found a place to stand in back with the other latecomers. The room was filled to near capacity with forty or fifty people seated in rows of folding metal chairs and others standing along the side and back walls. At the front of the stage, the Napa County Agricultural Board was on display, seated behind a walnut-flavored plastic table with matching walnut nameplates in front of them. They reminded Sunny of the labels on the cages at the pound. *Frank Schmidt, Commissioner. Friendly, loving. Great with children. ***Do not feed me snacks,*

*I am on a special diet.**** A pristine whiteboard spanned the back wall. The Napa and California flags hung limply from standing poles in opposite corners.

Sunny spotted Silvano Cruz sitting up off to one side near the front, wearing a striped Western-style shirt and bolo tie and looking agitated. His cheeks were rosy and he kept shifting in his chair, as if it were an effort not to leap up and seize the ag commissioner by the collar and give him a good shake. Charlie was up on the little stage with the board members, sitting in one of the few wood and fabric chairs. He'd changed into khakis and a bright orange button-down shirt and was wearing what looked like bowling shoes mated with cross-trainers. He had his head tipped to one side, listening.

A middle-aged man in a dingy white oxford shirt and stiff blue tie had stood up and was reading from a clipboard, describing, in the most technical terms possible, how pesticides were applied, whether sprayed from the air or ground or added to irrigation water for systemic uptake. His monotonous voice reminded Sunny that she'd had less than three hours' sleep. To make matters worse, the wall-to-wall carpeting and low ceiling made his voice sound round and soft. It was warm in the room and at least one attendee was already fighting a doze, his head intermittently lolling forward and then snapping back to attention.

The clipboard wielder flipped up a page and continued on to a detailed analysis of the toxicity of various broad-spectrum insecticides used against leafhoppers, making his way through Lorsban, Dursban, Baythroid, Provado, Admire, and Sevin at a wretched pace, hesitating over each word as though on the brink of lapsing back into silence. At last the sergeant at arms gave the one-minute warning. When the speaker had finally been cut off,

Commissioner Frank Schmidt cleared his throat and reached in front of the deputy commissioner for the microphone.

"Now, let's be clear about this," he said, directing his speech to the man who had just sat down. "Pesticides, being designed and engineered to thwart the growth and proliferation of pests, are by definition toxic. That is not in dispute. It is also not in dispute that we are in an unpleasant, worst-case-scenario situation here. I don't want to spray any more than you do. If we do decide to go ahead with a ground application, it will be judicious, it will be targeted, and it will be the last resort available to us. People, let's remember that a multibillion-dollar local industry is at stake, an industry we are all connected to, one way or the other. And that's just part of it. The almond folks, peach farmers, all the citrus guys are going to be affected. The glassy-winged sharpshooter spells trouble for a whole range of agricultural concerns. Even the residential folks are going to get good and fed up when they see what a mess these sharpies make once they're established."

There was a murmur as Schmidt looked around the room, considering which hand to call on next. "I'll ask everyone's cooperation once again in keeping their comments as succinct as possible."

He pointed to a man with long gray hair and a rangy beard like a wizard's. "Keith, why don't you go ahead."

The bearded man turned to the woman keeping notes and said, "Keith Spivy, Rising Star Farms, Yountville. I'd just like to say that I've spent twelve years creating an eco-friendly, productive, profitable organic farm run in harmony with the environment, using sustainable agricultural practices that actually improve the soil instead of depleting it. One dose of carbaryl will wipe out all of that in ten minutes. Poison my land, and not only is the land fouled, the fruits of the land are toxic as well."

A round of scattered applause interrupted him. "Carbaryl kills the honeybees we need for pollination, the ladybugs, dragonflies, earthworms, the good spiders, and all the other beneficials, not to mention the butterflies. Right now my farm can protect itself. If I allow you to spray, it will be as defenseless as the overstressed, chemical-ridden monoculture that's caused our vulnerability to this problem in the first place."

He sat down to more scattered applause. Frank Schmidt turned to Charlie. "Charlie, before we get much further into this, why don't you give us a quick recap of where we stand from the scientific point of view. Outline the situation briefly so everyone knows what we're talking about here."

Charlie nodded. "Charlie Rhodes, University of California at Davis, Napa County field research facility resident entomologist. While I haven't had a chance to examine the specimen or the area in which it was discovered personally as yet, my understanding is that it was a single glassy-winged sharpshooter discovered late on Friday afternoon in a yellow sticky trap located in an olive grove near the vineyard at the Maya Culpa Vineyard on Mount Veeder. I think we are all clear by now on the threat posed by the glassy-winged sharpshooter, but just to review, they're high-powered xylem tissue sap-feeders, and as such they vector all kinds of plant pathogens, notably the bacterium *Xylella fastidiosa,* a.k.a. Pierce's disease. The sharpshooter literally injects the bacterium into the plant as it's feeding, vectoring it directly into the plant's xylem tissues. There the bacterium multiplies and produces a gel-like substance that blocks the water-conductive xylem tissue and the plant starves.

"My team and I will be headed out there this morning to assess the degree of infestation and make a recommendation for treatment. It is possible, though frankly not likely, that this is a lone specimen or small pocket colony way out ahead of the general glassy-winged sharpshooter population. If that's the case, we may be able to take care of this with a localized application. I would urge the board to wait a day or two before taking any action while we gather the best and most complete information possible. We've had good luck in that this is a relatively low-activity time for sharpshooters. The cooler weather means less growth and development, and most important, less breeding."

The suits at the front of the room visibly bristled and Silvano Cruz stood without being called on. "Frank, may I?"

Schmidt looked annoyed. "Go head, since you're standing."

"Pierce's disease is one hundred percent effective at killing grapevines."

The sergeant at arms interrupted him. "State your name and affiliation or address for the record."

Silvano introduced himself to the stenographer, then said, "This is not a threat we in the wine business can tolerate. If there is any chance the shooter is here, the county must take immediate action or risk the total collapse of the grape-growing industry. This is an emergency situation requiring decisive, immediate action. We can't afford to wait around and see what happens. We need to treat the problem first and ask questions later. If the sharpshooter gets a foothold in the valley, we're done for."

The room rumbled. Schmidt called on a grape grower who supported Silvano's position, saying one sharpshooter was one too many and the county owed it to the grape growers to protect them in a time of crisis. A thin, brittle-looking woman stood next. She described how carbaryl caused respiratory problems, nerve damage, nausea, vomiting, and liver problems. Schmidt called on Ben Baker after that. He stood up in his padded flannel shirt jacket and introduced himself as the owner-operator of Hansen Ranch Organic Produce.

"The big wineries call this an emergency and a time of crisis. But is it really? The Hansen Ranch has been home to sharpshooters for millions of years, long before humans came along. The glassy-winged sharpshooter is just the new kid on the block. He's bigger, but he's still just a little leafhopper. Healthy vines growing in healthy soil rich with beneficial insects and microbial life can resist them as well as Pierce's disease, assuming the sharpshooters happen to vector it. Spraying my land would not only put me out of business and destroy the ecology of my farm, it would make the plants that survive that much more susceptible to disease, not to mention poisoning the birds, the reptiles, the fish in the streams, and the land my children play on every day. Short-term economic gain does not justify poisoning the land and all its inhabitants. Killing anything, no matter how small, has to be the very last resort, and I think anyone practicing sustainable agriculture will testify to the fact that we are not in a last-resort situation. Nerve poison is not our only option."

He remained standing for the boisterous round of applause that followed. For the next hour, Frank Schmidt pointed his gavel at raised hands, hearing testimony from a variety of perspectives, the majority against mandatory spraying. A massage therapist from Calistoga said, "I do not believe that forced spraying will lead to a more sacred and sustainable world," which provoked both soft laughter and a smattering of applause. The director of the local parks and recreation facilities claimed the host range under his purview alone was too big to spray effectively. "The GWSS," he said, using the bug's acronym, "will always find a home in the park system, if not elsewhere. We have hundreds of acres of riparian habitat dense with foliage. No amount of spraying will decimate a population in those conditions." An attorney from Napa said a forced pesticide application could be a violation of both civil rights and property rights, and a honey producer from Oakville said that the state of California was using $40 million in tax monies to subsidize the already lucrative wine industry's shortsighted and destructive farming habits, and driving people like him out of business in the process. A resident of St. Helena said door-to-door searches and forced spraying amounted to martial law. Most of what was said was common knowledge in the valley. It was just being repeated for the record. Most people also knew that if the bugs started to proliferate, the guys in the biosuits would not be far off. Finally Frank Schmidt banged his gavel.

"I think we have gained a good idea of the various concerns. We will be taking all of this under consideration as the board reviews its options, whether spraying or any of the other ideas we've heard here today. Meanwhile, I'd like to add that Napa County has more than a thousand traps out there collecting samples, and we're trying to find a way to improve them, using pheromones or scent or what have you, to attract the sharpies to the traps instead of simply gathering them at random. We've got close to a hundred California Conservation Corps personnel out there checking traps door to door. One thing we know for sure, the sharpie is coming, step by step. It's in Temecula, then Fresno, then San Jose and Sacramento, then Berkeley. Now we have our first known glassy-winged visitor here in our midst. We know it won't be long before they arrive in force. The question is how long and when to take action against them. We know that Temecula and Fresno waited too long. Nevertheless, this is no time to be rash or hasty just because we're worried. There is too much at stake for everyone concerned. Charlie, I'll be interested to hear your findings as soon as they are available. Motion to adjourn until eight A.M. tomorrow, when we will reconvene on the same topic."

Sunny filed out with everyone else, finding herself abreast of Ben Baker as they left the courthouse. She said, "That was a great speech you made in there. I hope they listen."

"It won't do any good," said Ben bitterly. "We lost this battle a long time ago. Everybody shows up when the drama gets hot, but where were they months ago, when the power to make this decision was handed over to Frank Schmidt in the first place, thanks to the manipulations of Jack Beroni and the big wineries? We'll see our land poisoned, all because nobody could be bothered to come out and try to protect it. Even you and your friend Skord, two people with such tangible interests in this valley's environmental well-being, didn't bother to come down to fight for the land when there was still a chance to save it. Everybody's too lazy to get off their asses and do something, but they cry plenty when it's too late. I'm sorry, it just makes me sick."

Sunny stopped, surprised at his anger. He shook his head and walked away.

PART THREE

Heavy Wine

12

What had begun with a suspicious dwindling of cookies, profiteroles, and candied citrus rinds had escalated to full-scale robbery in the dessert department. Everybody pilfered a shortbread or macaroon now and then, but to make off with an entire batch of almond crisps? Lighten the pantry of a two-pound tub of sugary orange peels? It took malice and daring, thought Sunny; it took a greedy heart. Who would do such a thing? Certainly it was too much for any individual to eat, even assuming a mammoth sweet tooth that persisted over several shifts. Aside from the annoyance, the problem was getting expensive.

Sunny perused the shelves of the walk-in for clues. Nothing else seemed to be missing, and the thief had left neither note nor calling card. Wildside employed a total of thirteen people in various capacities: a wait staff of three; one maître d' cum sommelier, who also tended the small garden in back; three busboys and girls; three dishwashers; a part-time prep cook; Rivka; and herself. It was safe to eliminate herself and Riv, since they were the ones inconvenienced by the heist. One of the waiters was on vacation during the days in question. That left ten possible suspects, assuming it wasn't one of any number of delivery personnel who came through on a regular basis, generally unannounced.

Perhaps one of them was running a sugar shack on the side and had found a crafty way to slip in and out with the goods unseen. Sunny imagined a makeshift roadside candy stand selling fresh hazelnut cookies and candied orange peels to passing motorists.

The issue touched on three long-overdue items on Sunny's to-do list, namely install new and better locks for the doors and windows, call a staff meeting to review policy and plan the semi-annual field trip, and hire a part-time pastry chef to relieve Rivka and herself of the dessert burden in the first place. Dessert had never been her passion, and she considered it the weak link in Wildside's repertoire. They made do with the standard fare of cookie plates, crème brûlées with candied citrus rind garnish, and fruit ices, plus her mom's special rum cake with vanilla bean gelato that Sunny knew was a culinary non sequitur in a restaurant known for traditional Provençal-Tuscan-Mediterranean-style cuisine but couldn't resist offering all the same. Only occasionally was there time to include a fig or pear tart or strawberry-rhubarb crisp, her specialty and Rivka's, respectively. Maybe this was the push she needed to get organized.

Sunny emerged from the walk-in intending to announce her idea about hiring a pastry chef but decided against it when she saw the look of concentration on Rivka's face. She was intensely focused on work or engrossed in some thought, or perhaps both. In fact, thought Sunny, she's been quiet all morning. It wasn't unusual for them to listen to music and go about their business immersed in the tasks at hand. There was a nice, meditative quality to working side by side without talking. But this morning Sunny had the feeling that something was wrong. There had been a notable lack of goofiness since she got back from the meeting, and Rivka hadn't demonstrated any of her usual gyrations to the music. She'd walked back and forth to the storage room and the walk-in numerous times without belting out a single lyric. Sunny assumed it would come out eventually; probably a glitch in operations with the new boyfriend. There would be time to hash it over later. For now, they were behind and they only had an hour until the lunch rush started. For motivation, Sunny made herself a double macchiato and dropped in two lumps of brown sugar.

About a quarter after eleven, Wade called to say he'd just walked in the door at home. He'd had to put Skord Mountain up for bail, which "was scary as hell" but wouldn't amount to anything more than a technicality, "as long as I don't get myself a one-way ticket to Rio." They agreed to talk later after he'd had a chance to check on the vineyard and take care of a few things around the house, maybe get some sleep on a bed that didn't feel like a piece of cardboard on a cement slab.

"To add injury to insult, this whole jailbird scene is costing me an arm and a leg. I don't even want to think about what Harry's bill is going to look like. He probably charged me for giving me the ride home."

"We'll figure it out later," said Sunny. "There are ways to make money. We can take Monty up on one of his partnership ideas or auction off coffee dates with Rivka. Get some rest and I'll call you in the afternoon."

She hung up the phone and shouted, "He's out!" to Rivka, who had her back turned as she sautéed a mixture of diced onions, carrots, and celery root for soup.

"Riv? Did you hear? That was Wade on the phone. He's home."

Something about her posture set off an alarm and Sunny walked over just in time to see two full-bodied tears run down Rivka's cheeks.

"R.C., what's the matter?"

Rivka turned off the fire and hiked up the bottom of her long apron, using a corner to wipe her eyes. She sniffed and retied the apron strings unnecessarily. "Um, I think I need your help."

"Anything. I am Dr. Freud and your humble sherpa all rolled into one. Want to go in the office and talk?"

"We don't have time. Besides, it's not anything to talk about. I have to show you."

"What do you have to show me?"

"You have to promise that when you see it you won't wig out, you won't get all upset or tell anyone or make any loud noises that somebody might hear."

"What are you talking about? You mean like scream or something? Riv, what on earth is going on?"

"Just promise me you'll stay calm."

"Am I always calm? Remember me? I'm the too-calm one. I'm like Mount Tam facing out to sea. I'm so calm I make the Dalai Lama look hyperactive."

Rivka smiled and cough-sobbed at the same time. "I know. That's why you're the only person I can trust with this."

She led the way out to the parking lot and up to her old Datsun two-door. Its yellow paint job was oxidized to a powdery matte finish, with rust highlights around the brightwork. Its tires, manufactured decades before the age of the SUV, looked far too small to be roadworthy. Rivka cast one last beseeching look at Sunny and unlocked the trunk, letting it spring slowly open of its own accord. Gym clothes, jogging shoes, magazines, Tupperware, an old metal change box, and jumper cables had been shoved back to make room for a rainbow-colored Mexican blanket, which lay neatly folded into a long, narrow rectangle. Rivka drew back half of it. There, stretched out on the blanket as though on display, was the last thing in the world Sunny expected to see. She stared down, struck dumb with shock, at Wade Skord's canvas rifle case. She sucked in her breath. "Ho-lee crap."

"You promised."

"I know. I'm not saying anything. I am very calm. Om mani padme hum. I assume that the contents are what I assume them to be?"

"Uh, yeah."

"Wade used his cork brander to burn the Skord Mountain emblem into the base of his."

"It's there."

"And the missing cartridge?"

"That, too."

"Holy crap. Holy friggin' crap."

"You promised you'd stay calm."

"I'm calm. I am very, very calm. I'm breathing, and I'm calm."

Sunny glanced behind her to confirm that there was no one else in the parking lot, then replaced the blanket and gently closed the trunk. The wait staff and dishwashers had already arrived and customers would be pulling in any second. She stared at the horizon behind Rivka and spoke softly. "I think it would be good if you told me where you got it and what it means, but not here. Somebody could be watching."

"Like who? You mean someone who works here?"

"No. I don't know. Don't look around. It sounds crazy, but there is a very small possibility that someone has been following me. Like, I think my house might be staked out. Just in case, let's casually have a look in the glove compartment, and maybe check the backseat like you lost something. Maybe smile a bit like it's no big deal. If you can find the something that you were looking for and bring it with you, whatever it is, that's a nice touch. Then let's walk back into the restaurant."

Inside, Sunny checked the front bar station and loudly confirmed that it needed to be restocked with the Cabernet Sauvignon they poured by the glass, as though evil eyes were watching her every move, even in the kitchen. "Better safe than sorry," she said, leading the way downstairs to the cellar with Rivka following woodenly behind. With a wall of cement at their backs and a clear view of the door, Sunny felt they could talk safely. If anyone came down the stairs, they would be able to hear footsteps long before their words would be audible.

"Okay, now what the hell is going on?" she hissed.

Rivka's eyes filled with tears and Sunny pressed her wrist. "Riv, this is not the time for tears. We can all have a nice, big nervous breakdown later. Right now you have to tell me exactly what is going on before things get a lot worse."

Rivka swallowed and took a breath broken by thwarted sobs. "Last night I stayed with, with Alex. He left for work early this morning, around five-thirty. I was getting ready and I dropped one of my earrings and I thought maybe it went under the bed. So I looked under there and there was a big box. Not an old cardboard box, one of those special storage boxes with the little metal piece on the end for the label of what's in there. I don't know what I was doing, snooping I guess, but I slid the box out. I probably wouldn't have done it if Alex kept a lot of junk around the house, but he doesn't. Other than his clothes and some dishes, his place is practically empty, so I was curious what could be in there. You know, what's special enough to merit going out and buying a special storage box? I wasn't going to go all through it, I thought I'd just have a quick look to see if it was pictures or what. I guess I assumed it would be full of photographs and letters. You know, the archives. Well, mostly what was in there were track and football trophies from high school, but I didn't see that at first because on top of the trophies there was a bath towel, and wrapped up in the towel was Wade's gun."

She seized up and started to cry again and Sunny put her arms around her. "Poor chicken. Now, don't go and be a freaker on me. You have to suck it up and deal, at least for a little while. We're going to figure this out."

Rivka snorted and sobbed at the same time. Sunny backed away so she could see her face. "So, how did it end up in your trunk?" she asked.

"I put it there. This morning. It seems like a bad idea now, but I didn't want anyone to find it at his house." She turned away and fought a losing battle with several wet sneezes.

"Riv, you have to tell me everything. Why was the gun in Alex's house?"

"I don't know," she sobbed.

"You know something. You suspect something. Tell me."

"I know Alex didn't do it. He was with me Thursday night."

"Ah. But Gabe wasn't. And he wasn't home watching a movie with his folks, either, was he?"

"No."

"Where was he?"

She looked up at Sunny. "I swore I wouldn't tell anyone."

"Riv, you don't have a choice. Do you realize that even if nobody we know is guilty of murder, you are already in serious trouble for tampering with evidence? In all likelihood you have the murder weapon out there in your car."

"I know!" She choked on a violent round of sobs and Sunny stood quietly until it subsided into soft little sniffs.

"You have to tell me so I can help you."

"Okay! Back off." She tucked a stray strand of hair back into the baby-blue kerchief tied over her braids and crossed her arms defiantly. "I know Alex didn't do it, but I don't know about Gabe. I was worried all along that maybe he did it, and then when I found the gun, it seemed like, like maybe they must have planned it together. I know in my heart that that's not true, that there is no way either of them could do such a thing, but I don't know what else to think."

"And?"

"And that's it."

"There's more."

"No, that's it."

"There's more. You didn't drop an earring. You were snooping around. Why?"

"You are such a bitch."

"Tell me. Rivka Marie Chavez, Wade Skord's butt is in a sling and so is yours. This is no time to be demure. Why were you snooping?"

Rivka sighed. "Because Gabe was at the Dusty Vine Thursday night getting drunk. He came by the house late, after we got back from the movie. It must have been close to midnight. He was ranting about how his father was a fool and the Beronis wouldn't own him the way they'd owned Nesto. He said Jack Beroni was never going to set foot in the winery again. Alex took him home and put him to bed. When he came back, he told me that his dad and Jack had had a fight that afternoon in front of everyone, and his dad had gone to see Al Beroni about keeping Jack in line from then on. Then later on after work, Nesto tried to convince Alex and Gabe that Al Beroni would take care of things, but Gabe said it was just lip service and that things would never be the same once Jack took over the operation, that he'd get rid of them as soon as he had control and Al was off golfing at Silverado every afternoon."

"Was Jack going to take over soon?"

"Probably. Al wanted to retire, but he wasn't sure Jack was ready to run things. He was trying to ease him into the business. That's what started the friction between Jack and Nesto in the first place."

Well, that explained why Nesto had lied about where Gabe was Thursday night, thought Sunny. He must have known that Gabe was drunk and ornery and in the wrong place. She stood quietly for a moment. "Hang on. I thought you didn't spend the night with Alex on Thursday."

"I didn't. After Alex got back he took me home."

Sunny braced her hands against the back wall and stretched forward until her back cracked. She stood up and met her friend's eyes. "Riv, I know what we are supposed to do, but we are going to do something very different. Normal, rational people would call the police right now, but we've already demonstrated in our own unique ways that we are not normal, rational people, so instead we are going to remove the item in question from your car and transport it here, taking great care that no one sees anything. I will disguise the item and lock it down here in the wine cage. You will then forget you ever saw it until I tell you. Until then, don't talk to anyone about it, don't even think about it, it doesn't exist. Steve Harvey has waited this long for it, it won't hurt him to wait a little longer. Even if Alex notices that it's missing, I don't think he'll ask you about it; he'll be too scared. If he does say something, you have to pretend you never saw it and you have no idea what he is talking about. Hopefully he won't realize it's gone for a while."

Rivka nodded. "Okay. Until you give me the word, it doesn't exist. How long are we talking about?"

"I'm not sure. Maybe a few hours, maybe a day or two. We'll have to see. One more thing. We have to act like nothing is wrong or people are going to start asking questions and then we'll have to make up little lies about why we're upset, and that's always a mess. Really solid lies, even the minor ones, are more complicated to sustain than anybody thinks. It's better not to say anything at all. Omission is the key."

"What makes you the expert on lying?"

"Strict parents and bad-girl tendencies as an adolescent. The combination practically turned me to the dark side before I could grow out of it."

Rivka closed her eyes in a deliberate blink. "Sunny, how did Alex get Wade's rifle?"

"I'm not sure yet. For now, let's just concentrate on getting it in here before we have a bigger audience than we do now."

By the time the day's fish delivery arrived, the rifle was safely stowed in the wine locker, and Sunny and Rivka had taken to the refuge of work. Rivka shelled fava beans while Sunny hefted a fifteen-pound side of halibut onto the fish board and went to work running a long, thin knife under its skin. She hacked a sizable worm out of its flesh and sliced the rest into tidy opalescent filets. When that was done, she collected the day's ducks and a meat cleaver. The cleaver made a blunt, heavy thunk as she removed the legs, wings, and breasts from each one with precision blows. How did Alex Campaglia end up with Wade's rifle? *Chop!* Either he put it there or someone else did. *Chop!* It would only be a matter of time, and not much time, until the police caught up with Gabe Campaglia. They were probably already tracking down everybody who was in the Dusty Vine Thursday night to find out if they saw anybody make that call. If Nesto told the same inadequate lie to the cops that he had told her, Gabe would soon find the inquiring light of justice shining on him. *Chop! Chop!*

What if Alex discovered that Gabe had killed Jack? Would a drunken Gabe have picked up the spent shell and carried it and the gun back home with him? Or did Alex go to Beroni after he left Rivka and find the gun and the shell in the woods? She remembered Gabe's face in the moonlight at the gazebo, equally startled as her own when she screamed, and the freshly oiled rifle set out on his coffee table. She thought about how Gabe's temper had flared for an instant at breakfast when she asked him why he hated Jack Beroni: "I guess I was just born to hate him." And Gabe had described Larissa Richards as a knockout and a high-society bitch, the only other strong words he'd used in their conversation. Sunny toyed with the idea that there was some other connection with Larissa that accounted for the heat.

Sunny finished with a duck and reached for another. Her imagination played out seductive scenes between Larissa Richards and Michael Rieder, who would not be able to resist telling her about the will that left everything to the Campaglias. She imagined Larissa, empowered by this new knowledge, scheming to get a share of the Beroni fortune using Gabe Campaglia as her agent. She might even have felt entitled to a share of the estate, which would have been hers if Jack had gone ahead and married her, and who knows what promises he made to keep her around for all those years. Gabe had his own motive, if he knew about the will. He didn't know Wade, but he might have heard talk about Al and Louisa's complaints to the police about Wade disturbing the local peace by shooting his rifle in the evenings. For that matter, Larissa would have heard as well.

Catelina Alvarez shook a finger at Sunny. She wouldn't like this line of thinking, all these assumptions. When she used to take Sunny with her to the farmers' market when Sunny was a child, they would select the week's fruits and vegetables. Catelina would hold up a peach in her gnarled hand and say, "Never trust the color on the outside, Sonya. A golden peach can be as hard as a stone or as grainy as porridge. The smell gives you a hint, but to really know, you have to slice one open and taste what is inside. Until then, you are only guessing." Then she would hand the peach to the grower and wait while he, grumbling, sliced it open for her. Catelina was the queen of due diligence.

Sunny whacked apart another bird and spun the facts again, despite Catelina's caution. She imagined Gabe getting lit up at the Dusty Vine, staggering out to the parking lot, calling Jack, stealing the gun, shooting him. But Jack's murder was far too complicated to be a drunken crime of passion. Plus, Jack wouldn't have left his party to meet a liquored-up Campaglia. Sunny tugged the last of the ducks onto the chopping block. It was even theoretically possible that Alex and Gabe had plotted the murder together. The timing was right, with Jack about to take over and edge them out. She scrubbed her hands. A couple of two-tops were already seated in the dining room, a party of three was lingering just inside the door, and there was still prep-work to be done. Nevertheless, she had a meeting to arrange. She worked quickly to pull together the last of the supplies Rivka would need to handle things for a little while on her own.

"Riv, would you do me a favor?"

"What's that?"

"Call Alex and get his brother's mobile number."

"Right now?" asked Rivka, glancing at the clock.

"I'm afraid so."

Gabe picked up his phone on the fifth ring.

"Gabe?"

"Yeah."

"It's Sunny McCoskey."

"Yeah." He sounded less than thrilled to hear her voice.

"I need to see you, right away. Is there someplace we can meet to talk? It will only take a minute or two."

"We're talking now."

"I need to see you in person."

She listened to him breathing. He seemed to be walking up stairs or a hill. "I'll meet you in the parking lot of the Dusty Vine," he said. "I'll leave in five."

"Right. I'll be there."

She hung up the phone to find Rivka staring at her. "I'm going with you."

"He won't say anything with you there. Besides, I need you to hold down the fort here. I'll be back in half an hour."

Gabe was sitting in his truck writing notes in a little spiral notebook when Sunny pulled in. Sunny's old Ford lurched up next to the late-model Toyota 4 x 4, the sort they seemed to hand out like sack lunches up at the Beroni place. She got out, and Gabe smiled at her like he thought something was funny. She felt suddenly self-conscious not only of the scarred-up old truck but of her checkered pants and white chef's jacket, an outfit Larissa Richards wouldn't be caught dead wearing in public.

"You weren't watching a movie with your parents Thursday night."

"Nope."

"You were right here at the Dusty Vine drinking."

"You're a smart one."

"Why did you lie?"

"I didn't."

"But you let your father lie for you. You didn't stop him."

"It's his choice. He can do whatever he wants."

She glanced across the parking lot at the phone booth under a street lamp. "Did you call Jack Beroni Thursday night?"

"No."

"Did you park your car up on the logging road, steal Wade's gun, and shoot Jack Beroni as he waited to meet with you?"

"No, I sure didn't." He smiled at her.

She watched his face. "You and Jack were about the same age, right?"

"Yeah."

"Did Jack have a girlfriend in high school?"

"He had plenty."

"No one in particular?"

He thought about it. The question seemed to interest him. "Yeah, I guess there was one in particular. He seemed especially fond of Claire Hansen all through high school. They broke up when he went away to college."

"Claire Hansen. As in Hansen Ranch?"

"That's right. I guess it's Claire Baker now. She and Jack were always close."

13

Sunny slid into the truck and fumbled the keys with quivering hands. She had the urge to shout or run. If there had been a river nearby, she would have been tempted to jump in, clothes and all, just to feel the shock of the water. She drummed at the steering wheel, waiting for Gabe to pull out of the lot and go on his way ahead of her. She needed time to get a grip on this new piece of information. If Larissa's hunch was right and Gabe's information accurate, the blond woman whom Jack Beroni was having an affair with was Claire Baker, and judging by what Nesto said, it was more than a fling.

She looked at her watch. Rivka was about to get slammed with the full force of a Wildside-sized lunch rush, admittedly minuscule compared with the traffic in the valley's name-brand restaurants, but it would still give Ms. Chavez a hearty workout handling it on her own. She'd have to survive for another hour or so.

At Oakville, Sunny made a right toward Mount Veeder. The truck chugged up the steep grade not far from Monty's place. Near the top of the ridge, she eased the truck over the lip of the pavement and headed down a dirt road to Hansen Ranch. Of the wide variety of dirt roads in the valley and the mountains that formed it, Hansen Ranch's road was perhaps the most picturesque. It was a genteel, pebbly brown roadbed worn smooth as any pavement by a century of use. On one side a white three-rail fence followed the road between sturdy Douglas fir trees with their lower limbs pruned to ward off wildfires. Even in late September, at the pinnacle of the dry season, the top of Mount Veeder was shades of green. No wonder so many people dreamed of rural bliss up here above the valley. If wine really was the expression of the spirit of the land, it was also no wonder that some of the most complex, articulate wines in California were made from grapes grown in the ripples and cul-de-sacs tucked around the mountain, the pièce de résistance and undisputed beauty queen of the Mayacamas Mountains.

The road dipped down and then popped up and rounded a sharp turn. Acres of olive, prune, apple, and pear trees came into view. A fringe of yellow sticky traps hung down along the edges, turning in the breeze. Further on, the trees gave way to a large vegetable garden covering several acres. Hansen Ranch grew at least ten varieties of organic greens, all the usual vegetables, an extensive array of herbs, asparagus, squashes, pumpkins, and anything else Ben and Claire could coax into taking root. Three scarecrows stood watch over the garden, and Mylar streamers, like the ones some vineyards used to keep birds away, flashed in the sunlight. At the end of the road was a white Victorian house with a swing on the porch and rosebushes around the sides. Behind it, parked in front of a separate garage, was a tan mid-eighties Land Cruiser like the one Gabe said he'd seen parked on the logging road near Beroni Vineyards.

Sunny idled the truck in the driveway. This was insanity. Even if it was true that Jack and Claire had renewed their high-school romance, it was none of Sunny's business. Even stretching "her business" to encompass events and situations vaguely related to Jack's murder, extramarital affairs of the deceased probably still weren't justifiably covered. And Claire was very much alive and very much married. On the other hand, Wade was in serious trouble, and now Rivka was involved. Was she going to let good manners stand in the way of helping them? She sat in the car, waffling.

Sunny turned off the engine and got out, praying as she walked up to the front door that Claire would answer instead of Ben. She had no idea what she would say to either of them, but at least she had a reason for coming to see Claire. She knocked softly, waited, then knocked again like she meant it. When there was no answer and no sound from inside, she made her way around back to the barn and outbuildings, hoping the Bakers didn't keep a ferocious guard dog who had been temporarily indisposed but would be trotting over shortly.

In addition to the garage, there were three good-sized outbuildings behind the house. Sunny called out and waited but heard nothing. It was a glorious afternoon and she scanned the needlepoint slopes of distant vineyards, wondering where Ben and Claire could be. She walked across the compound to the first building, a sagging white gabled shed just large enough to house a pickup truck. The side door had swung halfway open and she slipped inside. Her eyes took a moment to adjust to the gloom. The smell in there was sweet and musky, like rotting fruit and wet morels, and reminded her of winter days spent in the garage as a child, helping butcher the deer or elk her father never failed to bring back from his annual hunting trip. Sure enough, on a workbench straight ahead lay a possum, freshly skinned. Tacked to the wall behind it were numerous hides in various stages of processing, including a rabbit, a gopher, and a raccoon, its eyes dried to crackled slits. The wall to the left was covered with shelves, each burdened with a row of glass jars containing what looked to be mostly seeds, herbs, and insects, but also eggs of various sizes, feathers, soil mixtures, oily liquids, husks, peels, and bones.

Organic farming was getting weird, thought Sunny, opening one of the jars for a sniff. The fondness for composting and worm boxes seemed to have evolved into a general obsession with organic matter, and decomposed organic matter in particular. Those on the cutting edge in recent years had started whipping up fetid potions said to promote soil vigor or keep pests on the march. She knew someone who swore by a concoction he made out of a gopher buried for six months, then blended into a frappé and sprayed on his plants at the full moon. It lent yet more support to the idea that folks go a bit goofy out in the countryside on their own, soaking up a little bit too much nature for anybody's good. Still, she had to admit that the Hansen place looked bountiful, and there did seem to be some validity to many of the old folk remedies, such as using cat urine to keep away gophers and rabbits.

She closed the door and walked back to the open space between the buildings, listening. The largest of the three structures was a Victorian barn big enough to house an indoor tennis court, and she headed there across a rolling natural lawn. As she got close, she heard movement off to the right, coming from the furthest structure, an old storage shed another fifty yards away. She walked toward it, calling "Hello" so as not to arrive unannounced.

Like the rest of the farm, the storage shed was whitewashed, clean, and built decades earlier of sturdy, hand-hewn local timbers. At the back end, the double doors were flung wide open.

Claire had set up a packing station in front with crates of kale, squash, heirloom apples, celery root, carrots, potatoes, figs, and rosemary arranged in a semicircle around her. She was busy assembling boxes of produce that were delivered weekly or biweekly to individuals who subscribed. Claire looked up when she heard Sunny. Claire's cheeks were pink with exercise and her smile cheerful. She wore her pale blond hair pulled back in a ponytail.

"Sunny! What a nice surprise! My goodness, what brings you way out here?"

"Hi, Claire. I'm sorry to pop in on you like this. I haunted the front house for a while, but when nobody came to the door, I figured I'd come to you." She stalled. "The farm looks great."

Claire pulled off her gloves and gave Sunny a kiss on each cheek. "Doesn't it? You remind me of how lazy I've been at getting people out here. When was the last time you visited?"

"Last fall? Maybe October. Rivka and I came out. I remember you made an amazing pumpkin soup."

"With way too much heavy cream and jalapeños. That's the secret to really good pumpkin soup, make it incredibly fattening. I hear you were at the sharpshooter meeting this morning."

"Yeah, I was there. Ben did a nice job speaking against pesticides. I didn't know he was such an eloquent public speaker. I've never known him to talk much." Sunny stopped. She was starting to feel like a hypocrite; this was not a social visit. She decided to get to the point. She looked around, checking to see that Ben was nowhere within earshot. An assortment of upturned log sections stood nearby waiting to be split and Sunny tipped her head toward them. She and Claire went over and sat down. A knot formed in Sunny's stomach. This was a dreadful topic to bring up. Claire looked at her expectantly.

"I don't know how to say this. It's really none of my business. If it weren't for Wade needing help—do you know about Wade? That he was arrested?"

"I heard. I can't believe it."

"He's out on bail, and I assure you that if it weren't for his situation, I wouldn't have any interest in sticking my nose into other people's . . . business."

"What is it?" She frowned and Sunny saw worry come into her face. Was it her imagination or did Claire look like someone accustomed to bad news?

"Claire, how close were you to Jack Beroni?"

She opened her mouth in shock, then closed it and looked away, shaking her head with what seemed to be successive waves of indignation, anger, and resignation. She worked a long splinter of wood off the log next to her and poked at the ground with it.

"You weren't just having a casual affair," said Sunny. "You've been in love with him since high school." Sunny was becoming more experienced at eliciting information from people, and she'd realized that making a statement often got them talking more easily than if she'd asked a question.

Claire smiled, warmly at first, then her lips slid into a straight line. "Yes, but I was never good enough for Jack's family. Not much is. And there was a time, years in fact, when I loved Ben just as much."

"What happened?"

"I don't know. I'm not sure you ever really know about these things. They're gradual. Ben and I wore each other down, I suppose. The farm has never been a financial success and it's been hard on both of us. Over the years, struggling constantly to make this place work, he got more and more introverted, more distant.

We've spent most of a second mortgage and used all the money I inherited when my mother died. The next step is to sell. This ranch has been in my family for five generations." She dug a trough in the ground with the splinter of wood, absentmindedly scraping as she talked. "The taxes alone are several times more than we made last year."

"You shouldn't have to sell. This land is so valuable, you could get financing to put in your own vineyard. I wouldn't be surprised if Cabernet Sauvignon grown where we're sitting right now sold for fifteen hundred dollars a ton."

"I know. Believe me, I've tried to get Ben to go along with that idea. He's absolutely against it. You know how he feels about the wine business. It's a matter of principle with him. He says he'd rather go broke than turn booze farmer. He feels like they've ruined the valley, cutting down the forests and orchards so they can plant more grapes, causing erosion, eating up habitat for animals."

"How much of that is about being jealous of Jack?"

"He's never had anything to be jealous of. I fell for Ben in college, a few years after Jack and I split up. Ben doesn't know there was ever anything between us." She sighed. "No, Ben's abhorrence of the wine business has come from all those county meetings he goes to. He's been on the opposite side of the fence since the winery definition battle in the eighties."

Claire's expression made her face look hard in a way Sunny had never seen before, as if she'd grown used to being unhappy. "Once he said if I ever asked for a divorce, he'd get a lawyer and make sure I lost the girls. I don't think he was serious, but you never know. He's changed over the years. I do know we wouldn't get out of it without selling this place, and I won't do that until I've exhausted every other option." She started scraping a new trench. "I used to be in awe of him, the way he devoted himself to this place. The way he loved to watch things grow."

Sunny twisted the toe of her shoe in the dirt. "Where is he now?"

"Out making deliveries."

"And Thursday night?"

She smiled. "Come on, Sunny, don't be ridiculous. He may not be the happiest man alive, but he certainly didn't kill Jack. He's not cold-blooded. Ben still cries every time he has to shoot a gopher. I see him. He'll watch the hole and pace for hours until he finally decides to do it. Then he's upset for days. This is not a guy who could commit a murder. And anyway, he didn't know anything about Jack and me. Even if he did, I don't think he'd care that much. Ben stopped loving me in the romantic sense years ago. Staying together has been about the girls and the farm for a long time now. I don't think he particularly cares who I sleep with, as long as I keep it a secret."

"I'm sure that's not true."

"Marriages are not always what they seem, Sunny. Forever is a long time."

Sunny bit her lip. "You were home Thursday night?"

"Me? Yes."

"The whole night?"

"Yes."

"And Ben, too?"

"I assume so."

"You don't know?"

"We don't sleep together. He works at night sometimes. After dark is the best time to do certain applications. To be honest, I don't always know where he goes and I don't want to know."

"Applications?"

"Biodynamic solutions. You know, to keep pests away or balance the soil."

"So there are times when he leaves at night and you don't know where he goes?"

"It's usually the west orchard. If I know Ben, the other woman has leaves and bark, not feathered hair and big boobs."

"Does he drive over there?"

"Usually. It's too far to walk carrying equipment."

"Did you hear him leave Thursday night?"

"Sunny, stop. Ben was here on the night of Jack's murder, miles away from Beroni Vineyards." Claire stood up. "I think this whole conversation has gone far enough. I need to ask you to give me your word you won't talk to anyone about this, any of this, and then I think you'd better leave."

Sunny felt her face heat. She hadn't been asked to leave anyplace since she was a kid passing notes in school. "Just one more thing and I'll go. And I won't speak of any of this to anyone, I promise. Did Jack ever come here to see you?"

"Of course not," she snapped. "He would never come anywhere near this place."

Claire stood and put her gloves back on, giving Sunny a pained, disapproving look before turning back to her work.

Sunny walked back to the truck. The midday sun warmed her shoulders and the guilt and shame she'd momentarily felt lifted with each step. None of this mess of lies and secrets was hers, and she wasn't about to start carrying it around. Now that Jack was dead, Claire might be able to find her way back to Ben. The best way for that to happen was for the past to evaporate, starting with what Sunny knew. She unbuttoned her chef's jacket and stripped down to her T-shirt, longing to grab the old blanket she kept behind the seat of the truck, stretch it out on the grass, and have a nice long nap. Instead, she needed to get back to the restaurant pronto and see if there was anything left of Rivka after a solo battle with the hungry gourmands. On the drive back, she lined up the new questions she had, starting with whether or not Ben had found out about Claire's affair. Next up was what Jack was doing up here Wednesday night, if it wasn't to see Claire. Monty had seen Jack's Jaguar racing down Mount Veeder on Wednesday night. She pictured Claire's face when she'd answered that last question, about whether or not Jack ever came up here. Sunny was willing to bet she was telling the truth as far as she knew it. In fact, it seemed painful to Claire that Jack didn't want to come near the ranch.

Claire said Ben didn't like to kill things, but barn number one seemed to scream the opposite. Still, farm life involves more killing than anybody likes to admit. All farmhouses get overrun by mice and wood rats from time to time, and rattlesnakes take up residence under the porch and in the garage eventually. Gardens attract a host of quadrupeds eager for a meal, not to mention birds by the flock, and anyone who keeps chickens has a problem with coyotes, possums, and raccoons, not to mention predatory birds and mountain lions. And then there were all the little lives, the insects and the microscopic life. It was like Nesto said, there were plenty of pests in the valley, depending on your perspective. "Getting rid of them" was usually a euphemism. Farmers tried alternatives, but often enough getting rid of a pest meant killing it. That barn was just Ben Baker being as efficient as possible by using every part of the animals he killed.

As she drove, she ran Ben through the steps it would have taken to kill Jack. He would have had to find out about the affair. In such a tight-knit community, there were plenty of ways that could have happened. It was hard to believe he wouldn't object to her sleeping with another man, no matter how far their relationship had slipped. How well did Claire Baker know her husband, anyway? It was even hard to believe it would be enough to drive him to murder in genteel Napa. But Ben had been boiling with anger after the hearing. Could years of frustration have been channeled into a hatred of Jack Beroni? Ben could have made that call to Jack Thursday night from the Dusty Vine. Maybe he confronted him about the affair. But why would Jack agree to meet him? What could they have to say to each other? She thought about the list she and Wade had made of people who knew that he kept a rifle in the winery. Ben and Claire were on it. They'd been at Wade's house the night they played Assault Golf after dinner. Even if Ben hadn't seen where Wade kept the gun, it wouldn't have been that difficult to find, knowing it was stashed somewhere reasonably accessible in the winery. Still, it didn't explain how Alex ended up with the gun or how Mike Rieder's business card came to be outside the winery.

The gravel parking lot at Wildside was packed when Sunny finally got there. She parked on the street a block down and jogged back, throwing on her chef's jacket as she came in the rear door. Rivka gave her a look.

"You better have one hell of an excuse, McCoskey."

"Damn straight." She looked over the open counter at the dining room, which was filled with customers, both seated and waiting. Most looked like they were on their second course, a few were eating dessert. "How bad is it?"

"Let's just say we don't have a whole lot of time to chitchat."

Berton, the maître d', strolled over to the zinc bar and leaned against it as if he had all the time in the world. That was his expertise. No matter how busy the tiny dining room got, he always maintained an air of professional ease and competence, as though waiting an hour for a table was exactly the way it should be. Sunny whipped around her prep station, putting up four salads while he stood watching.

"So, what happened? Did you decide to call it quits after nine holes?"

"Does my jacket say *Chef?*" she said, giving him her best haughty look. "Table five needs water."

"Bite me!" he replied, without emotion.

He cruised away, overseeing the diners like a director scrutinizing a dress rehearsal. The next hour and a half sped by in a blur of mixed greens, pasta, grilled vegetables, roasted meats, seared fish, and braised duck breasts. Just before three o'clock, Charlie Rhodes came in and took a seat at the bar. Sunny felt an involuntary flutter in her stomach. What was she, twelve? she thought. Wasn't she a bit old to be having crushes on cute boys? Still, there were his hands, each fingertip pressing the zinc, hands of a rock climber or flamenco guitarist, and the little white scar on the right index finger.

"Am I too late for lunch?"

"Yep, unless you happen to hold certain degrees. We're running a special late lunch service for area entomologists. In honor of harvest."

"Wow, that is such a coincidence."

"Chef's special?"

"Sounds good."

She put together a plate of various leftovers from lunch and slid it across the counter.

"Did you go out to the Maya Culpa yet?"

"Yeah, I was out there all morning."

"What'd you find?"

"Not much. Well, not anything, at least not in the way of glassy-winged sharpshooters. Whole lot of dead bugs stuck to a whole lot of bug traps. The usual assortment of winged critters, plus a few blue-greens and that one glassy-winger they located on Friday." He cut himself a piece of roasted meat and swiped a layer of mashed potatoes on top of it.

Sunny poured them each a glass of Wildside private label Cabernet Sauvignon, a joint project with a winery down the road that she'd spent far too much time and money on last year. He took a swallow.

"You know," he said, "just when I think I get these little guys all figured out, they go and throw me a wild card."

"How so?"

"Well, first of all, the glassy-winged specimen in the trap turned out to be a stage-two nymph, which is weird because those traps normally only catch adults. You've seen them, right? They're sticky strips that hang down from a limb. You generally have to fly or hop to land in the middle of one, and stage-two nymphs don't do either. They crawl, and they don't even do that very well. For another thing, it's the wrong time of year for stage-two nymphs around here. It's like finding a fawn with spots in November, or butterflies in January. I can understand finding a stage-two in a year-round breeding ground like Southern California, but up here they should be dormant right now. I wouldn't expect anything but adults until March or later. It just goes to show you that nature is always stretching the rules. Just when you think you have it all figured out, you find an exception. But that still doesn't explain how a non-hopping, non-flying leaf grubber landed in the middle of a sticky trap."

Sunny stared at him. "Oh my God."

"What?"

"Nothing."

"That's not a nothing face."

Her mind raced. She thought of the silver Jag screeching around the corner, brake lights flaring in the dark Wednesday night. That would be the same day he'd canceled lunch with Ripley Marlow so he could make a last-minute trip to Los Angeles, the night before he was killed.

"When was the last time those traps were checked?"

"Friday afternoon."

"I mean before that."

"Tuesday afternoon or Wednesday morning."

At that exact moment, the back door yawned opened and Ben Baker appeared, wearing his usual flannel jacket and jeans and hoisting a hand truck loaded with produce up behind him. He stacked the boxes inside the walk-in and gave Sunny a wave. She put on a casual smile.

"Hi, Ben. You look tired. Can I make you a cappuccino?"

"Love one, thanks." He pulled off his gloves and tucked them in the pocket of his jacket, resting against the hand truck. He acknowledged Charlie with a nod.

"Mr. Rhodes."

"Ben."

"Any word from the board?" Ben asked.

"Nothing yet," Charlie said.

"Hi, Rivka," Ben said as she came back into the kitchen.

Rivka waved and flashed a smile before turning back to her work.

Sunny went to the bar and poured cream in a stainless-steel pitcher, steamed it, and fired two shots of espresso. She gave Charlie a look and raised her index finger ever so slightly, hoping to convey a desperate plea for him to say nothing, whatever it was he might want to say. She poured the shots and added a splash of liquid, spooning a blanket of creamy foam on top.

Ben took the cup and sipped. "I need to apologize about this morning, Sunny. You caught hell for no reason. Those meetings set my pants on fire."

"Don't worry about it." Sunny watched his reaction to the cappuccino. The secret to perfect foam is fresh cream from a dairy where they let the cows graze instead of keeping them in stalls and feeding them fish meal. In her head she recited what she told the wait staff. *Pour only what you need and hit it once with steam. Cream should never be overheated or reheated unless you intend to give your patrons the trots.*

"I was reading an article about biodynamic farming the other day," said Sunny, seeing if she could lead him to confirm a piece of the Thursday-night puzzle. "It's pretty interesting stuff."

"Definitely. I've been experimenting with it for a few years now. I have one solution that seems to work pretty well with aphids."

"But you have to spray that stuff at night, right?"

"You don't have to, but people tend to think it works better. The plants are dormant at night, so the solution stays on the surface longer, which is where you want it."

"Isn't that a huge hassle, going out in the dark?"

"You get used to it, and it's just every once in a while, mostly at the beginning of the growing season." He finished the cappuccino and set the cup in a bus bin. "Thanks."

"No problem. Hey, I'm having some people over for dinner tonight. I'd love it if you and Claire could come."

He frowned and then caught himself, relaxing his face with an effort. "Tonight? That sounds great, but I'll have to check with Claire. What time?"

"Around eight?"

"We'll be there, unless I let you know different after I talk to the wife."

Charlie watched her with an amused look on his face. When Ben left he said, "What was that all about?"

"Just a sec. Riv, is he gone?"

She glanced out the window. "Yep."

Sunny exhaled and let her shoulders relax.

"What's going on?" asked Rivka, looking from Sunny to Charlie.

Sunny held up a finger signaling for them to wait and quickly dug her planner out of her bag. She flipped to the back where she'd written down Michael Rieder's phone number and dialed.

"May I please speak with Mr. Rieder?" asked Sunny when the receptionist picked up.

"He's with a client," said the young man on the other end in a carefully mannered voice.

"I see. Well, maybe you can help me," said Sunny. "This is Detective Jessica Thompson. I spoke with Mr. Rieder over the weekend in regard to—"

"Jack Beroni?" The young man finished the sentence for her.

"Exactly."

"I'm sorry, I don't think I recognize your name," said the receptionist. "Are you with the Napa police?"

"I'm not local," said Sunny. "I flew up from Los Angeles Homicide to help out the St. Helena Police Department. They're officially handling the case. I'm afraid we have a good deal more experience investigating homicide in my neck of the woods."

"I'm sure," said the young man.

"I was just having a bite to eat and a thought occurred to me, a small detail I should have confirmed with Mr. Rieder yesterday. Did a man named Ben Baker happen to phone your office last week at any time?"

"Ben Baker? Yes, I spoke to him last week myself. He called to ask about the Hansen Ranch paperwork, but his wife had already picked it up."

"I see. She had already picked up the paperwork." Sunny paused. "Do you happen to remember what day that was?"

"It would have been Tuesday—no, Wednesday morning."

"Got it. Thank you very much for your help, Mr. . . ."

"James. Steven James, with a V. My pleasure. Shall I have Mr. Rieder return your call?"

"No, thank you. That won't be necessary. I think I have everything I need now."

Charlie watched her in amazement, his eyebrows crowding his forehead and an incredulous look on his face. He said, "Sunny, what are you—"

"Shh!" She flipped more pages in the planner and dialed Gabe's cell phone. After several rings he picked up. When she'd persuaded him that he did not need to get some rest but in fact would like nothing more than to come to dinner at her place that night, she hung up and stood thinking, a pencil in hand hovering over her planner. Rivka stopped what she was doing and stood watching her.

Sunny ticked off her fingers, then looked up and pointed at Charlie. "You'll be there, eight o'clock sharp," she said. She turned to Rivka. "You, too. With Alex. You have to bring Alex. This is important and I'm not joking. I can count on you to be there tonight, right?"

They nodded, bewildered.

14

Monty Lenstrom was easy. In the five years she'd known him, Sunny couldn't remember a time when he had turned down an invitation to dinner, especially on a dull Monday night. The last call she placed, made from the semi-privacy of her office, was to Wade Skord. He sounded understandably unhinged from his usual frame of mind. His voice was thin and frayed with anxiety. He said he'd spent the day pacing around the winery, alternately working with a manic fervor and then noticing that he'd been staring off into space for who knows how long. Wednesday would be harvest day, he figured. He said he didn't feel like having dinner with anyone, that even his friends would stop talking when he came in, and everyone would look at him like he was Charles Manson on parole.

"Maybe, but you have to come anyway," Sunny said.

"Why?"

"Because I need you there."

"I don't get it."

"Indulge me. Please. Wade, who fed your cat while you were up the river?"

"You."

"Well, it's payback time."

"There's payback for pouring dry cat food in a bowl? You are a sick woman."

"Just be at my place at eight and don't give me no lip. This is about more than dinner."

"I surmised as much."

After lingering over a final bite of Mama McCoskey's rum cake and the dregs of a latte for forty-five minutes, the last of Wildside's customers waddled out the door at ten minutes to four, followed soon after by the last of the wait staff. By five the dishwashers had gone home, and Rivka and Sunny had restocked the pantry for the next day. Rivka tossed her apron in the laundry and reached for the ceiling, stretching up, side to side, and down. She threw one foot up on a window ledge and executed a deep, lunging stretch.

"You know that nonexistent item we discussed this morning?" said Sunny.

"I've been wondering about it."

"It still doesn't exist. I'd say it should rematerialize sometime tomorrow morning at the latest."

Rivka placed her hands on the toe of her cross-trainer and bent forward, her face tucked to the side of her calf. Her voice sounded muffled. "Okay. I hope you know what you're doing." She turned her head toward Sunny, looking at her from under her arm. "You do know what you're doing, don't you?"

"Of course."

"Really?"

"No, not really. I'm sort of winging it."

"Oh, good. That's a big relief. Because I was a little worried that maybe we were in over our heads."

"We are, but I have a plan, or at least an idea for a plan. All you have to do is be yourself."

"Just like Mom always said."

"And don't say anything about the item."

"Right. Be myself but don't mention the most important thing on my mind."

Sunny stuck around after Rivka left, killing time until she figured Nesto Campaglia was likely to be home. She made a minor dent in the heap of unopened mail in the office, and at a quarter to six, she raided the pantry and packed the truck full of supplies for the dinner party, fitting the perishable stuff into a cooler with a few slabs of ice. Then it was finally time to drive over to Nesto's house. As she pulled up into the shade, she spotted him out back in the garden, which was a relief because it meant she could skip knocking at the door and having to get past Mary Campaglia. He watched her walk over, letting water pool up from the hose he was using to water a section of bell pepper plants. An orange sunset backlit his form.

They exchanged greetings and Nesto continued with his watering. Sunny waited to see if he would turn his attention back to her. He did not.

"Mr. Campaglia," she said, "I know Gabe wasn't with you and Mary here on Thursday night. He was at the Dusty Vine, drinking."

She waited again, and when he didn't respond, she went on.

"I also know that you met with Al Beroni on Friday, and he told you about the will he'd written up, specifically that Alex and Gabe stood to inherit Beroni Vineyards if Jack died without any children. This part is just a guess, but my idea is that he suggested you make sure the boys had solid alibis because the will gave them a motive, and when the cops found out about it, it wasn't going to look good."

Nesto walked to the side of the house and turned off the water, then came back. His long, antenna-like eyebrows rode together in a somber frown. He said, "Al is a good man. He figured if his own dynasty died out, the Campaglias ought to take over. I don't think he ever really thought that would happen, of course. The main part of the will makes it clear that he believes the Campaglia family is crucial to the success of the winery. There's a clause in there about retaining Gabe, Alex, and even their children in key positions, not that it would have held up in any legal way if Jack wanted to do otherwise. Al's a sound businessman. He knows the value of experience, and stability. I guess he hoped Jack would come around to his way of thinking eventually."

"I have another guess," said Sunny. "You weren't here at home with Mary Thursday night, either."

"You're wrong there. I was home all night after about six."

Sunny expelled a theatrical sigh and dug her hands into the back pockets of her baggy black-and-white chef's pants. "Mr. Campaglia, your son is in serious trouble. On the night of the murder, he was drunk and belligerent in front of witnesses, to whom he expressed a violent resentment of Jack Beroni. He was at the Dusty Vine at the time when somebody, probably the murderer, used the pay phone in the parking lot to arrange the fatal meeting with Jack. He's a good shot with a rifle, and he has an extremely compelling motive. And that's not even all of the evidence against him, Mr. Campaglia. I've left out the part that could insure that both he and his brother are sent to prison for a very, very long time. Maybe their whole lives."

The color came up in Nesto's face and he began to puff. "I've had enough of this. I've had just about enough. My sons are innocent. Gabe has never been an easy spirit, but he wouldn't hurt anyone, let alone kill Jack."

Sunny looked away and stole a moment to think. She wanted more. It was risky to push him—she was all but accusing one or both of his sons of murder—but she didn't have many other options. "If that's the case, tell me why Wade Skord's rifle was hidden in a box under Alex's bed."

"What the devil are you talking about?"

"Wade Skord's rifle, which I think we can safely assume was the murder weapon, was found under Alex's bed wrapped in a bath towel in a box, lying on top of a bunch of old high-school trophies."

Nesto seemed to stagger, and Sunny formulated a quick action plan in her head in the event that he started reaching for his heart right then and there. She fought the urge to reassure him. He had to break. He walked over to the side of the house and leaned against it momentarily, then began methodically re-coiling the garden hose he'd been using. She could see his mind working as he did it, trying to figure out if she was lying, and if not, how Alex could have become involved. He would be asking himself how well he knew his sons, how much they might be capable of. He was probably remembering all the times they'd schemed together as kids and run into trouble, and the times he'd seen the grown-up Gabe drunk. He'd be wondering how sensitive the balance was between passion, anger, and self-control in Gabe, and in Alex for that matter. He knew his boys, but how well did he know them as men? Finally he came to the confused and desperate place she had, regrettably, been hoping to lead him. Assuming she was telling him the truth, and being unable to explain why Alex had possession of the murder weapon, he had no choice but to tell her his entire story in the hope that something he said might somehow absolve his sons. He turned the water back on and rinsed his hands, then wiped them dry on his pants and walked slowly back over to her.

"On Thursday afternoon, Jack and I had a disagreement," he said. "You know that part already. Jack even threatened me. I was still angry, so I went to see Al about it later that day. We talked about Jack's position now and in the future, about my role, and about how Gabe and Alex fit in. He seemed to understand my point of view across the board and said he had no intention of allowing Jack free reign until he was confident that he knew what he was doing, that unfortunately he didn't trust his son's temper or judgment to date, and it might be years before Jack could assume an independent leadership role at Beroni. He said meanwhile he'd make sure Jack stayed out of the winemaking decisions entirely. From my perspective, we'd come to complete agreement and I was satisfied.

"That evening, the boys came by around six-thirty. I told them what Al had said, assuming it would put their minds at ease, same as it had mine. It didn't. Gabe in particular was still very angry. He said that Al had his head in the clouds, that Jack told him whatever he wanted to hear, and that Al was getting old and as soon as he retired, which might be any day, Jack would be running the operation and we would have no say about it. He said we needed contracts to guarantee our salaries and positions right away—even the houses we live in. I told him I've lived in this house for forty years without a contract and Al's word has always been good enough for me. I tried to calm him down, but he was upset and he was making me upset. He stormed out and, I'm told, spent the rest of the evening at the Dusty Vine, like you said. Alex stayed and tried to convince me we should see a lawyer, more nonsense in my opinion. Then he went out to see your friend Rivka—she'll vouch for that, I'm sure.

"After supper, Mary cleaned up and I went into the living room. I sat down and I thought about the whole business. I'm not ashamed to admit I got melancholy thinking about how the Campaglias have always seemed to do all the work and the Beronis seem to reap all the rewards. I thought about my father, and how he worked and worked and came out of it with nothing. He died without savings, without owning anything more than a car. Mary tried to show me the positive side, but the past was all stirred up inside me and I couldn't think straight. I'd had a couple glasses of wine at dinner, and I opened another bottle after Mary gave up and went to bed. I was ready to wallow in my feelings that night, feeling sorry for myself and my boys, feeling sorry that I hadn't done more to make sure they had a future. Miss McCoskey, the truth is, I got good and drunk sitting there alone in my living room." He waggled a finger at Sunny's nose. "I only do it once in a blue moon, and let me tell you, it's not a good idea for me or anyone else. You let all the demons out and they start to run around and take over. It's trouble waiting to happen."

Sunny held her breath and waited for him to go on. Nesto raked his weathered old hands through the dense turf of gray hair on his head. His eyes flashed.

"I went out and I got in my car. This was maybe ten o'clock. I decided I was going to go over there and give Alberto Beroni what he had coming. I was going to tell him how the Campaglias had lived long enough as hired hands on their own vineyard.

Four generations of Campaglias have worked this land so the Beroni family could get rich. I was finally going to do something about that."

The force that had propelled Nesto on his tirade seemed to suddenly falter and diminish. He stood quietly, looking at the sky to the west with its canary-yellow and orange streaks fanning out from the mountains.

"I drove over there. I went all the way up to the house and I turned off the engine and was about to get out. Then I noticed that I could see them through the window, sitting in the living room together. Al and Louisa were sitting there just like they had on any night for the past forty years. I could see the back of Al's head and the newspaper he was reading. Louisa was sewing something, probably one of her embroidered pillowcases. All of a sudden I couldn't go in there for any reason. I realized that that was their house, not mine. History is history, it's over, and I had no more right to that house or the vineyard than any other man. They lived in their home, the same way I lived in mine.

"I sat there for a while thinking about things. I thought about being a kid and how Alberto was like a brother to me, and then I turned around and drove right back out of there. I never even got out of the car. Anyway, I must not have been paying much attention to the road because the next thing I know, I just about run over Jack. He's walking right in the middle of the road, dressed head to toe in black, and the bumper was practically on him before I stopped."

"Did you talk to him?"

"No. I just gave him a wave and drove on."

"What time was that?"

"About ten-thirty or quarter to eleven, I'd say."

"What happened after that?"

"Not a thing. I went home and went to bed. The next day it was just like you suggested. When I got to work, the police were already there. Al was very quiet. Very controlled and very quiet. I'd say he was in shock. He sent word down that he wanted to talk to me right away, and when I went up to the house, he took me into his office and showed me the will. It was the most amazing thing I have ever seen. He said I had always been like a brother to him, and I'll tell you that made us both cry like a couple of babies. He made me swear not to tell anyone about what he'd shown me, and then he said I'd better be sure the boys both had good, solid alibis because the police were bound to find out about the will. He didn't want them to have any trouble. He knew they didn't kill his son."

He gave her a searching look. Sunny thanked him. Nesto walked her out to the truck. After she got in, he closed the door for her and stood with a hand resting on the roof of the cab. She rolled down the window and he ducked his head to make eye contact. "I've told you plenty that I haven't even told Mary. What about that other business you mentioned?"

"Nothing we've said today goes beyond you and me as far as I'm concerned. About that other business, I'll be in touch."

She turned the key and the truck roared to life. There was barely enough time to get home, shower, and disinter a few buckets of delectable roasted duck legs from their protective nest of fat before her guests were scheduled to arrive.

Back at home in the shower, she closed her eyes and let the water drum against her forehead. It would have been heaven to stand there for another ten minutes letting the heat unravel the tension in her neck, if it weren't for the eight dinner guests slated to arrive in half an hour. She cut the water and stepped out, releasing a great round cloud of steam. They would feast on roasted duck legs cooked slowly until the rich, dark meat fell easily off the bone; fettuccine with Wildside's trademark mushroom cream sauce; butternut squash soup with a big garlic crouton floating in the middle of each bowl; and a salad of arugula, Fuyu persimmons, Gorgonzola, and candied pecans—plus as much red wine as possible. If she could get everyone to drink cognac afterward, they'd really be in business. Most of the food was ready and waiting in cardboard boxes in the kitchen, thanks to owner's privileges at Wildside, but she still needed to get the hot stuff hot and throw the salad together.

At ten minutes to eight, Sunny stood in front of her bedroom closet, pushing hangers back and forth. She chose a calf-length skirt made of velvet the color of dark chocolate and as soft and sleek as a cat. For shoes, she picked out a pair of dark brown riding boots. She pulled on a mottled moss-green sweater and had just selected small gold earrings with tiny topaz stones and a slender gold chain bracelet when the doorbell rang. Charlie Rhodes stood at the door with a wine bottle in one hand and a bouquet of white and yellow roses in the other. Elated, Sunny took the flowers and smelled them, wondering what kind of flowers they were intended to be. Were these "I find you enchanting and irresistible" flowers or "Let's just be friends" flowers? Rivka would know.

"Come on in. You're the first," said Sunny. He took off his jacket and they headed for the kitchen, where Sunny hunted for a vase. The fact that he brought flowers at all was a good sign, she figured.

"I'm glad I've got you alone," he said. "I was hoping we'd get a chance to talk."

Her heart hit a pothole. "Really. What about?"

"I guess I'll just come out with it. I've been sort of worried about you. This thing with Wade and Jack Beroni seems to have you all worked up. At the restaurant today you seemed sort of, well, manic."

She winced but made a quick recovery. So much for any subtle romantic message with the roses. "Don't worry about it, I'm fine. It was just a busy day and service was running late." She gave him a reassuring smile laced with a fierce look she hoped would curtail any further concerns and went back to assembling dinner.

Charlie opened the bottle she handed him and he poured them each a glass of a Pinot Noir as clear and bright and rosy as a garnet.

"About my manic state. I need to ask you a favor," she said, chiming her glass against his. "I might say something tonight that you will know is not true, but I want you to pretend that it is and go along with it. It's very important, and not just to me. I can't say what it's about right now, other than it's not nonsense or drama or insanity. I'll explain everything tomorrow."

He hesitated.

Sunny smoothed her velvet skirt and pushed her hair behind her ears, glancing up with a studied look of composure. She said, "I'm asking you to trust me."

Charlie studied her. "Okay. I'm not sure what's going on, and whatever it is, I don't like it, but I guess I'm in."

The doorbell rang again. "One more thing. You can't say anything to anyone about this. No side remarks or insinuations about going along with my nonsense, okay? Tonight is not a joke."

"You're not exactly putting my mind at ease."

"I know, I'm not trying to. Just bear with me for tonight."

Rivka and Alex arrived, and right behind them, Ben and Claire Baker. The quiet kitchen turned boisterous. Rivka kept herself busy taking everyone's coats and bags and putting them in Sunny's bedroom. Rivka had pointed Alex out once at a party before they were dating, but this was the first time Sunny had ever seen him up close. He was tall and wide shouldered with a plain, handsome face and the shadow of a beard on his pale skin. His hands were hidden in the pockets of his cords, and he'd shoved himself against the far wall of the kitchen, looking extremely uncomfortable. These Campaglia boys weren't much for social occasions, thought Sunny. The look of barely contained hysteria on his face was echoed on Claire's.

Sunny wondered if Alex had discovered that the gun was missing from his room and decided that he had. It must be perplexing for him to wonder who could have broken into his house and found it. He might wonder if it was Rivka, but he would probably be afraid to ask for fear of giving himself away if it wasn't her. It occurred to her for the first time as she turned the fires down and prepared to dress the salad that if she was wrong and Alex was actually guilty of murder, she had placed Rivka in considerable danger by asking her to keep the gun a secret. Her heart thumped, pulsing under her ears, and the lights seemed to wink. She stepped back suddenly, just catching herself before she fell, but not before she caught a damning look from Charlie out of the corner of her eye. She took a deep breath. He was right, she needed to calm down.

Monty showed up and pulled two bottles of Cabernet Sauvignon out of a paper grocery sack. The first was a 1992 Caymus Special Select that made everyone say *Ooh,* followed by a 1986 bottle of Dunn Howell Mountain that provoked an awed hush. Sunny looked over Charlie's shoulder at the label. It was a rare find even for someone who saw as much wine as Monty did. The Dunn operation was even smaller and more eccentric than Skord Mountain, and its wines generally sold for a good deal more money, being Cabernet Sauvignon to Skord's less marketable Zinfandel.

"I figured we ought to celebrate tonight. Carpe diem," said Monty.

Sunny bussed him on the cheek and handed him the wine opener. "You're a brave and generous soul, Lenstrom. Let's get those things open before you change your mind."

At half past eight, the doorbell rang again and Sunny ducked out of the kitchen to open it. Gabe Campaglia stood on her doorstep smelling like aftershave and hair products. So, thought Sunny, he has a streak of vanity after all. He came in and they lingered by the door in a brief, slightly awkward silence while he took in her house.

"There is absolutely no way he could tell the difference, but do you think he would admit it?" came from the kitchen, Monty's voice. Gabe let her take his suede jacket, which she quickly deposited in the darkened bedroom. When she came back, he followed her toward the sounds of conversation. She introduced him around, then he took up a silent post beside Alex.

There was a flurry of appreciative exclamations when Wade arrived, in some cases expressing relief that he was safely home, in others expressing joy that everyone could finally move to the table. Monty and Charlie shook his hand, and Sunny made her way over to embrace him. She could hardly believe he was really there in front of her. She rested her hands on his shoulders fondly, running her fingers over the fabric of his gray wool jacket. There was a rough spot on one shoulder where the fabric was snagged up. She smoothed the spot, and Wade slid out of the jacket. Holding the jacket in her right hand, Sunny flicked her nail over the spot again, wondering what might have caught the fabric.

"It's an abrasion from that rifle stock of his with the crack in the bottom," Claire said, as if reading Sunny's mind. "There's nothing you can do about it, unless you want to reweave the whole shoulder. There was that night you all went out to shoot, and I noticed a snag on Monty's sweater in the same place when he came back in. Monty's sweaters never have snags on them." She winked at Monty.

Sunny's blood suddenly ran cold as she stood facing Claire in the overly warm kitchen. The dead animals in the shed at Hansen Ranch. Claire could have been the shooter. It could be Claire's anger that lead to murder. Anger at Jack for a love that survived twenty years but never amounted to more than a secret. Frustration at having been devoted to him despite his snubbing her and his family's disdain for Hansen Ranch. Maybe Jack had told her he was ending the affair to marry Larissa, maybe Claire had given him an ultimatum, maybe Claire blamed him and Beroni Vineyards for the ranch's financial problems. Maybe Claire was tired of being the one who made sacrifices so they could be together. Claire's motives were as good as or better than Ben's.

Sunny feared that she had looked too hard at the wrong partner. Oh God, what was she trying to do at this dinner party? She thought she knew, she thought she had it almost all figured out and could squeeze out the rest by bringing everyone together. But if she'd misinterpreted all those facts as pointing to Ben, what else had she gotten wrong? She held on to the counter so the room would not start to sway. She was in it now, everyone was here. There was nothing to do but go ahead with the plan. Only now she wasn't so sure how it would turn out.

On the surface, the evening progressed in an ordinary fashion. Each guest's unease was not visible to the others, but Sunny knew it was not a happy gathering, and the thread of conversation was always just barely adequate to keep the party going from one topic to the next. The bottle of Dunn had been dispatched in the kitchen while their palates were pristine, and the Caymus soon met the same fate, followed quickly by a bottle of the Carneros Pinot Noir. Sunny reached across the table and refilled Charlie's glass from another bottle of the Pinot, saying, "I can't stop thinking about what you said about that glassy-winged sharpshooter they found over at the Maya Culpa. It just doesn't sound right to me."

"They found one?" Wade said.

"On Friday," said Charlie. "A solo specimen. We went over the area thoroughly this morning, but there didn't seem to be a local population. At least I wasn't able to find anything. I don't know where that little guy in the trap came from."

"Probably somebody's grandmother brought home a new rosebush from the garden shop," said Wade. "They're up to their belly buttons in sharpies down in L.A., and they're shipping them up here with every hothouse flower. No amount of inspecting is going to catch every one."

"We thought of that," said Charlie, "but there's nothing nearby that's newer than thirty years. It was found in a mature olive grove far from the house and the winery, far from any of the ornamentals. In fact, I didn't see much for ornamentals on the whole place. They've kept it pretty au naturel up there."

Wade grunted, a sound somewhere between mere acknowledgment that something had been said and agreement with it.

"Tell him about the part where it's the wrong kind of sharpie," Sunny said.

Charlie explained the oddity of finding a stage-two nymph in a trap designed to catch flying and hopping insects.

"It sounds fishy to me," said Monty.

"I started thinking after you left this afternoon," said Sunny. "And so I gave Frank Schmidt a call." She looked at Monty. "That's the county ag commissioner."

"I know who Frank Schmidt is."

"Ex-*cuse* me. Anyway, I was following up on what you said this morning, Ben. How everybody just sits around on their duffs, letting whoever shows up at the meetings decide what happens to the land. I figured I would give Frank a call and let him know my position on the matter, as the proprietor of a local business dependent on locally grown organic produce. He listened, but then he told me that they're going to start spraying carbaryl in a broad radius around the find starting tomorrow morning even though Charlie's team didn't locate any more sharpies in the area. He said there's nothing he or anyone else can do about it; the decision has been made. Apparently the ag board felt they couldn't risk an infestation, no matter how small the chances. He said they're getting big-time heat from Sacramento."

"They can't start spraying tomorrow morning. They have to hold a public hearing before they can do anything like that," said Ben, his voice rising angrily.

Sunny threw Charlie a look. "Not this time. They have an executive order from the governor. It's been declared an emergency situation."

"I heard about that," said Charlie, pouring himself another glass of wine. "They passed a bill last week that gives the state's sharpshooter task force the right to move on a decision without a public hearing. That's why they upgraded the glassy-winged sharpshooter to a class-one pest. Special rules apply because they consider catastrophic losses to be at stake."

"And what exactly is a broad radius according to Frank Schmidt?" asked Ben, dropping his fork down with a clatter.

"I'm not sure. Charlie, do you know?" said Sunny.

"I don't. I suppose I'll find out tomorrow."

"Do they plan on letting the property owners know about this, or are they just going to show up?" asked Ben caustically.

"He said a guy will go around ahead of the spray crew and let the occupants know what's going on," said Charlie.

Ben was fuming. Sunny said, "I'm as upset about this as you are, but I don't know what we can do about it at this point. At least it won't affect your organic status anymore. They also passed a bill saying that organic produce that gets nuked as part of an emergency effort can still be called organic."

"They passed that law quite a while ago," said Ben.

"That's awful," said Rivka. "So the organic produce I'm buying could be even more toxic than the nonorganic stuff and I won't even know it."

"That's right," said Sunny. "It's a serious blow to the credibility of the word *organic*. It's one giant step closer to the now-meaningless *natural* on packaging." Sunny looked at Claire, who was nodding in agreement but didn't seem upset. She was watching her husband's face.

Ben was flushed with anger. "That's not the worst of it. It's not just that the produce won't be organic anymore, the land won't be. The land will be poisoned. There'll be carbaryl in the soil, in the plants, in the water. It takes years for it to dissipate, let alone for the soil to build back the natural defenses and strike the right balance of beneficials and microorganisms. If they spray like that, the whole concept of an organic farm is over, and we can thank our friends at Beroni Vineyards for the service." He glared at Alex and Gabe.

Alex looked at Rivka. Gabe looked at Ben. Gabe's eyes were red and he looked as though he was fighting to stay awake. He wrestled his shoulders back. "It's not Beroni Vineyards," he said. "It's all wineries. There is no cure for Pierce's disease in grapevines. It means certain death. The glassy-winged sharpshooter vectors Pierce's disease right into the heart of grapevines. If the sharpshooter gets established, we are out of business, and so is every other grape grower in town, until they can engineer a plant that resists it, and that could be years. The local economy would crumble. The wine industry would never grow back because all the land would be strip malls and suburbs, built over the best grape-growing land in the world."

Gabe fell silent. Ben looked around the table in frustration, his cheeks plum red and his glare darting from one of them to the other. Eating had stopped, and the tension was unbearable. Sunny fought the urge to flee to the kitchen or at least nibble a nail. She checked Claire, then focused on Ben. The longer the silence at the table went on, the closer to exasperation he got.

Finally Ben spoke. "Charlie, you have to stop them. That sharpshooter is a phony. It was planted in that trap. I caught Jack Beroni planting one in a trap on my land last week. On Wednesday night around ten o'clock. It was the same as the one you found, a stage-two nymph. He must have put one in the trap at the Maya Culpa at the same time."

Claire stared at her plate, holding one hand at her forehead like a visor.

"That can't be true," said Charlie vehemently.

"It's true. I didn't say anything because I didn't want to risk them not believing me. I couldn't prove it. I figured there was a chance they'd spray anyway, just in case, even if I told them it was planted. I knew Beroni would deny it, of course. So I just let him get away with it. It didn't occur to me until now that he might have planted more than one."

"Why would he plant a sharpshooter on your land?" asked Charlie.

"To drive me out of business. He'd been trying to force me to give up on the farm and grow grapes in partnership with Beroni Vineyards. He even offered me my own boutique label. He knew that if the county sprayed my farm with carbaryl, we might as well quit organic farming. He loved to wave his money under my nose. He actually thought I could be bribed into ripping out hundred-year-old fruit and olive trees so I could grow grapes for a bunch of wine snobs in a glutted market. He thought he'd encourage the county to destroy my farm, and then come around with his wallet and take the place off my hands or force me into a partnership. He even tried to seduce Claire into selling to him."

Claire looked mortified under the shield of her hand, and her face was tightening up. Sunny wondered if Ben's word choice was coincidental. She also wondered how much of this Claire knew and when.

"Are you sure it was him?" Rivka said.

"I'm sure. I was out in the orchard Wednesday night doing an application of a treatment that keeps off the leaf curl when I heard that cell phone of his."

"At night?" asked Rivka.

"That's the best time. His cell phone plays a few bars of 'O Sole Mio' instead of ringing. No one else's phone plays that song. So I went down there, and as I got closer, I heard a car drive off down the service road. There were fresh footprints around the trap, and it didn't take me long to figure out what he was up to. Sure enough, there was a shooter planted there in the trap."

"I saw him driving down Mount Veeder late last Wednesday night," said Monty with excitement. "Remember, Sunny? I told you about it. I was coming home from dinner and his silver Jag with the 'Wine Guy' plates flew by me going about eighty."

"Sounds about right," said Ben.

Monty shook his head. "What a thing to do. Christ, it seems like Beroni never had an ethical thought during his entire existence."

"How can you say such a thing?" cried Claire, her voice trembling with rage. She shoved away her chair and stood up, glaring at Monty. "You didn't even know him. You're all vicious. You can't even be nice to him after he's dead." A stream of angry tears ran down her cheeks as she glanced around for her purse and jacket. No one moved while she walked into the bedroom, collected her things, and left without another word. The sound of the doorbells jangling and her heels clicking on the brick steps outside seemed to rouse Ben from a meditative state, and he pushed back his chair, got up, and silently followed after her.

15

"I guess I said something wrong," said Monty nervously. His eyes darted from Sunny to Rivka to Wade, seeking reassurance. "Claire's right. I didn't even know the guy. I have no right to come down on him, especially now that he's dead."

"We've all been out of line," said Rivka.

Sunny held her glass and studied the faces at the table. Alex looked even more gaunt and haunted than he had when he arrived. Ben Baker's revelation about Jack planting the sharpshooter on Hansen Ranch seemed only to have intensified his distress. Gabe, on the other hand, looked nothing more than slightly bemused by the Bakers' sudden departure. He eyed the bowl of fettuccine sitting just out of reach, considering seconds. Rivka had her head tipped to one side and was turning the silver post in her ear round and round, a habit of hers when she was thinking. Rivka missed nothing. She knew about Claire and Jack just from the look on Claire's face.

Charlie said, "It's feasible," as though there had been no break in their conversation. "It's certainly not difficult to procure a sharpshooter. Half the counties in California are up to their apricots in them. And all you'd have to do is stick one to the trap. That's not a problem."

"He waits until he's sure everyone is in bed," said Monty, abandoning his contrite posture. "He drives up there, leaves his car down on the service road, walks up to the orchard, sticks one of those sharpies in a trap, then takes off like a bullet when his phone rings, even though he probably never imagined Ben was around to hear it. Either before or after that, he goes over to the Maya Culpa to put down another bug, in case nobody spots the first one, or in case Baker finds it before Charlie's people do. He probably figures Baker wouldn't report it anyway and risk having Frank Schmidt's minions crawling all over his land. No offense intended, Charlie."

"None taken."

Wade had been pushing his food around on his plate. He looked at Sunny and said, "And why would Jack want Mount Veeder sprayed if there weren't actually any sharpshooters"

Sunny hefted the heavy ceramic bowl of pasta down the table, setting it in front of Gabe Campaglia. He gave her a hint of a smile and dug in.

"Don't you get it?" said Monty. "Beroni wanted to make a splash for his pop, do something that would prove he was savvy enough to run things after Al retired. And all of a sudden there is little Claire Baker on his doorstep looking lonely and doe-eyed, with her perky bottom parked on the hottest Cabernet Sauvignon property in the county, and he thinks, Ben Baker won't sell, but Claire might. She just needs a little nudge. So he gets himself a sharpshooter or two and loads up Charlie's traps, only he doesn't count on Baker scooting around out in his orchard at ten o'clock at night like a madman. He also doesn't do his homework, so he doesn't know he's got the wrong sharpshooters." Monty was about to go on when his eyes settled on Wade. There was a flash of recognition and he closed his mouth abruptly. Sunny watched him, wondering what thought had changed his mind about what he was about to say.

Alex put his napkin on the table. He'd had as much as he could take. He put a hand on Rivka's shoulder and whispered something in her ear.

She said, "You go ahead. Sunny can drop me."

"I'll leave you the truck," Alex said. "Gabe, you drove, right?"

"Me? Sure." He worked his plate while he talked, twirling pasta onto his fork without looking up. "What's the rush?"

"I gotta get home and get some rest before I pass out," said Alex.

Gabe stared. "You ready right now?"

"If you are. I have to get up early." Alex tapped his wristwatch and gave Sunny a sheepish look. "Sorry to eat and run. Dinner was great."

Gabe sighed and put down his fork. "Well, I guess I'm ready then."

When they'd gone Sunny surveyed the survivors. "Anyone for dessert?" she asked skeptically.

"Not me," said Monty. "In fact, I'd better be getting home as well." Sunny made a token effort to dissuade him, with no success.

"What's his problem?" said Wade after Monty had jogged down the front steps and raced out to his car.

"You want my guess? He can't quite decide if you're guilty or not," said Sunny.

"What?" said Wade.

Rivka and Charlie averted their eyes and said nothing.

"Well, I'd say he was just about to suggest that Ben Baker killed Jack Beroni when he looked at you and remembered Jack might have tried the same trick at Skord Mountain, and you might have decided you'd had just about as much as you were going to take," said Sunny.

"Except that spraying my vineyard with pesticides isn't going to put me out of business," said Wade. "Probably the opposite. It would be a terrible thing that I would hate to have to do, but it wouldn't be nearly as bad as looking at a bunch of dead vines with sharpshooters sucking the life out of them. Pierce's disease will put me out of business long before carbaryl will."

"What about Alex and Gabe?" said Charlie cautiously. "They weren't too excited about staying for dessert. Do they think Wade is guilty, too?"

"Alex is just tired," said Rivka quickly. "They get up at the crack of dawn."

"Bullshit," said Wade. "They're up to something, or at least Alex is."

"Such as?" said Rivka, lifting a protective eyebrow.

"I wouldn't know," said Wade. "But I do know that this conversation is giving me heartburn. McCoskey, I will expect a full explanation in the morning or I'm boycotting your dinner parties indefinitely."

Sunny started clearing the table, trying not to see the fear and disappointment in Wade's eyes. She had cajoled him into coming, and just what he'd wanted to avoid had happened: He'd been reminded of his predicament and subjected to scrutiny. She said, "Don't go yet. Stay and have a cognac with us."

Wade emerged from the bedroom pulling on his jacket and headed for the door. "Nothing doing. I don't know what you're up to, Sunny, but it's certainly not helping. I'll thank you for not cooking up any more schemes." He closed the door solidly behind him, leaving her standing halfway to the kitchen.

Rivka looked at her. "What's he talking about?"

"He thought tonight was part of some elaborate plan to help clear him." Sunny struggled to regain her own confidence, fighting a wave of fear that he was right and she had been just mixing up more trouble, not even sure of what she was doing.

"Did it work?" asked Charlie, ruefully.

She thought about it and smiled for the first time all night. "Yes. Dessert?"

"Not for me," said Charlie. "Unless I'm still part of your plan, I think I'll head home, where at least I know what's going on. Anyway, I need to figure out what I'm going to tell Frank Schmidt tomorrow morning."

"So you believe what Ben said?" said Rivka.

"I'm not sure. It does explain some things that are hard to account for otherwise."

When Charlie had gone, Rivka went to the front door and peeked out, then closed it and turned the bolt. She collected a stack of dirty plates and silverware from the table and came into the kitchen, where Sunny was putting away leftovers.

"So, Claire Baker was in love with Jack Beroni," said Rivka.

"Yes."

"And they were having an affair."

"Correct."

"Which Ben was not aware of."

"Not if what he said tonight is true. I don't think he was covering. He did a good job if he was."

"And Jack wanted Hansen Ranch."

"I believe so. I think he tried to persuade them to enter into some kind of partnership to grow grapes. A new contract for Mayacamas-grown Cabernet Sauvignon would be a major coup for Beroni Vineyards. It was going to be Jack's opening act as the new chief. Ben would never agree, but it wasn't necessarily his decision. Claire inherited Hansen Ranch from her father."

"So, being a slimeball, Beroni decides to force the issue. He plants a sharpie on the Baker place, and another on the Maya Culpa to guarantee that they spray the area."

"That's what I'm thinking. But we have to back up a bit to see the whole picture," said Sunny. "The Bakers are having serious financial trouble. Jack knows this—I'm guessing that's how he first reconnected with Claire; she came to him asking for a loan—and he takes the opportunity to propose a partnership. Claire tries to persuade Ben, but he won't go for it. On Wednesday, Ben gets desperate enough to actually consider the idea of going over to the enemy. Or at least that's my guess, because he called Jack's lawyer, Mike Rieder, to ask about the deal Jack Beroni had been pushing. Rieder's receptionist couldn't be more friendly to Ben. He says the papers are all set, your wife picked them up this morning, all we need is your signatures and we're in business. Well, Ben didn't know anything about signing any papers. That's during the day on Wednesday. That same night, he discovers Jack planting the shooter. Are you okay?"

"I'm not sure. I just think that if we really believe Ben did it, we need to call the police right now. I mean, the man just had dinner in your house."

"We don't want the police right now, not until we know what happened for sure."

"We know what happened. Ben found out what Jack was doing and he killed him."

"We can't prove it. Steve Harvey will just think it's a crackpot theory of mine to help Wade." Sunny hesitated and then laid out her alternative theory. "There is also the possibility that Claire did it."

"What?!" said Rivka. "You think little blondie Claire with the frosted pink fingernails did it?"

"Claire may be little and cute, but she's tougher than you think," said Sunny.

"But she was in love with Jack, she wouldn't kill him."

"Love and hate are two sides of the same coin," said Sunny.

Sunny rummaged in a cabinet for a bottle of cognac and took down two stemless glasses shaped like smooth, heavy stones with a depression at one end. The cognac was a very good one that Monty had brought back years prior from a summer in Provence. She tipped a thin stream of the amber liquor into each glass and handed one to Rivka.

"Fortes fortuna juvat," said Sunny, touching her glass against Rivka's.

"What does that mean?"

"Fortune favors the brave. Somebody wrote that in the sidewalk outside my house in college."

Rivka took a few whiffs of the cognac's fumes and threw the shot back, holding it in her mouth like a delicious medicine. She swallowed and let out a breath with an *Ahhh*. "Okay, let's cut to the chase. How did Alex come to possess the nonexistent item?"

"I'm not sure yet," said Sunny. "Speaking of Alex, we need to review Thursday night. What time did he arrive at your place?"

"About seven-thirty."

"And what time did you separate?"

"About one in the morning."

"What about all that business with Gabe coming by after his stint at the Dusty Vine? When did that happen?"

"That was just before midnight. Alex wasn't gone very long. Maybe twenty minutes max."

"Think about every minute of that night up until the time you went back to his place. Was Alex out of your sight at any time?"

"Only long enough to hit the toilet at the restaurant and buy a box of black licorice and a root beer at the movies. What are you getting at?"

"I just want to be sure I've closed all the loopholes."

Rivka yawned. "So what are we going to do about that non-existent item we made disappear this morning?"

"Nothing. It does not exist."

"I can't torture Alex like this forever. Did you see him? He's losing his mind trying to figure out what happened to it. If he gets any paler, I'll be able to see through him."

"He'll have to survive for a few more hours. By tomorrow morning, the police will have it."

"How?"

"Just you leave that to me."

"What are you going to do?"

"I'm going to call Steve Harvey. I just have to confirm a hunch first."

"What hunch? You're driving me crazy with all this evasive talk, McCoskey. You never used to keep secrets."

"Maybe you just never knew before."

Rivka sneered and Sunny poured another round of cognac. Dwight Yoakam sang his heartache songs while they finished the dishes. It was only ten-thirty when Rivka gave up trying to get her to talk and went home, but by then Sunny was punchy with sleep. Could it only have been last night when she was at the restaurant until two-thirty? And this morning when Charlie knocked on her door at six-thirty? It seemed as if days had passed since then, and she longed to lie down on her bed and sink into the sweet oblivion of sleep. She locked her hands behind her and stretched back, then twisted side to side, popping the overworked vertebrae between her shoulder blades. There would be time for sleep later.

She found her address book in a drawer by the phone and flipped to the Bs, found the number, and dialed. Ben Baker answered on the second ring.

She put on her firmest voice and said, "I have something that will interest you. Meet me at the gazebo in town, the one in the park, at eleven o'clock sharp. Don't pretend you don't know what I mean. I'll have it with me. And if you think you can just ditch your jacket, I took a sample of it tonight. It's already in the mail to Steve Harvey."

She hung up without waiting for an answer and dialed Steve Harvey's mobile phone. After a few rings the voice mail picked up. She said, "Hi, Steve, it's Sunny McCoskey. I hope you check this thing because I need you to meet me at the gazebo in town, the one in the park next to the police station, at eleven-fifteen tonight. Oh, and by town I mean St. Helena, of course, and by tonight I mean Monday. See you there, I hope. Thanks."

She grabbed her pea coat out of the closet, winced at the navy-blue wool next to the brown velvet of her skirt, hung the coat back up, considered the other options in the coat and jacket department, remembered what she was supposed to be doing, and grabbed the pea coat again, hoping there was enough cogent thought left in her head to finish what she'd started.

One light, golden with old age, shone weakly at the entrance to Wildside when she drove up. Sunny got out and crunched around the side of the building and unlocked the back door to the kitchen. Inside, she flipped on the lights, jogged downstairs, and unlocked the door to the wine cellar. She hung the padlock on its hook beside the door and flipped on the light inside, letting the door close behind her. The wine cage was tucked in the far left of the cellar, where the light was poor. The key to the wine cage looked like several others on her key ring and she tried a number of them randomly, didn't find it, and decided to be more methodical. In her haste she forgot which way she had been working, from the silver key forward or from the bike key backward, and had to start over. It was at that precise moment that she realized she had made a serious mistake in her planning. Ben could guess that she had hidden the gun at the restaurant.

As if to corroborate her suspicion, a board creaked overhead. She froze. There was another soft creak, then another. This was not her imagination. Somebody was upstairs in the kitchen, moving toward the cellar door. She looked around frantically. The wine cellar was twenty by thirty feet, with tall wine racks lining the back and side walls. Not a lot of options. Three more racks were arranged in rows in the middle, all filled floor to ceiling with sleeping bottles. The wine cage, where the old and valuable wines were kept, stood in the far corner. There was only one way out of the cellar, and unless she planned on edging past the intruder on the stairwell, she was trapped. If only she'd relocked the kitchen door. Or if she had only brought her bag with her cell phone. Now that she thought about it, it must have been obvious: The restaurant was the most natural place for her to hide the gun. Once she revealed that she had it, there would have been little doubt where she would keep it. She flipped through her keys as quietly as she could, listening to each cautious step overhead. She tried one after the other in the padlock on the wine cage. If she could get it out in time, she might be able to use it as a bluff. It wasn't loaded, but guns didn't always need to be loaded to be effective.

She thought she heard the door at the top of the stairs open. There was no time to get the gun now, and besides, it might be better to leave it in there where at least no one else could get to it. It was her only bargaining piece left. Moving as quietly as she could, Sunny slipped up to the door and flicked off the cellar light. The room was pitch black. Feeling her way, she used the struts on the metal wine rack closest to the door to climb up to the bare overhead bulb, imagining with each movement the shattering crash if she pulled a wall of wine down on herself. The bulb was still just out of reach.

She raised her right foot up to the next strut and slowly shifted her weight onto it, hoping the slender metal band would hold. Her fingers wrapped around the warm bulb and she twisted it, listening to the stairs creak under the weight of footsteps. She twisted the bulb around one last time and it released. She could hear steps coming toward the door at the bottom. She pushed the bulb into her pocket and climbed back down the wine rack, which rocked perilously. Just as she pressed herself against the furthest wall, the cellar door opened.

Very faint, soft light filtered into the cellar from the light in the kitchen at the top of the stairs. A shadowy figure stood in the doorway groping for the light switch. Sunny heard the clicks as the switch was flipped up, down, up. She hardly breathed. Her last hope had been dashed. She had held on to a sliver of hope that it was Steve Harvey snooping around, checking up on her, but he would have called out as he came down. She heard a metallic click, a sound she'd only heard in movies, and knew the safety on a handgun had been released.

"I know you're in here, Sunny," said Ben. "Why don't you come on out."

At the furthest corner of the room where Sunny had wedged

herself, a barely gray dimness made it difficult to see. It was too dark and shadowy to read, but not dark enough to prevent Ben Baker from spotting her as soon as he walked around the last wine rack. Sunny fingered the lightbulb in her pocket nervously.

"Sunny, I know you're here. I don't want to hurt you. I just need that gun and everything will be fine and we can all get back to normal around here."

She could hear him moving down the corridor along the end of the racks. He was making his way toward her, moving slowly. "Not all of us," said Sunny in a quivering voice. Her heart was beating so hard that her words sounded far away in her own ears. "Jack Beroni won't be getting back to normal anytime soon, and neither will Wade if he's convicted of a murder you committed."

Ben appeared around the end of the last wine rack and Sunny met his eyes in the gloom. The pistol in his right hand was leveled squarely at her.

"I'm sorry about that," said Ben. "Old Wade's not a bad guy. But you have to admit he's part of the problem. He doesn't fight for what he believes in. He makes big threats, then he rolls over like a puppy for them. He figured somebody else would take care of defending the land. There's no excuse for that kind of laziness. You have to protect what can't protect itself."

"Killing me is only going to make matters worse," said Sunny. "That snip of your shirt is in the mail already. When Steve Harvey receives it, he's going to know exactly who killed me and why."

"I don't want to have to kill you, Sunny, you know that. And all Steve Harvey is going to have is a scrap of fabric from my jacket. It doesn't prove anything."

"It does when he matches those fibers with the ones that you and I both know are caught in the crack on the stock of Wade's gun."

Ben glanced around and spotted the large package on top of the rack in the wine cage. He smiled with satisfaction. "I'll need the key."

Sunny stared at him, trying desperately to think of some diversion or response.

"The key, please," said Ben. He stepped toward her with one hand outstretched for the key and the other holding the pistol.

"Even if you manage to get rid of the gun, there's still the tire tracks off the side of the road over at Beroni. And your gardening gloves," said Sunny.

"Doesn't prove anything. It's not a crime to drive off road, and it's not a crime to shoot a gun. I'm not going to jail, Sunny, get used to that. I'll kill you first if I have to. There's no reason for me to go to jail. All I did was get rid of a destructive force upsetting the balance of nature. Jack wasn't happy cutting down his own forests and turning his own half of the valley into a monoculture, a distortion that's unnaturally vulnerable to every pest in creation. He had to attack what's mine. My land. My wife. Jack Beroni is the one who should be in jail for all the things he tried to do. Enough talk. The key, please."

The blood pounded in Sunny's temples. She couldn't think straight, but she hoped he wouldn't shoot if she kept talking. "I'm not giving you the key, Ben. You'll have to kill me, anyway. I know everything. I know how you parked on the hidden road and walked to Skord Mountain, stole Wade's gun out of the winery, hiked overland to the lake at Beroni Vineyards, and shot Jack Beroni. You'll have to kill me, but even that won't do any good because I'm not the only one who's figured it out. How long do you think it's going to take Wade and Charlie and Alex to put it together? And what about Rivka and Claire and Monty? Not to mention Gabe. They'll all figure it out when I'm found dead."

"Maybe. And then they can sit around for the rest of their lives talking about it, because they can't prove anything without the gun. Now give me the key."

Ben's outstretched hand was only a few feet from Sunny. The resolve seemed to harden on his features.

Out of the corner of her eye she saw a shadow move. Her mind cleared. "I, I don't know which key it is," said Sunny. "I might not even have the right key ring with me—that's why I hadn't taken the gun out yet."

"No more talk! Give them all to me!"

Slowly she moved her hand toward her pocket, hardly daring to breathe or look as Rivka drew up behind Ben. Rivka was holding a bottle of wine by the neck. Sunny showed no expression as she drew the lightbulb out of her pocket and dropped it on the cement floor. The sound of the shattering glass distracted Ben, who looked down at the floor and back at Sunny just as Rivka smashed the bottle down on the back of his head. The gun went off with an ear-numbing explosion as he crumpled to the floor. Sunny buckled in response to the deafening noise and a searing hot pain in her leg. A gush of wine flooded from the rack behind her, surging out in a widening puddle around her feet and filling the close space with the heady smell of well-aged Cabernet Sauvignon.

They stared down at Ben's face, slack and unconscious. A panicked look on her face, Rivka let go of the bottle in her hand and it smashed on the floor, the sound of the crash mixed with the continuing ringing of the gunshot.

Sunny flinched and let out a gasp of pain. She leaned against the wall of wine, struggling to stand. Not a foot away from her, she saw where the bullet had shattered several bottles of wine. It was only then that she felt the warm, wet sensation on the back of her thigh. She braced herself and turned to look. There was a tear in her skirt. Sunny reached behind her and lifted it, careful to hold it away from her skin. About six inches above the back of her knee a chunk of green bottle glass that looked about the size and shape of a large arrowhead stuck out of the back of her leg. She let her skirt drop and looked back at Rivka, afraid she would be sick. The room whirled.

Just then they heard someone jogging down the stairs, and a second later Steve Harvey appeared around the corner of the wine racks, carrying a huge flashlight in one hand and a pistol in the other. "Freeze!" he yelled, and trained his gun first on Rivka and then Sunny. Then his eyes went to Ben Baker, who was curled on the floor, with blood-red wine soaking his shirt.

16

Wade Skord saved the best for last. His crew of volunteers had arrived hours before dawn, bundled up and shivering against the night cold. They'd strapped headlamps on over their stocking hats and shouldered the old wooden crates, heading out into the vineyard with Wade leading the way with a lantern. They sliced clusters of berries free by the misty glow of their headlamps until the sun came up. By noon, most of the vineyard had been harvested and boxes of perfectly ripe berries were being upturned into the crusher-destemmer. Stems tumbled out one side and the thick, scarlet must gushed out the other into the fermentation tanks, sending up the smell of fresh Zinfandel grape juice, an aroma of dusty jam and boysenberry and a hint of clove.

By the time Sunny and Rivka arrived in the early afternoon, the only area of vineyard that still had fruit hanging from its vines was half an acre of woody oldsters, primitivo planted in the late 1880s, around the time Ernest Campaglia was producing his first vintage at the Cortona Winery next door. Wade had lived at Skord Mountain for five years before he discovered these vines, tucked away in the hillside behind the house. They'd gone wild and unruly, twisting up into the encroaching oaks and Doug firs. He had spent three years coaxing them back into yielding the kind of fruit he could use to make a wine worthy of the *terroir*. "My own little piece of Beroni Vineyards," he used to say. "History in a bottle."

The harvest crew, or at least those with the stamina to make it through the entire day, lay scattered on the dry grass in front of the winery like broken toys, all of them stained, dirty, sunburned, and exhausted. A woman Sunny recognized as a line cook at an upscale grill in Napa was in her socks walking on Monty Lenstrom's back while he grunted and twitched his legs. Gabe and Alex Campaglia were stretched out against either side of a pine tree with their arms folded under their heads, looking like a couple of muscular bookends. Wade walked over when he noticed Rivka and Sunny making their way down to the winery.

"Well, if it isn't Hercule Poirot and her sidekick, Crouching Chavez," said Wade. He gave Rivka a friendly kung fu chop.

"Elementary, my dear Skord," said Sunny, feigning a puff on a pipe.

Wade stood with his hands on his hips, looking ridiculously pleased with himself. His face and T-shirt were smudged with shades of purple and red, and his hands were stained nearly black with juice. A pungent, sour smell like a truckload of recycling seeped out from the shady opening of the winery. Tanks were being scrubbed down and young wine was being racked from barrel to barrel. A whiff of sulfur drifted from the fermentation tanks. The juice was already beginning to heat up.

"How's the leg?" asked Charlie, barely lifting his head from the ground, his voice thick with fatigue.

"Getting better, but my career as a swimsuit model is probably over. I'm going to have a scar the size of Wade's belt buckle."

Wade thumbed his trademark buckle, a rodeo prize as big as a tea saucer that they'd bought together at a flea market in Petaluma.

"It'll be great. It looks like a three-pointed star," said Rivka.

"A scar is the natural man's tattoo," said Wade.

"You're the toughest chef on the block now," grunted Monty, his face turned to the side and shoved into the ground.

"Great, that's just the reputation I was going for." Sunny limped over and eased herself down onto the grass next to Charlie.

"Let's see that hand," he said.

Sunny held it out and he lifted up an edge of the bandage. "Ew. Have you been cooking with that thing?"

"I wear gloves."

"It's still gross."

"Thanks."

A gust of cool air heavy with moisture wafted up the draw.

"I think we got that fruit in just in time," said Gabe. "I looks like it might want to rain tomorrow."

"I'm glad to see you here, Gabe," said Sunny. "I've been meaning to ask you something."

"What's that?"

"Why, exactly, were you stalking me? It was you, wasn't it, Sunday night?"

Alex snickered and Gabe looked off at the vineyard self-consciously. "I saw you leaving my place," Gabe said. "I was up the road cutting firewood when you came by. I figured whatever you wanted, it had something to do with Jack, and I thought you might get into trouble."

"So instead of calling me, you waited outside my house, tailed me to Wildside in the middle of the night, and tried to give me a heart attack by pressing your face up against the window like a psychotic killer?"

"That wasn't actually intentional. I just wanted to see what you were doing in there."

Alex made an L with his thumb and index finger and held it up to his forehead. He mouthed *loco*. Rivka laughed. Monty, released from his trial of pleasure and pain, rolled himself closer to them. "I still need to know one thing, too," he said to Sunny. "How did you manage to end up with Wade's gun in your wine cage?"

"Simple. I got it from Rivka, who lifted it from Alex, who I'm pretty sure found it in the woods by the lake at Beroni, when Silvano went to phone the police on Friday morning after he found Jack." She looked at Alex, who'd drawn up his knees and had his face tucked under one arm. "Alex arrived at work a few minutes after Silvano Friday morning. When he saw what had happened, he thought he'd better take the precaution of removing the murder weapon, just in case the homicidal maniac turned out to be his brother—or his father, for that matter. Better safe than sorry. Unfortunately, Silvano caught a glimpse of him hiding something away in his truck. That's why he figured Alex or one of the other Campaglias did it. If Silvano hadn't been so amenable to the idea of getting rid of Jack himself, he might have gone to the police."

Monty flipped over on his back. "What I don't get is how you knew it wasn't our pal Gabe, here."

Sunny smiled at Gabe. "I knew he didn't do it."

"What made you so sure?" asked Monty.

"Well, aside from his character, which I observed to be rather sensitive and gentle despite the gruff exterior, because he is left-handed. Thanks to Farber, I found Michael Rieder's business card to the right of the winery door. Left-handed people put their gloves in their left-hand pocket, and when they pull their gloves out to put them on before they reach for a metal door handle, for example, the business card that they forgot they had tucked in their pocket falls out to the left."

Monty stared at her with a dazed look. "You scare me."

"There is still one mystery that no one has solved," said Rivka.

Sunny looked at her inquisitively.

"The cookies. Who has been stealing the sweets from Wildside's pantry?"

"That is a very odd question for you to ask," said Sunny, giving her a sidelong stare.

"Why do you say that?" asked Rivka.

"Because *you're* the one who's been taking them," said Sunny. "I can't believe you can maintain that poker face when you know you're guilty."

Rivka burst out laughing and rolled backward. "Oh my God. I am so busted! How did you know?"

"Well, I might have guessed when I saw hazelnut cookies in Gabe's lunch box that morning, but I didn't really think about it until you mentioned the orange rinds were missing. I knew you were lying about something because you implied it might be Heather who took them when you knew Heather was in New York and had been for days. The Rivka I know would never make such a mistake."

"I didn't want to accuse someone who would actually have to take the rap."

"Exactly. But the real proof was that metal change box I saw in your trunk. That says 'bake sale' loud and clear. Who gets the money?"

"The Calistoga 4-H Club."

"Why not just ask?"

"Last time I asked you said no."

"I did?"

"Remember? I wanted to sell cookies at that fund-raiser for the juvenile hall?"

"They were collecting money to send kids on a field trip to the Sears Point Raceway. I nearly went over there to picket them."

"I was going to tell you, sooner or later," Rivka said.

"Sure," said Sunny, smiling. "I'm going to have to keep a closer eye on you."

"Are the cookies why you were at Wildside last night in time to clobber Ben Baker?" Alex asked Rivka.

"I knew Sunny was up to something when I left her place after dinner. I called her as soon as I got home, and when she wasn't there, I figured she was at the restaurant. When I saw Ben's car parked down the street, I knew there was something funny going on."

"And Steve Harvey? How did he end up at Wildside?" asked Alex.

"I called him before I left home," said Sunny. "I asked him to meet me in town, where I was supposed to meet Ben. But just like Baker, he went by my house and Wildside first, hoping to intercept me."

Wade emerged from the winery with two glasses in one hand and a couple of wine bottles in the other. "I need two volunteers," he said, coming over. "Chavez, you just keep your hands where I can see them. We don't want any trouble."

"I'll try to contain myself."

"Are you ready to bottle?" asked Sunny.

"Oui, ma petite cochone. Il est l'heure de l'assemblage. Another baby vintage is just about to be born."

"Yum. Let me at it."

Wade poured a splash from the first bottle into each glass and handed them to Sunny and Rivka. "Personal saviors first."

They swirled, sniffed, studied, and sipped. Sunny said, "Earthy. Dirt clods and briar patch, but in a good way."

Rivka said, "Loads of black pepper, black cherry, clove, a bit of tobacco. Nice."

"Nice, Miss Chavez, is not what we are about here at Skord Mountain." He tossed what was left in their glasses on the ground and poured from the second bottle. Sunny sipped and held the wine on her tongue, drawing air over it so the vapors went up her nose, then handed her glass to Monty.

"Well?" asked Wade.

"Big, solid blackberry foundation, plenty of black pepper for kick. Slight mushroom, and probably more to come later. Healthy dash of licorice and some chocolate to finish. Very nice."

Monty sipped and held the glass up to the failing afternoon light. "Yep. Hazelnut, some molasses. It's classic Skord. I'd say this one is a contender."

"Chavez?"

"Love it."

"That's better," said Wade. He took a glass and poured for himself, smacking the chewy, tannic young wine. "I'm getting 1958 Chevy Bel Air all the way. Racy, but built to last. Two-door, tuck-and-roll upholstery. Flames, but nothing overstated. No chrome, no fuzzy dice."

"Brando circa *On the Waterfront*," said Monty.

"Exactly," said Wade.

Monty held out his glass for a refill. "I can't help thinking how sad it is that Jack spent his life being in love with his high-school sweetheart and she was married to someone else the whole time."

"You're such a little girl, Lenstrom," said Rivka. "He didn't really love her. It was a land grab."

"It makes it easier to think so," said Sunny, "but that's not how Nesto described what he saw. He said he'd never seen Jack put his arms around Larissa or anyone else the way he did with Claire. He thought they were in love."

"Love will get you every time," said Wade.

A pensive silence fell over the group. Things had worked out well for Wade but not for Claire and her two little girls, or for Larissa, or Al and Louisa Beroni. They had all lost so much.

Wade trudged off toward the winery for more glasses. Sunny lay back and looked at the eggshell-blue sky directly overhead. To the west, thick gray clouds were forming, and already the temperature was dropping. The parched land would smell wonderful when the first drops hit it and all the plants woke up. She wished the rain would come now, but tomorrow would be soon enough. That would give Wade time to get in the last of his harvest. She thought of the gray light of a rainy day and the sound of the drops thrumming on the roof.

"You know," she said, rolling up on one elbow, "a nice, dull rainy day sounds great to me right about now."

"Me, too," said Charlie.

"My favorite thing is to put on some music, like Segovia or Peter Tosh or just about anything, and make grilled cheese sandwiches and tomato soup, grab a book, and open a bottle of good, cheap red wine," said Sunny. "You know, nothing fancy, so you don't have to pay attention and you can just slug it down."

"I'll be over at noon tomorrow," said Monty.

"Me, too," said Rivka.

"Doesn't anybody around here have to work for a living?" asked Charlie.

"It's probably going to keep raining until dinnertime," said Sunny, tipping her head back to smile at him and feeling a gust of cool air brush her cheek.